Gathering Storm

Lyn GALA

Dreamspinner Press

Published by
Dreamspinner Press
4760 Preston Road
Suite 244-149
Frisco, TX 75034
http://www.dreamspinnerpress.com/

Gathering Storm
Copyright © 2010 by Lyn Gala

Cover Design by Mara McKennen

ISBN: 978-1-61581-556-2

Printed in the United States of America
First Edition
August, 2010

eBook edition available
eBook ISBN: 978-1-61581-557-9

Many thanks to Kimberley and Stella Omega.
Your willingness to read rough drafts
and your unique views on sexuality
have given this story life.

Chapter One

THE afternoon sun stabbed across the sky, and Vinnie narrowed his eyes against the glare. The wide lawns had been mowed today, and the smell of cut grass made his nose itch, but he couldn't scratch it. He needed both hands to scramble high enough into the oak tree to hide in the dense leaves.

The school's bells chimed at two p.m. exactly, the same as every day. Even though the sound drifted out through state-of-the-art speakers, the sound was actually a recording of old fashioned church bells. Vinnie wondered if the headmaster thought it would give the military school more dignity.

Whatever the reason, the sound of a dozen old brass bells chiming slightly out of time with each other had grown to be Vinnie's favorite aphrodisiac. Who would have thought that simple bells could be so kinky, and yet they were. Sometimes Vinnie felt like one of Pavlov's dogs, only instead of drooling, he got hard every time those slow, solemn bells rang.

He shifted on his branch and pushed on a higher limb to get a few more leaves out of his way. They would be coming soon: the runners.

Two years ago, Vinnie had been one of those runners. He'd listen to those bells and dread the coming order to fall out into companies. That had been before Joshua Sawyer Charleston had come. Rumor had it that wasn't his name, although Vinnie couldn't imagine why someone would choose a name like that, so it was probably his.

Considering the amount of time he and his classmates had spent discussing Commander Charleston and his mysterious identity, Vinnie found it more than a little ironic that now he really was living under an assumed name. No one at this school had ever known him as Vinnie, and the desperate little boy he'd been all the way up though his junior year had vanished along with his long-forgotten name. Of course, if Charleston really did have some reason for changing his name, he'd have a better reason than Vinnie. His story would involve gangsters and witness protection or foreign wars and enemy spies. Charleston was the sort of man who walked around with this air of leading-man confidence that made him seem larger than life.

Sometimes Vinnie had fantasies about finding Charleston's secret identity. Hell, most of his fantasies included Charleston in one form or another. But some of his favorites focused on finding some hidden clue to Charleston's mysterious past. Back when Charleston had just been one more instructor ordering him to do pushups, the fantasy had included blackmailing him. Oddly, even in Vinnie's fantasies, Charleston had kicked his ass rather than pay. However, by midterms Vinnie had pretty much fallen for the guy, and he'd grab his cock late at night and imagine some gangsters showing up on school grounds.

If Vinnie's real name showed up in this neck of the woods, it wouldn't be nearly as interesting. Oh, his father was sure to come looking. Lawyers and psychologists would descend on him along with threats about being cut out of the will, but Vinnie tried not to worry about that. He preferred to stick his head in the sand and hope that his past would just give up and move on. He was proud of his new name, though; he chose a name to show off his pride in his Italian heritage. Vinnie. It was a solid name with a long history of tough guys, and it gave him more confidence when he stepped out into the night or when he trespassed on school property to climb up a tree and watch a company running past.

Settling himself down in the crook of the branch, Vinnie slipped a hand inside his pants and watched as the company crested the hill. The upperclassmen were in front, their packs sticking up like hunchbacks. The front one was the captain, a pimply-faced boy with strong legs that Vinnie vaguely remembered from his own inglorious days in the academy.

Behind that group, came the middle-classmen who were allowed to run without packs. These were the ninth and tenth graders, and a few female faces appeared in this group. Vinnie always had good eyesight, and even from this distance, he could see the horror on one girl's face. Her hair had come loose and was winding around her body in long blonde waves that were definitely going to earn her demerits for being out of uniform. However, she kept running. And the reason for her unwillingness to break formation crested the hill.

Commander Joshua Sawyer Charleston. He was wearing shorts today, the summer heat beating down so that his shirt was already showing the first signs of sweat stains, and Vinnie groaned. Oh god. This was so worth risking getting arrested. Charleston ran at a steady pace beside the pack of students, his long legs hitting stride while younger ones scrambled to keep up.

Vinnie couldn't decide why he was so obsessed with the man, but the very sight of his gray hair and his strong body made Vinnie start to harden. The others whispered that he'd been a war hero—some sort of special forces or sniper, and Vinnie could believe that rumor. Charleston moved with power, without doubt, without fear. When the headmaster had walked in, and every other academy instructor had gone stiff with either respectful fear or fearful respect, Charleston had simply looked over with a lazy gaze before going right back to counting off the pushups he'd ordered Vinnie to do.

Fuck. Charleston did love giving orders. He had certainly loved giving Vinnie orders, and Vinnie had been shocked to find that he actually reveled in getting ordered around. For seventeen years, his father had tried ordering Vinnie to stop fucking up, ordering him to stop torturing nannies or soon-to-be stepmothers or soon-to-be ex-stepmothers. It turned out that Vinnie wasn't particularly good at orders until it was Charleston with his ice-cold gaze ordering him to hit the ground and keep doing pushups until he was permitted to stop or until his arms fell out of their sockets.

Vinnie stroked his thumb along his cock and groaned. Charleston was staring straight ahead, his gray hair streaked with the last remains of black that refused to fade away. That was the perfect metaphor for Charleston. He was just too stubborn to yield, even to time. His body certainly hadn't yielded. It was hard, curving muscle, and as the company jogged closer, Vinnie could see the way Charleston's body shone with sweat. He imagined his hand sliding over the smooth flesh and Charleston smiling at him with that odd, crooked smile that always looked just a little sarcastic. Charleston would reach out and grab the invading hand. Maybe he would pin Vinnie against some wall with his body, or maybe he would twist Vinnie's arm around and slip his other arm around Vinnie's neck, trapping him.

Vinnie's cock was hard now, hard and hot and ready to come, but Vinnie denied it. *Permission denied*, he told himself with a low chuckle. Instead, he slowed his strokes, torturing himself as the group jogged closer. The path was a good fifty yards from Vinnie's tree; he'd chosen it for its safe distance as much as for the view, but every time Charleston brought his company to that bend in the path closest to the tree, fear added its own spice to his lust.

What if Charleston caught him? Would the man remember him as the punk recruit he had taken in hand his first year here? Had Vinnie become one more faceless student who had taken a little more discipline than the others to bring into line?

That was a fear Vinnie always pushed to the side as fast as he could. He didn't want to be invisible, not to Charleston. He'd rather have the man hate him than forget him. He wanted to believe that Charleston had truly seen him every time the man had ordered him to do pushups in the center square or do pull-ups until his shoulders screamed with pain or ordered him to run the obstacle course in the pouring rain. He'd endured all that just to get one look of respect from those storm-gray eyes Charleston had. Some days he'd even earned it.

By the time Charleston was done running Vinnie ragged, Vinnie had been too tired to raid the girls' dorm or the kitchens. He hadn't even considered stealing the gardener's car and taking it for a quick ride that was sure to piss his father off. He hadn't even bothered cheating on his Latin exam by scaling the side of the main building and going in a half-open window the way he had his junior year. Of course, it helped that Charleston would quiz him on everything from Latin verb conjugations to the military history of Blackfoot Indians while making him do pushups, something about a good soldier being able to think and work at once.

Honestly, Vinnie hadn't given a shit about being a good soldier, but he had found himself considerably invested in pleasing Charleston. The man was sexy. And unlike most people, he didn't fall for Vinnie's charm or take an almost instant dislike to him.

Vinnie found most people had a pretty visceral reaction to him the moment they met him, and that reaction rarely had much to do with anything he'd done. It had to do with his green eyes and his dark hair, his broad shoulders and tanned skin and sultry good looks. People wanted him or they envied him, and Vinnie had learned to manipulate both of those responses. However, Charleston had been something new—something unexpected. He had charmed Vinnie instead. Vinnie had worked so hard, that every night he'd just fallen asleep until morning came, and Charleston roused them from bed with quiet threats of extra miles for anyone too lazy to get himself moving.

By the end of the year, Vinnie had been toned and hard—in more ways than one. He'd won three medals in the interscholastic athletic competitions his senior year, and even his father had been forced to express something that came close to pride at Vinnie's accomplishments. Of course, that had made it even more delicious when Vinnie refused to go to college. The old man's spluttering and Charleston's single raised eyebrow were forever linked in Vinnie's memory.

The group was approaching the bend now, and Vinnie held his breath, his hand wrapped tightly around his hard erection. The lack of oxygen played games with Vinnie's balance until the whole earth seemed to buck and heave under him. With his free hand, he hugged the tree limb while taking soft, panting breaths.

"Company halt!" The voice was so loud that it made Vinnie jump in his hiding place. Shit, shit, shit. What if Charleston caught him? Oddly, Vinnie's cock only grew harder as the danger increased. "Kestler, get that hair secured. Adams, either fix that shoe or head back to the barracks, and you and I can do our own run after chow."

Vinnie rested his forehead against the rough bark and groaned. He remembered Charleston's private runs. Run double-time some, get ordered to the ground for a dozen pushups, run double-time more, get ordered to do two dozen sit-ups with Charleston holding your legs. Equal parts heaven and torture.

Someone must have said something, because Charleston's commanding voice answered, "I don't care how you do it, but secure that hair or head back to barracks and report after chow for a private run with Cadet Adams."

Vinnie slowly allowed his hand to run up and down his hard cock. The end had wept enough precum that his shorts clung to his skin, and the pain of his delayed orgasm turned into a living creature that wrapped around him, squeezing until coming was all Vinnie cared about.

"Robinson, set pace. Quail, pick it up or you'll be third on tonight's run." Charleston's voice demanded obedience—unquestioning, immediate obedience, and Vinnie ached to be one of those cadets under Charleston's command again. Leaning to the right, Vinnie watched while Charleston paced the group, his sharp gaze watching as the company formed straight lines. Robinson called out for the group to start, and the students fell into a slow jog and started down the wide path. Charleston stood and watched them, critical, evaluating. God help anyone who fell short of his demanding standards.

Vinnie couldn't control his breathing anymore. He gasped for air, gulping it hungrily as his lust rose up around him, uncontrollable and uncontrolled. Oh God, he wanted to come. Fuck. If he could only come. However, Vinnie had never been a quiet fuck. He cried out, shouted, flailed and fucking sang soprano if his partner was good enough. Right now, his body was tingling and his cock aching so bad that he felt on a knife-edge, ready to come with a fucking scream, and if he did that, Charleston would see him… would know. But he had to come. Vinnie clung to the last of his control, his arms shaking. The last cadet jogged out of sight, and Vinnie devoured his last look at Charleston.

Then, without warning, Charleston turned and storm-gray eyes found Vinnie, pinned him to the tree as neatly as a butterfly pinned to a collector's page. Vinnie cried out, coming all over his hand and his shorts in a burst of need so strong that it wiped away all common sense and fear. One eyebrow twitched up, and that half-sarcastic, twisted grin graced Charleston's face for just one second, and then, it was like nothing had happened. Charleston turned and headed down the path, running double-time to catch up with the others, and Vinnie was left, panting and clinging to the tree-limb and still lost in that gray storm.

Chapter
Two

THAT moment haunted him as he wandered through his day, dazed…
and oddly sated from his orgasm. After he'd slunk home, he'd
half-expected Charleston to come pounding on his apartment door. Hell,
he had fantasies about it. In half his fantasies, Charleston had pushed him
back into the wall and pinned him there while he quietly rattled off rules
about how Vinnie's ass was his. One call to the police, and Vinnie would
be in a world of shit for trespassing and public indecency, and that sort of
police report would definitely attract the attention of Vinnie's father.
Charleston would lay the blackmail out in simple terms that Vinnie
could not debate, and Vinnie would be so very neatly caught in a trap of
his own making.

In the other half of his fantasies, Charleston had pushed him back
into a wall and then introduced him to Officer Friendly who promptly
arrested him for public indecency. That one wasn't as much fun. He'd
watched the afternoon courtroom shows with dread and hope curling in
his stomach.

He tried to tell himself that he was safely hidden. His new identity
had kept his father's goons off his back. Either the old man hadn't
bothered to hire top of the line private eyes, or the forger who had sold
Vinnie the papers had been as good as he'd bragged. However, Vinnie
had the odd feeling that Charleston could still find him. He wasn't sure if
he was being realistic about how screwed he was or romantic and stupid
by trying to make Charleston out to be some kind of superhero, but his
gut was twisted up so badly that Vinnie jumped every time the
downstairs neighbor slammed a door, and he kept going to the windows,

scanning the quiet street for some sign of either Charleston or Officer Friendly.

The sun had eventually started to sink, staining the sky pink, and Vinnie slipped out of his apartment slowly and cautiously. Every step, he'd looked around for Charleston, certain the man was going to leap out at him. In school, it seemed like Charleston had some sort of odd kink for sneaking up on him.

Just days after Charleston had first shown up to take over for the old physical trainer, Vinnie had been in back of the garage taking the headmaster's car apart. He'd had most of the bolts for the door off when he'd caught a flash of green against the stone wall. He'd turned, and Charleston had simply been there, leaning, watching. He wasn't standing near any door. In fact, the only door to the area was through the garage and Vinnie could see that. If Charleston had walked around the garage, the dogs would have made a god-awful racket, and they'd been silent.

To this day, Vinnie still couldn't figure out how Charleston had managed it—not unless he tunneled up through the ground or rappelled down from the roof, and those seemed a little extreme. Okay, they seemed a lot extreme. Charleston had ordered him to reassemble the parts and had promptly ordered Vinnie to the ground for about a million pushups. But then he had escorted Vinnie back to the dorms without telling anyone—not Vinnie's father or the headmaster. That had been the first time Vinnie had truly understood that he was out of his depth with Charleston. The man couldn't be manipulated or predicted.

And that belief that he was out of his depth followed him as he walked down the dark streets, searching every shadow for Charleston. He wasn't sure if he was relieved or disappointed when he got safely to work.

"Vinnie," RJ greeted him, her feet sticking out from under the counter, so he was guessing that the beer hoses were acting up again.

"How are all my favorite pervs?" Vinnie greeted the room enthusiastically.

The bartender pointed at him with the towel. "Speak for yourself. I happen to be a very normal faggot." Dan laughed at his own joke.

Vinnie laughed too. "You'd better watch the language in front of the boss."

RJ's only response was to reach out from under the counter and show them both her middle finger. Vinnie opened his mouth, right on the verge of saying something about how unladylike that was, but he liked his cock and balls still attached to his body, so he closed it without being a smart ass. "So, any big news tonight?" he asked instead. Dan was already pouring him a Coke.

"The toilet in the third stall keeps running."

"Ah, but that is definitely boss-lady's thing. I clean the toilets, and given my charm and good looks, that is clearly a waste of my considerable talents, but trust me, you do not want me touching anything mechanical."

"After the mess you made out of the register tape, I can believe that." Dan's snort made his disgust clear, but Vinnie just smiled prettily, and the man shook his head, a grin already tugging at the edges of his lips.

RJ pulled herself out from under the counter, her shirt streaked with gunk that Vinnie just did not want to think about. "I still feel like putting you over my knee and spanking your bare ass for that mess." Standing up, she wiped her hands on her jeans before testing the beer tap.

"Mmm. I've never turned down the offer of a good spanking," Vinnie said. RJ's narrow-eyed look sent him into full retreat, but he still managed to give her a little hip wiggle and a wink as he went. He might not have the genitals that she preferred, but if he had been a woman, he would have thrown himself at RJ and bared his ass. She scared him nearly as much as Charleston, and he liked scary.

"You're going to get yourself into trouble, boy," she warned. "Get the damn wall cleaned." She turned and headed for the back, and Vinnie sighed as he faced his work for the evening. No wonder he was so bored that he was off spying on really hot ex-teachers. The chalk wall was covered in graffiti, the floor had layers of broken chips and dust and general disgusting gunk that Vinnie did not want to think about, and the bathrooms... Vinnie sighed again. He should probably start there if RJ was going to have to fix a toilet. RJ in a bad mood was a tsunami; all you could do was get the fuck out of her way. He definitely didn't want to contribute to her bad mood.

Wrinkling his nose and letting himself feel one second of longing for the trust fund and inheritance he'd walked away from, he headed for the back where he kept the cleaning supplies. He'd finished cleaning the bathroom and was moving tables to sweep before RJ headed into the men's room with her toolkit.

Vinnie was scrubbing at chalk with an eraser when she came back out. The back wall of the club was a chalkboard that, by the end of the night, was usually full of stick-figure pornography. It amused the drunker patrons, and RJ was all about keeping the customers amused and drinking. He swiped the eraser through a pink stick figure of a man getting taken by three stick-Doms at once.

"I'd fire you, but then my wall would never get cleaned," RJ said as she came up behind Vinnie.

Vinnie gave her one of his charming smiles—one that worked on juvenile court judges and young women and customers in the strip club. RJ just looked at him. She was a little like Charleston that way. "Right. On it," Vinnie quickly said, scrubbing the stick lovers into oblivion. When Vinnie had first started working here, he'd been on the mortified side of embarrassed. He'd worked through that and reached lustfully interested, and now it was just all too boring. And when Vinnie found sex boring, his life was truly on the wrong path. He rubbed the wall a little harder and faster.

"Hey," RJ reached out and caught his arm, stopping him. Vinnie stopped and looked at his boss. She was a proud, dyke, cock-woman who loved to embarrass the shit out of virgins and loudly debate the physical attributes of just about anyone. The first night Vinnie had slunk into the bar—back when he was still using his real name and going to the military academy—RJ had found him and promptly started discussing how large his cock might or might not be. Then she'd found out he was underage and promptly kicked him out with a well-placed boot to the ass.

"Don't make me do this emotionally supportive shit," she sighed unhappily. "Just tell me what bug crawled up your ass and died." She ran her hand over her short, spiked hair, plopping down on top of one of the tables Vinnie had dragged to the side so he could sweep and mop easier.

"You're just sweet talking me because you want to get your cock up my ass," Vinnie told her with an impertinent wink. RJ might be gay as they came, but she'd been known to throw a few men over a tabletop before pegging them with her favorite strap-on harness. She wasn't an Amazon of a woman or even particularly large, but her five-foot, six-inch frame was all muscle and scary as hell. Vinnie had eight inches on her and a longer reach, and he still wouldn't tangle with her... not unless he was in a mood to lose and get pegged. Looking at her strong arms and her dark hair just starting to gray at the temples, Vinnie realized that it might not be half-bad to get pegged by RJ.

For a second, she just looked at him. "Babe, I could get my cock up there any time I put my mind to it. Your kinks are not exactly state secrets." RJ slid off the table and strode toward Vinnie so fast that he didn't have time to move out of the way before RJ had him backed up to the wall. Bringing her knee up, she put it into his crotch and then leaned forward into it. Vinnie froze. Right now he was pinned and uncomfortable, but one inch to the right, and that knee was going to make him sing soprano.

Bringing her hand up, RJ caught Vinnie by the back of the neck. "Get your head on straight or get out of the bar. With those big wounded eyes of yours, you're going to smell like catnip to any abusive son-of-a-bitch that walks through that door right now. Sometimes I swear you are too pretty for your own good." With a light slap to his face, RJ turned and headed back to the bar. "I'm not kidding," she said over her shoulder, "if you can't get your head out of your ass, finish the cleanup and head home. I'll find another dancer to take your shift."

"Great, I do all the shit work and someone else gets the glory." Vinnie thought he'd muttered that softly enough that no one would hear it, but RJ stopped near the bar and turned around to give him a murderous glare.

Vinnie cringed. "Which would be only fair if I couldn't get my head out of my ass, but my head is well on its way out, RJ!" he finished with a bright smile. RJ rolled her eyes. Turning back to the wall, Vinnie erased with feigned enthusiasm. Even if RJ was right, Vinnie resented her just a little. Maybe he wanted to be a bit abused. Besides, it wasn't like he was any of her business. She was just his boss. Once he reached the end of the wall and the very last pornographic stick figure—this time a man doing something that would not be advisable with a horse—he looked over.

She was doing the books, but her gaze kept slipping over toward him, and Vinnie gave her another bright smile. There wasn't anything that a good old-fashioned Vinnie smile couldn't fix. Her eyebrows drew down, and Vinnie took that as a signal to get the hell out of dodge, at least until the boss-lady was busy elsewhere.

Taking the two erasers he'd used on the wall, he headed out to the side entrance where the liquor came in.

"Hey, Vinnie," one of the others greeted him as he trotted up the side stairs, a bag with this dance outfit slung over his shoulder. He was just a dancer—he didn't do the clean-up or prep work Vinnie did. He danced a few nights a week and then went to school to be some hot-shot lawyer. He had student loans to make up for what dancing couldn't provide, so no scrubbing toilets for him. Vinnie felt a flash of unfamiliar jealousy. Of his many faults, that generally wasn't one.

"Hey, Tom. What's hanging and how low?" Vinnie asked with a salacious eyebrow wiggle. Tom just shook his head and went inside. As the heavy service door drifted closed, Vinnie groaned at his own idiocy. Tom was one of the few dancers who definitely weren't gay or even bisexual, so he was probably not the one to make low-hanging testicle jokes with. Damn it. Vinnie was totally off his game today, and he could not get back on it.

Leaning over the metal railing around the low stairs, Vinnie prepared to beat the erasers together when the bar's cat came wandering down the alley, hunting or patrolling or whatever he did when he wasn't getting spoiled by the cook who left scraps for him outside the kitchen doors. Vinnie pounded the erasers together, and a pastel cloud of chalk dust rose into the air. Whites and pinks and yellows swirled together before they slowly settled toward earth. The leading edge caught the cat's shoulder, and the animal darted forward, scattering the rest of the cloud with his tail; however, a long streak of pink was left along the animal's black flank. The cat gave Vinnie a yellow-eyed stare and then strutted past, feigning indifference to the pink chalk that dusted its coat.

Vinnie could practically hear the animal accuse humans of being juvenile.

"Nope, not humans, just me," Vinnie confessed. He watched the cat vanish behind the dumpster with an angry tail twitch. "Just me." Gaying up the cat with a little pink dust was nothing compared to this afternoon's escapades.

What if Charleston contacted his father? The school would have that contact information; after all, his father hadn't moved his fat ass in over forty years, so he sure as hell hadn't moved in the last three. No, the old man would only move if forced, and if Vinnie's mother hadn't been enough to shame him into moving, Vinnie doing a runner sure as hell wouldn't.

Turning his back to the rail, Vinnie leaned back and wondered if he shouldn't call his mother and check to see if that bridge was still open and ready for him to make a full retreat. While he hadn't seen her in close to fifteen years, she took his collect calls. She cared... in her own drunken way. Then again, after being married to Vinnie's father, the woman deserved to indulge a little. Richard Martello had married her, humiliated her, driven her into the bottle, and then divorced her without sharing one cent of his many millions.

Family trust money was not actually owned by family members—only held in trust. Vinnie remembered his father coming home from court and bragging about that bit of legal maneuvering that had left Vinnie's mom penniless and homeless. His father had celebrated that night, and a couple of very well-endowed women had been happy to help him spend the money that Richard had not been forced to turn over to his ex-wife.

If Charleston called his father, Vinnie's whole life just might unravel in a series of angry accusations and blackmail. If his father couldn't control Vinnie's life, he'd ruin it, and Vinnie didn't have a whole lot of doubt on that front. Shit. He never should have taken such a risk. His mom would take him in and give him a home, if by home he was willing to accept a musky and ready-to-be-condemned apartment in the worst part of Fort Worth. Vinnie liked his life here. He liked dancing for men. He loved the look of lust that came into men's faces when they saw Vinnie on stage.

And he'd risked it all. For what? Vinnie felt a wave of self-loathing. He'd risked everything to indulge in a stupid fantasy about a man who was probably straight as a fucking ruler. Even worse, his cock was hardening even now at the very memory. Charleston's blue-gray eyes captured him for that one moment, and Vinnie was just pathetic enough that one second of life caught in that stare was worth all the risk.

"RJ's right," Vinnie said softly to the universe at large, "I am so headed for a fall." But sadly, Vinnie had no idea how he was supposed to avoid hitting the ground at full speed. In fact, he was already falling, and catching himself midair... well, the cat might be able to do that, but Vinnie had always been more for falling on his ass and then charming everyone with a smile to convince them it hadn't hurt at all.

"Vinnie, move your cute ass," RJ's voice snapped him back to reality.

"Coming!" Vinnie called, not willing to push RJ's buttons. Plenty of nights he had fun with that, but tonight he didn't want to get eaten alive by the boss-lady. "Am I doing the warm-up show, oh grand queen of my world?" Vinnie asked as he trotted into the back of the club with his best grin on his face. If his life fell apart, he'd deal, but right now, he wanted to feel the power of making others helpless with lust. RJ kept telling him he could be a headline stripper if he learned to work the crowd, but Vinnie preferred to find one poor sap and pour all his charm into making one man lose all coherent thought.

RJ gave him a dirty look that made it perfectly clear he was on her shit list. "Do the food runs," she ordered him. Vinnie's grin faded as he faced his punishment.

"RJ, come on," he pleaded. She turned around and pinned him with a look that promised pain. He was starting to wonder if she was Charleston's long lost sister or something, because they did share one seriously cold glare.

"You know the law. You keep yourself fully covered. You do not touch patrons, and you do not make any offers that could be construed as prostitution."

"Hey," Vinnie objected, but RJ's glare shut him up. Once or twice he had been tempted into a little side work, but it wasn't the money.

Sometimes he just wanted to know that he had the power to make men pay for it, but he'd always kept any business far away from RJ's place.

"I get one fine, and it's coming out of your backside. Not your pay—you. And if I put you over my knee, I promise that you are not going to enjoy it for even one second. Got it?" RJ demanded.

"Got it," Vinnie agreed, hiding his frustration. At least he thought he was hiding it; from the evil look RJ was giving him, maybe not. Damn. He'd needed the control tonight. He'd needed to walk the stage and manipulate some middle-class jerk who came to a gay joint to get his rocks off before going home to the wifey and pretending to be straight. He needed men to look at him with desire.

The memory of a single, curious raised eyebrow flashed though his mind. He needed to erase Charleston, and he couldn't do that if he got stuck carrying chip bowls and emptying ashtrays. It wasn't exactly a glamorous job. And RJ wasn't a woman who backed down once she gave an order. Vinnie sighed as he went to grab cheap tortillas out of the pantry. Count on RJ to know if one bowl went empty tonight, and Vinnie did not need that grief.

Chapter
Three

BY THE time the music started and the first dancer slunk out on stage in a sequined outfit straight out of RuPaul's wardrobe, Vinnie was in a serious funk. "Oh well, if you can't beat 'em, join 'em," Vinnie told Dan before he headed for the dressing room. Dan looked at him oddly, but just kept filling drink orders from the growing line of men at the bar while Vinnie darted into the back. RJ had ordered him to stay fully dressed and fill chip bowls; he planned to do both. He just thought he could find a way to get what he needed at the same time.

By the time he came out of the back, Vinnie had changed into an outfit that would have gotten him into the hottest clubs in New York. His jeans were just tight enough to hint at everything without giving anything away, and his red silk shirt was open to his belly button. That showed off a nipple ring that laid against his pale skin. He'd added just a hint of glitter, enough to catch the eye without the customers noticing he was wearing glitter. The same was true with the makeup. He had on just enough to make his eyes and mouth a little larger, a little more sensuous, but he avoided being obvious. Around his neck, he'd looped a length of chain he'd pulled off the back fence. The two ends dangled in front, a beautiful contrast against the silk, and the slight edge of rust where the chain wrapped around his neck looked really hot. To finish off the look, he stood in bare feet, just like a good little subby boy should.

Vinnie surveyed the room through his lashes, ducking his head to simulate the sort of innocent charm that turned men into big piles of stupid. He already had the eye of a half-dozen men and even a couple of the women who regularly showed up to ogle the dancers. With a roll of his hips, Vinnie headed back to the bar. He'd stashed a dozen chip bowls under there, and he grabbed two before carefully heading into the crowd of men.

With his bare feet, Vinnie had to keep his eyes on the floor in front of him. One stubbed toe could ruin his evening, but the eyes on the floor worked for the persona he was projecting. The bowls were set on high tables around the stage area. RJ wanted the guys eating and getting thirsty and ordering more beer, so Vinnie's job was to keep those bowls full. If she didn't like how he did it, that was her problem. Vinnie grabbed the first bowl only to find it full. Before he could even put it back, a huge hand reached in and grabbed a whole handful of the chips.

Most of the chips crumbled and fell to the ground, sprinkling Vinnie's toes, and Vinnie tried to look suitably cowed as his new friend ate the others. His new friend had two friends of his own, and Vinnie watched as they closed in from the sides.

Desire and danger sang through Vinnie's bones. This was a scary game he was playing, and these three looked like good old-fashioned leathermen who could take him over their knees and spank him into tears, but right now, they were playing on Vinnie's territory. The tallest one moved around to stand behind Vinnie, and Vinnie let him, perfectly willing to be trapped.

"I haven't seen you before," the man commented, slipping an arm around Vinnie's waist.

"I should…." Vinnie let his words trail off as he twisted, mimicking a break for freedom. As he moved, the guy's hand slipped under the open shirt and stroked over Vinnie's hot skin.

"You should what, boy?" the man in front asked. Reaching out, he lifted the two ends of the chain and closed his fists around them. Vinnie sucked in a breath. He wanted this. Fuck, he wanted this… needed this. Letting his gaze fall to the floor, Vinnie waited, stiff with tension as the guy pulled on the makeshift leash, forcing Vinnie to step closer to him. The bowl was trapped between their bodies until the third guy reached in and plucked it away.

"I…." Vinnie's eyes came up to the third man's face, but he didn't know how to read the guy's expression. The first guy soothed him, whispering in Vinnie's ear from behind. His hand slipped down, sliding into the waistband of Vinnie's jeans.

"I would have remembered you," he confided in a stage whisper loud enough for his friends to hear. Vinnie gave them a small and frightened version of his famous smile.

"I should go. RJ's not going to be happy with me," he said. Looking up while keeping his head bowed submissively, he studied his three captors. The man in front reached his hand up and put his palm on Vinnie's cheek in an intimate gesture. Pulling Vinnie's face toward his with the chain leash, the man leaned in and kissed Vinnie—not a tender kiss, but a commanding kiss. His tongue reached out and slipped under Vinnie's upper lip, pulling it out far enough for the man's teeth to close over it firmly enough to earn a gasp from Vinnie. At the open invitation, the man's tongue quickly moved into Vinnie's mouth. Vinnie squirmed, the hand in his jeans slid dangerously low, and the leash grew uncomfortably tight. After a couple of minutes, the man pulled back and held up a twenty-dollar bill.

"Very nice," he commented as he slipped the bill in the front of Vinnie's jeans so far down that the paper brushed the top of Vinnie's slowly hardening cock. Shit, he had really needed this. Giving his captors a wide-eyed and dazed look, Vinnie looked around the room as though searching for rescue. They moved in on him, predators protecting their prey. So very predictable. Vinnie gave a little shiver, and the one in back pulled him close so that Vinnie could feel the guy's cock against his ass, even through his own jeans and the guy's leather.

Several of the patrons were watching with undisguised lust, and RJ.... She looked ready to come over, grab Vinnie by the leash, and beat him senseless. The way Vinnie felt tonight, he would probably let her. He never could seem to make her understand the thrill he got out of watching powerful people lose control. When they wanted him or even when they hated him, he could break their will—force them to react to him. That was the sexiest thing in the world for Vinnie, and right now, he needed to feel sexy. Vinnie squirmed and made a little whine deep in his throat as he returned his gaze to his three captors.

After the leatherman with the leash had deposited his money, he left his hand beneath Vinnie's jeans, his splayed fingers stretching across Vinnie's lower stomach scant centimeters from Vinnie's now painfully enlarged cock. This gave the guy in back a chance to let go of Vinnie's jeans without risking an escape, as if Vinnie had any interest in escaping.

"My turn," he announced as he placed his hands on either side of Vinnie's face and pulled Vinnie's head to his own. This time Vinnie opened his mouth before the lip bite could be repeated. "Eager," he approvingly mumbled before covering Vinnie's lips with his own. Vinnie left his lips parted, and the invading tongue attacked immediately. Vinnie didn't have to fake the uncomfortable squirming now. The power of these three men holding him, wanting him—that was enough to put him on the edge of orgasm. The guy sucked at Vinnie's mouth, inviting Vinnie's tongue to explore in return. Vinnie complied happily.

Before Vinnie could retreat, the man's teeth closed even as the suction continued. Vinnie flinched, startled at the trap. He tried to withdraw his head, but a hand latched on to the back of his head and pulled him forward. He tried to pull back his tongue, but the teeth tightened, and Vinnie froze. As soon as Vinnie froze, the man's teeth eased up, and he felt the other man's tongue stroking along the underside of his tongue in rhythm with a stroking that now began on his left nipple.

Vinnie relaxed. These three knew their game. Vinnie wondered what they could do with rope. A nail raked his nipple, and he groaned as his body sent so much blood to his cock that it closed the distance between it and the fingertips of the man in front who still had his hand down Vinnie's jeans. When Vinnie felt the head of his cock nudge the warm finger, he groaned into the mouth that still held his tongue captive. "Nice hardly seems adequate," the kisser commented after he finally released Vinnie's mouth. He held up his twenty dollars, and the first man finally pulled his hand out. Vinnie held still as the hand with the money disappeared down the front of his jeans. This time, the hand didn't stop until it had pushed the money between Vinnie's cock and his lower stomach, allowing the man to run his finger down half the length of his cock, which twitched approvingly.

Vinnie now turned his attention to third guy. "Let's take this somewhere private," he suggested and nodded at the other two.

"I'm all in favor of private, but three on one?" Vinnie looked up. For the first time, fear was starting to win out against desire.

"I didn't ask for your input, boy," the first guy said, tightening the chain leash. Vinnie made a little squeaking sound. Two more men detached from the shadows and started wandering toward them, and for the first time, Vinnie felt a spark of real fear. Most leathermen were polite, careful to not go past negotiated boundaries, and sometimes even a little easily manipulated. Vinnie had dated one for a few weeks, and he'd learned the right wiggle could get the guy to demand exactly what Vinnie wanted to offer, but five on one was feeling more dangerous than he was willing to try. The two new men were older than the three who had already "captured" Vinnie.

"You're going to make that noise a lot tonight," the first man who'd kissed Vinnie promised darkly. If it was just the one guy, Vinnie would have been tempted. His cock loved the attention, and he loved the fact that he had successfully distracted this man from the floorshow. Now, he had eyes only for Vinnie.

"Maybe later," Vinnie said with a shy smile. He really didn't need to piss these guys off. Even if RJ tried to pull him out of this mess, he wasn't sure she could with this particular group. Menace drifted off them in waves like the stink of old beer.

"I don't think so. I don't appreciate a cock-tease."

"And I'm just trying to put out chips," Vinnie said, trying his best not to choke on his own lies. Or maybe that feeling was from the chain leash pressed tight against his neck.

"That so?"

Vinnie sighed. "Okay, so maybe I was putting out a few signals, but RJ doesn't let shit happen in here. So let me go before things get ugly." Dropping the submissive body language, he crossed his arms and stared at the man still holding the impromptu leash around Vinnie's neck.

The guy laughed. "You think I give a shit about some cock-woman? Fucking penis-wanting freak."

RJ appeared at Vinnie's side. "And this penis-wanting freak will toss you out on your ass if you don't let him go."

For a second, the five looked at each other incredulously. "You and what army?" The man finally let go of Vinnie and squared off against RJ.

He had to be twice her size, but she still looked him up and down with the sort of disgust that made Vinnie's guts twist in fear, even if he wanted to laugh at the guy for the cliché.

RJ gave a smile that made Vinnie shiver. Looking them up and down, she seemed to sum them up and dismiss them utterly with one glance. "Me, Smith, and Wesson," she said slowly. "And if you're really stupid, we can call the cops and have this discussion with them," she said firmly. "Vinnie, get your ass in back, and if I see you within the next twelve hours, I am going to put you over a spanking bench and turn your ass bright red, understand?" RJ pinned him with a glare that made it clear she'd do it.

Vinnie nodded and headed for back.

"Wait a second," one of the leathermen protested.

"Oh, we will be waiting a second. The six of us are going to have a little conversation while Vinnie gets his ass a ride home with Danny," RJ said. Vinnie turned, and Dan was already tossing his apron at the bar and coming around to the kitchen door. Vinnie cringed. Shit. He was in so damn much trouble that he wasn't even sure he'd have a job tomorrow.

"Come on, Romeo," Dan said, catching Vinnie by the arm.

"I should get—"

"Your ass out to my car," Dan finished for him. Vinnie didn't even have a chance to point out that he'd rather wear his street clothes home before Dan was pulling him out of the club.

Chapter
Four

PICKING at the edge of the car seat where the stuffing was just starting to peek out, Vinnie stared into the night. Dan hadn't even given him a chance to grab his keys out of his locker, so he'd be shimmying in through the bathroom window. Again. Vinnie sighed.

"Oh don't start that. You can twist the tops around forward and backwards, but I've been at this game too long for a pretty little face and a sigh to work on me," Dan warned.

"What?" Vinnie looked over at Dan.

"I'm not a top. Those little tricks just piss me off, Vinnie." Dan looked like a top—all muscles and tattoo—but looks lied. Vinnie had seen him kneeling for more than one man, and RJ treated him like a personal servant, which seemed to make him almost as happy as kneeling.

"I'm not trying to play you," Vinnie promised. Dan glanced away from the road just long enough to give Vinnie a dirty look. "I'm not. I'm just naturally manipulative without trying." Vinnie gave Dan his best grin.

"Fuck. Does that ever work?"

"More often than you'd think."

Dan shook his head. "We need to find you a better quality top, then. You pull that shit on RJ, and she'd string you up on the wall and then leave you there for the night to think about the error of your ways.

Actually, now that I think about it, she really may do that after tonight's little performance."

Vinnie scrubbed his hand over his face. "Yeah, yeah," he sighed. The fact was that he really did dream about a top who couldn't be manipulated. His problem was that the people he liked generally didn't like him.

"Going after that group was not the smart move." Dan kept his voice carefully neutral.

"Hey, they were strong tops."

"They were stupid tops who didn't notice you had them wrapped around your finger."

"I—" Vinnie stopped. Okay, he sort of was manipulating them. "I was enjoying myself," he finally finished.

"Fuck." Dan stopped at a red right. "I know there are lots of guys that don't use the hanky code, but even without a flag, I could tell those guys were all flagging black, and you're not a pain-slut, Vinnie."

"I can put up with a little pain if it makes someone happy." Vinnie suddenly felt like he was being insulted.

"You don't get off on it," Dan said firmly. "Those guys were more my speed than yours, and even then, I would start putting out signals until I had talked to them and established some sort of backup plan. Five on one may sound like a fantasy, but it could turn into a nightmare quick enough."

"I don't need the safe subbing talk, Mom. Thanks anyway."

"Brat."

"You like brats."

"I like to be the brat and get turned over someone's knee," Dan corrected him. "That's why you can't play me. Seriously, though, that kind of shit is going to get you hurt or fired."

"Yeah, yeah." Vinnie rested his head against the seat and closed his eyes. Instead of finding some sort of relief, he was going home with only a half day of work in, and his whole body was tight as a fiddle string.

"Whatever's eating you, you need to get it straightened out." Dan pulled the car up to the curb in front of the old house Vinnie lived in. Like a lot of houses in the area, it had been converted into four apartments. Vinnie didn't move.

"Have you ever really fallen hard for a straight guy?"

"Well, shit." Dan slammed the car into park and stared out the front window. "Welcome to reality. It sucks, but it does seem like everyone has to have that one unforgivably straight guy somewhere in their past. Think of it as God's initiation joke for all gay men. Is that why you had your head so far up your ass?"

"Yep." Vinnie shifted and reached down his pants to rearrange the bills the leathermen had slipped down there. "What the hell am I supposed to do?"

"Masturbate."

Vinnie glared at Dan. "I'm serious."

Dan looked over and gave a good-natured shrug. "I am being serious. Masturbate. Find yourself a couple of really good fantasies, and then masturbate like a thirteen-year-old with his own bathroom. You'll eventually get over him."

"It'd be more fun to have help getting over him," Vinnie said sadly. The truth was that a little part didn't want to give up his fantasies of Charleston and those strong hands holding him against the wall while Charleston explained in very soft words exactly what he expected from Vinnie. The man hadn't even given an "or else." He'd just given the order, and for the first time since he'd been five, Vinnie had wanted to obey.

"There's always the hard way." From the tone of voice, Dan had done it the hard way and had more than a few regrets about it.

"What's that?"

Dan looked over. "Tell him you're gay and you have a hard-on for him. If you survive the hospital visit, you'll be over him." Dan's expression faded like he was lost in the past. It was an oddly vulnerable expression on a man that looked like an extra from a biker movie.

Vinnie cringed as he thought about how much damage Charleston could do. Whether the man was special forces might be up for debate, but everyone knew he'd been a military officer, and they were all guessing he'd been a serious bad-ass. He could do physical training six hours a day with six different classes and still keep up with them, push-up for push-up. "I think I'll skip that part," Vinnie offered.

"Smart boy." Dan smiled, and the past seemed to slip away. "Just get your head out of that pretty ass of yours, or you're going to land on RJ's bad side."

That made Vinnie shiver.

"You have no idea." Dan shook his head. "That woman is more man than all five of those bikers put together, and my guess is that they're learning that right about now. You, however, do not want to have an up close and personal relationship with her bad side. It's not pretty. So go masturbate, get this guy out of your head, and come ready to kiss RJ's boots so she doesn't kick your ass tomorrow."

"Sir, yes sir." Vinnie tossed off a messy salute, and Dan reached over and shoved his arm. Smiling, Vinnie got out of the car and trotted toward the side of the building so he could climb the oak and shimmy in his bathroom window. He could hear Dan's car still idling outside the house as he climbed. The engine finally roared and the car pulled away only after Vinnie had landed in an inelegant heap of limbs on his bathroom floor.

Chapter
Five

VINNIE knew he was way past stupid out into the land of completely fucking insane. Actually, any time he voluntarily got out of bed at five in the morning, he was questioning his own sanity. The hills around the academy rolled gently, and he let his car coast down one and right off the shoulder into the grass between two big elms. The lightest touch on the gas, and his old clunker settled behind a knoll of grass where the wide, green branches of the trees would hide it.

He'd blown every penny of the money he'd been saving to buy an old Mustang, but he felt good because he had a plan. Four days of masturbating and sucking up to a very pissed RJ hadn't cured his little Charleston obsession, so Vinnie was going for one of the classics—gorge until you couldn't eat another bite. Oh, he wasn't dumb enough to actually walk up to Charleston and make the big gay announcement, but he figured that a few weeks of heavy stalking and some video recordings so that he could watch them at home, and his libido had to get tired of wanking to the same image over and over. Oh, with his fucking Adonis looks and gray hair, Charleston was hot, but Vinnie had never been a fan of monogamy, not even in his fantasies. So he just needed to wear himself out on this particular image.

He fingered the warm plastic and cool metal of his newest toys. The man behind the counter at the electronics shop had given Vinnie so many winks and nods that it was really pretty clear this equipment was just this side of illegal. If Charleston caught him… well, punishment would be sure to follow. Vinnie's cock hardened as he considered the punishments he'd endured his last year of military school. Charleston would quietly count off the pushups, and if Vinnie worked hard enough, if he sweated and groaned and kept pushing himself through the pain of fatigued muscles, he just might earn a, "Not bad, Martello." Martello. Vinnie hadn't even thought of that name for almost a year. He wasn't that little rich kid scrambling after his father's attention and twitching every time his father dangled the inheritance in front of him and then jerked the bait just out of reach.

No, he was Vinnie Bernardi, a gay dancer and part-time janitor who liked to read, surf the Internet, and spy on certain well-built instructors at the local military academy. He just had to be a little smarter about it now. Getting caught in the tree had made for some nice fantasies, but Vinnie really didn't need a police record.

Deer had made a path up to the top of the last hill, and Vinnie ducked down as he approached the crest. The spot where he'd laid yesterday was still a mat of grasses surrounded by the slowly swaying stalks all around it.

It only took seconds to set the tripod into the same three dents in the earth from yesterday. The black dual day/night high resolution IR camera snapped in place on top of that, and then Vinnie plugged the cord into a small monitor.

The sun was just edging up over the horizon, fingers of pink stretching into the sky, and Vinnie focused the camera on the door at the back of Charleston's cabin. Any second now, he was going to come out in shorts and a T-shirt and head over to the obstacle course. Before Vinnie had invested in the equipment, he'd come out to make sure it was worth the money. It was. Vinnie had complained that Charleston ran them too hard, but he drove himself even harder.

Yesterday, Vinnie had lain on the hill in the weak morning light and watched as Charleston swung through the ropes. He threw his body from one point to another with a power and flexibility that reminded Vinnie of a cat. Watching on the small screen back door to the cabin, Vinnie remembered yesterday and imagined the heavy grunt as Charleston landed on the hard-packed ground on the far side of the ropes. Today, he'd have an even better view. He'd be able to zoom in on the straining muscles and see his back arch. As soon as he could afford it,

Vinnie was going to buy a directional mike that would catch every grunt and groan.

Vinnie's cock was already starting to harden, and he pressed himself to the cool morning ground and squirmed in his little hidden nest. Where the hell was Charleston?

"Problem, Martello?" a cool voice asked. Vinnie sprang up and turned, his heart thumping painfully against his ribs. Charleston was there, his arms crossed as he leaned against a tree.

"Commander," Vinnie breathed.

"You never did watch your six, Martello." Charleston pushed away from the tree and started strolling toward Vinnie like this was just two men running into each other on the street. Light was smeared across the sky, and Vinnie could feel himself breathing, but he seemed to have lost all control over his body. "So I know you're not using the name Troy Martello. What are you going by these days?"

Vinnie even stopped breathing as Charleston moved into his space, the scent of his spiced cologne and mud clinging to him. One eyebrow went up as Charleston considered Vinnie's equipment, then he looked at Vinnie, his body close enough that Vinnie couldn't move forward without touching Charleston, and he couldn't move back without hitting about five hundred dollars worth of surveillance equipment that he really couldn't afford at all, much less afford to break.

"Funny, I don't remember you being this quiet." Charleston crossed his arms and settled back on his heels. Vinnie had seen that body language before… usually right before Charleston settled in for an hour or two of watching while cadets suffered under him.

"I should go," Vinnie stepped to the side and started reaching for his camera. Charleston did a neat sidestep so that Vinnie was left choosing between retreating without his equipment or touching a man who was equal parts exciting and downright terrifying. And the longer Vinnie was here, the more the terror was starting to win over the excitement. Forgetting his equipment, Vinnie gave Charleston his best smile, full of boyish charm and forgive-me innocence as he backed up through the tall grasses. The long stalks tangled around his ankles and clung to him, but Vinnie steadily retreated with Charleston in slow pursuit.

Reaching into his pocket for his keys, Vinnie fumbled and looked down, and before he could look up again, strong hands caught him by the arms and thrust him backwards. With a hoarse cry, Vinnie tried to windmill his arms, but Charleston's grip was too firm. Balance gone, Vinnie sailed helpless back, turning midair as Charleston yanked on one arm, and then Vinnie slammed chest-first into a tree with enough force to drive the air out of him. Without a word, Charleston wrenched his arm up behind his back, forcing Vinnie onto his toes, and then frisked him.

"Hey, if you're into these games, you only had to ask," Vinnie said, trying for a flippant tone. His voice was pitched a little too high, but he still expected some sort of reaction. Whether Charleston punched him or retreated in a heterosexual panic, Vinnie's words should have stopped him. However, the man was annoyingly focused and continued his pat down until he found Vinnie's billfold tucked into the lower leg pocket on his khakis. "Okay, I think you've made your point now," Vinnie tried to jerk his hand away, but it was like trying to move a rock. Charleston leaned in closer, his knee pressed up against the back of Vinnie's leg so that Vinnie was pinned to the tree.

"Oh, I don't think I've even started making my point," Charleston disagreed. He reached into Vinnie's front pocket and pulled out the car keys. Resting his forehead against the rough bark, Vinnie tried to order his cock to stop getting the wrong ideas, but being held helpless in the woods was too close to his fantasies.

Charleston released his hand, and leaves rustled as he backed away, but Vinnie didn't have his keys or his wallet or his expensive toys, and Charleston was about to discover his new identity. He didn't bother turning around or even lifting his head away from the rough surface. The small digging pain of the sharp-edged bark was a welcome relief from the reality about to come crashing down around him, and still his cock was hard. He was such a sick, sick boy.

"Vinnie Bernardi," Charleston said slowly. The sound of plastic flipping told Vinnie that Charleston was busily going through all his cards. "Not bad. Social security, driver's license… even a Blockbuster card. New ID this good doesn't come cheap."

Vinnie finally turned around and leaned back against the tree. That was about all that was holding him up.

"Which makes me wonder why you're risking everything to watch me." Charleston threw the wallet at Vinnie, who plucked it out the air and tucked it away with as much cocky swagger as he could muster given the circumstances.

"Who says I was watching you?" Vinnie grinned.

There went Charleston's eyebrow again. Vinnie's cock ached at the memory of the punishments that eyebrow used to promise.

"So, you were watching the students?" Charleston asked. His voice was almost amused, like there was some hidden joke that Vinnie hadn't caught onto. Pushing away from the tree, Vinnie squared off against the older man.

"Maybe. There are more women now. All that jiggling flesh when they run." He put on his most salacious expression and moving his hands up and down to suggest merry bouncing breasts, even if the women on the run had been noticeably lacking in that department.

Charleston nodded, his expression even more amused. "So... Vinnie... how do you feel about a pedophilia conviction?"

Vinnie's eyes grew large as he realized he had just stepped into a big, steaming pile of stupid. "Okay, so I was looking at you," he quickly admitted. He did not need to go to prison for ogling underage girls, especially when young and tender did absolutely nothing for him. Now some women, like RJ, could get him interested as fast as a gray-haired man with a powerful body and confidence in spades. But girls were just not his thing. "Look, I'm sure you don't exactly appreciate all this—"

"Just figured that out, did you?" Charleston interrupted. Vinnie flinched. Okay, he was hoping Charleston would take it as some sort of compliment, but clearly he wasn't.

Vinnie took a second to really study Charleston. The man was fingering Vinnie's keys and had an expression of almost amusement. Understanding him was like trying to read a foreign language, because none of this made any sense. He should be furious and throwing punches or horrified and calling the police or maybe, in Vinnie's wildest fantasies, he should be complimented and forcing Vinnie to the ground. Standing and just staring with faint amusement was not a normal reaction.

"What do you want?" Vinnie asked. If games and charm weren't going to work, maybe he needed to try a more direct approach.

"Better," Charleston said, and Vinnie couldn't control the flush of pleasure at that single word. Fuck. The man's compliments still had a way of sliding through all the cracks in Vinnie's self-defenses. "I want to know what you're doing up here."

"I thought that was obvious." Vinnie swept his hand out toward the hill where, on just the other side, Charleston had his small house at the edge of the academy's property.

"No other reason other than watching?" Charleston walked back toward the camera and stopped when he could just see over the crest of the hill to his own backyard. "Nice vantage point. A little on the obvious side, though. When you're tracking a target, always assume they know their vulnerabilities and have taken steps to minimize the risk."

Vinnie opened his mouth to ask what that meant, but Charleston bent down and quickly pulled the cord out of the monitor and picked up the tripod, camera and all, and collapsed the legs. "Grab the rest," Charleston ordered with a casual tone that suggested that he didn't have any doubt at all that Vinnie would obey him. For a half second, Vinnie wanted to argue. He wanted to make Charleston work for that obedience that he seemed to assume was his natural right. Then Charleston walked past. "Now, Martello," he said, and Vinnie found himself hurrying to obey.

"It's Bernardi," Vinnie said. He could at least rebel that much. Charleston stopped and looked at him for a second.

"Now, Bernardi," he corrected himself. "Before I get any older." With that, Charleston headed to the car and slipped in behind the driver's side, tossing the camera in back.

Fuck. What had he gotten himself into now? Vinnie scrambled to collect the cords and the monitor and slip it all into the bag, afraid that at any second Charleston was going to take off without him and equally terrified that the man would wait for him.

By the time he stumbled up to the car, Charleston sat in the driver's side, his hands resting on the wheel. Vinnie swallowed as he looked at the fingers curled around the wheel so tightly that the knuckles were turning white. In school, when Charleston had put his large hand on Vinnie's knees during sit-ups, Vinnie had fantasized about them. They were strong with long fingers and neatly trimmed nails. Vinnie had imagined red prints from those hands decorating his ass, and now they rested on the wheel of his car.

"Bernardi."

"What?" Vinnie snapped to attention as he realized he'd been staring at Charleston's hands. The man looked amused as he snapped his fingers.

"Get in," Charleston said firmly.

"Oh, right." Vinnie hurried to the passenger side, setting the equipment on the backseat floor before getting in next to Charleston. "Um, we aren't going to the police, are we?" Vinnie asked.

"Since when have you ever known me to let someone else handle the discipline?" Charleston asked. The tone and the words were enough to make Vinnie shut up. If he didn't keep his mouth closed, he was going to end up babbling because this was entirely too close to every fantasy he'd had since he was seventeen years old and Charleston caught him with the headmaster's car. Instead of offering up his dignity and his first-born child, Vinnie stared out the front window and tried to not squirm as the man of his dreams drove them back to Vinnie's apartment.

Chapter Six

THE second Charleston opened the door, Vinnie could feel his face turn red. Yeah, he couldn't afford the nicest place in the world, but he could have at least cleaned it up. He half expected Charleston to order him to start cleaning, and sadly, he would be more than willing to follow any order Charleston gave. Instead, Charleston just pushed Vinnie toward an open bit of wall on the far side of the couch.

"Assume the position, Bernardi." Without waiting to see if Vinnie would obey, he headed toward the one closed door, which led into the bedroom.

Vinnie leaned his hands against the wall and watched curiously. Charleston had always given off seriously dominant vibes, but having the man here was twisting Vinnie's guts into all sorts of knots. Lust was there, but so was sheer terror. This guy could strip Vinnie of every defense mechanism and disguise and lay him bare; Vinnie instinctively knew that. Of course, that was part of Charleston's charm. He was a hard man, a man who said very little and could glare a person to death. He was exactly the sort Vinnie always fell for.

He watched as Charleston walked behind him. Without warning, Charleston kicked the insides of his feet, and Vinnie gasped in surprise before widening his stance. Clearly they would not be using the bed. "Shouldn't you take my pants off first?" Vinnie asked with a sweet smile. With his legs spread so far, Charleston wouldn't be able to get them down far enough to fuck Vinnie.

"Nope," Charleston answered. Putting his hands on Vinnie's hips, he pulled. Vinnie had to put more of his weight on his hands as he stuck his ass out.

"Is Daddy going to punish me for being a bad boy?"

Charleston's face twisted like he had bit into a lemon. Fuck. Clearly the man wasn't into daddy-kink. "Feel free to gag me any time," Vinnie offered along with a weak grin. When Charleston didn't react, he turned his face toward the wall. Shit, he really was a dork.

"Make a comment like that again, and I will," Charleston promised. Then his hands were feeling up Vinnie's legs, squeezing and testing. Vinnie tried to stand still under the examination, but he couldn't avoid some squirming. Charleston's fingers came to the outline of his cock, and Charleston took extra time to feel along Vinnie's bulge, reaching down to press his balls right through the fabric of the jeans. Vinnie sucked in a breath and struggled to just keep his mouth shut. Hell, right now he wanted a gag. Just when Vinnie was about to beg Charleston to strip him naked and fuck him already, Charleston moved on, running hands over Vinnie's chest and up his arms.

Vinnie was quickly discovering a new kink. Charleston's touch felt almost clinical, like the man was examining a new horse and trying to decide if it was worth riding. Vinnie half-expected Charleston to pry his mouth open and check his teeth, and Vinnie would not have protested.

Instead, Charleston took one of Vinnie's wrists and pulled it away from the wall and behind Vinnie's head. His other hand grabbed Vinnie's shoulder so hard that he hunched up from the pain.

"You don't need force, well, not unless you're enjoying it," Vinnie amended himself. Oddly, Charleston marched him to a corner instead of into the bedroom.

"Kneel," Charleston ordered.

Still not understanding the game, Vinnie did. Charleston grabbed his other hand and pulled it back behind his head as well. "Interlock your fingers." Vinnie obeyed. Charleston then pushed his head forward. "Your forehead will not come away from that wall and you will not move your hands, understood?"

"Yes, sir," Vinnie answered immediately. Oh shit. He'd thought Charleston had dominated him before, in school. He'd thought that having Charleston order him to the ground and do pushups was about the most helpless feeling in the world. Hell, Vinnie'd had men tie him hand and foot, and he still hadn't felt as totally helpless as he had when Charleston had been his commander in that damn school. But this... this was the most helpless Vinnie had ever felt in his life. He couldn't have moved if his life depended on it. His cock was so hard that it hurt, and he had to keep blinking away the tears that gathered in the corner of his eyes, but he kept his forehead against the wall as Charleston did something behind him.

Vinnie would have left the bondage equipment out if he'd known this was going to happen. Hell, he would have gone out and bought bondage equipment. Still, if Charleston wanted a scene, Vinnie had some interesting tools. He had several lengths of good rope. True, he'd been using it to tie a chair back together while the glue dried, but they were lying in the corner. And that chair he'd just got from the thrift store and fixed—it had solid wooden arms and a straight back that would be uncomfortable as hell if Charleston tied him tightly against it. His handcuffs were sitting on the glass and brass entertainment center, and those were high-quality, expensive ones. Vinnie hated the cheap play cuffs—he could always break them.

However, with his head in the corner, Vinnie couldn't see anything Charleston was doing. An odd thumping noise made him frown. Tilting his head, he tried to see something out of the corner of his eye. "Eyes forward," Charleston snapped, and Vinnie hurried to obey, but not before he'd seen Charleston thumping his boot along the baseboards like the apartment was a car and he was kicking the tires.

Charleston moved to stand right behind Vinnie, one hand resting on his head. "Can I trust you to hold position?"

Vinnie took a deep breath. "What are you going to do?" he asked carefully. As much as he wanted to obey, he wasn't sure he could if Charleston planned anything too adventurous. Vinnie was a wiggler, and he couldn't stop himself no matter how much he tried.

"Check out your bedroom," Charleston answered.

Vinnie groaned as his cock threatened to explode with lust. "Probably not," Vinnie admitted. He wanted to feel Charleston's bonds, and now he would. Was Charleston the sort to use the handcuffs or the rope? It said a lot about a man, which medium he chose to do his work. Handcuffs were fast, but not as versatile or artistic. Rope allowed for more creative tying, but a good submissive could wiggle free given enough time.

Charleston grabbed his wrists and pulled them around to the small of Vinnie's back. The sound of little ratcheting clicks warned Vinnie a half second before plastic pulled tight. Charleston had brought his own bondage equipment. Vinnie liked a man who came prepared. Plastic ties—just as secure as metal cuffs just as long as Vinnie didn't get to a pair of wire cutters, and less likely to over tighten and cause real damage. On the bad side, Vinnie couldn't wiggle and strain without really marking up his skin. Charleston pulled up on Vinnie's feet, and he was shocked when Charleston secured his ankles and then connected the two ties, effectively hogtying him.

"Can't use much other than my mouth like this," Vinnie pointed out with a smile over his shoulder. Charleston stood up and backed up enough to study Vinnie.

"Then try not to say something stupid enough that I have to gag you," Charleston advised him before heading into Vinnie's bedroom. Vinnie sighed as he found himself alone. With Charleston in the other room, Vinnie could look around. Every box was open, several books were laying out, the television and DVD player had both been moved enough for Vinnie to see the line of dust tracing their old positions. If Charleston was doing a military inspection, he was going to find a hell of a lot to complain about.

Vinnie shifted on his knees. Damn this was hot. Charleston hadn't even told him what he expected of Vinnie. No negotiations, no discussions. Yeah, Vinnie knew all the stuff about safe and sane. He knew he should have discussed a safeword and negotiated his lists of "wills" and "wont's." He knew that, but those sorts of negotiations always killed the mood for him. Truth be told, those leathermen in the bar were far more Vinnie's speed. If there hadn't been five of them, he would have been seriously tempted to wait out back and hook up for the night, no matter what RJ and Dan said.

Smart? Maybe not. He'd had one bad scare. When he was eighteen and still half-scared every time he'd wandered into a bar, a guy had tied him up and then insisted on barebacking. Vinnie had cried and begged. He'd gone to the clinic the next day and pleaded with the doctor to give him antibiotics to help him fight off the HIV virus if the asshole had passed it on to him. He'd lived in fear for five or six months. But he hadn't been able to deny his nature. He wanted to be dominated. Barebacking was about the only activity he put on his red list even though there were plenty he didn't particularly enjoy. The enjoyment was in watching a top lose all control and wallow in his own pleasure. Vinnie wondered what Charleston would look like when he came.

He watched as Charleston came out of the bedroom. "I don't bareback," Vinnie blurted.

Charleston looked at him with surprise, that one eyebrow lifting up. "Isn't it a little late to be negotiating terms?" he asked.

Vinnie smiled and gave a half-shrug that he aborted in the middle because of the hogtie. "I'm not one of those subs who negotiates. If you want it, I'll do it, but I'm not going to make it easy for AIDS to get me."

"At least you have some sense," Charleston said. He turned his back and headed for the kitchen. Vinnie could hear cupboards opening and closing.

"Are you going to leave me out here all day?" Vinnie shouted over all the banging. Charleston looked through the opening at Vinnie.

"I could always gag you. Actually, gagging you has been a fantasy of mine since you were a mouthy seventeen year old trying to talk your way out of punishment."

"Then do it," Vinnie said invitingly. Clearly Charleston was the sort of Dom who needed a little encouraging to really get into the groove, and that was fine. Vinnie was good at encouragement. Charleston walked out of the kitchen and into Vinnie's bedroom. Vinnie cringed at the wide range of possibilities for gags. Yeah, he had a nice ball gag in his toy drawer, but he knew some guys like to get really serious and use things like dirty underwear. Vinnie braced himself to just accept it and not throw up if it came to that. After all, getting fucked by Charleston would make about any price worth paying.

Charleston appeared with a scarf in his hand. Vinnie raised his eyebrows at that. No matter what the movies showed, scarves didn't make good gags. You could still talk—you just sounded like an old man with loose bridgework when you did it.

"Open up," Charleston ordered. Vinnie stomped down on his urge to complain and opened his mouth. In Charleston's defense, he did tie it tight enough that Vinnie left his mouth partially open to ease the strain on the corners of his lips.

Charleston turned to head back into the kitchen. "I can shtill talk," Vinnie said, his words muffled but understandable.

"Yep, and you can still breathe which is the bigger point, but that should remind you that I asked you not to," Charleston said. "And that ball gag is too large for your mouth. Get that jammed in behind your teeth during a jaw cramp, and you're going to be in for more pain that you really want to deal with, Bernardi."

Vinnie narrowed his eyes and was ready to argue that point, but Charleston pointed a finger at him. "Now be silent or you're going to be making up for aggravating me, and you probably won't like it." Vinnie sagged in his bonds and waited as Charleston went back to rummaging through his kitchen. This was definitely the oddest scene he'd ever had, and he'd had some odd ones. RJ always complained that the weird ones were drawn to him like a moth to a flame. Vinnie liked to point out that he was hot enough to qualify as a flame, but this time he was starting to wonder. Charleston hadn't even stripped him before hogtying him.

Charleston spent quite a bit of time in the kitchen before he came back out. He took one look around the room and then walked over to stand next to Vinnie, his hand resting on Vinnie's shoulder. Vinnie looked up, wondering what was next. When Charleston pulled out a knife, he sucked in a sharp breath.

"Now you're worried?" Charleston asked. "You need to worry before you're helpless, Bernardi, not after." Reaching down, he slipped the point of the knife in under the plastic ties and gave a sharp jerk. Vinnie grunted as the plastic dug into his wrists before it broke. His ankles were still tied, but his hands were free. Vinnie brought them around to the front and rubbed them, wondering if Charleston wanted some form of foreplay. Instead, Charleston stuck his knife back into his pocket. "Try and steer clear of trouble, Bernardi. I'd hate to go to your funeral." Without another word, Charleston turned and walked out. For several long minutes, Vinnie could only stare at the door and blink, wondering what the hell had just happened.

Chapter
Seven

IT TOOK Vinnie almost an hour to get everything back where it should be, but most of that was due to his own lax housekeeping. Charleston had systematically touched just about everything in the apartment, but most everything ended up within one inch of where it had started. He'd pulled boxes out of the bottom of Vinnie's closet and rifled through old Halloween costumes. The man had fingered his underwear, and Vinnie was trying very hard to not think about that.

"Buddy, you have got to get that guy out of your head before we really, truly fuck ourselves, because we will fuck ourselves long before he will fuck us," Vinnie told his own recalcitrant body. It didn't matter. His cock knew what it wanted. Vinnie could feel the deep ache as his desire sank so deep into him that he considered a quick trip to any bar other than RJ's. She might look out for him, even while pretending not to care, but there were bars where he could find cheap and abusive sex easily enough.

Reaching out to stroke his finger along the police cuff, Vinnie sighed. That wasn't what he actually wanted, though. "Right, time to pull out the old fantasies," Vinnie told himself firmly. Like Cary Grant as the devilishly handsome liar in *Suspicion*. That was a man he could lust after with abandon.

Stepmother number four or five had been into classic movies, and Vinnie was fairly sure she'd figured out he was gay long before he had. They'd sit on the couch together when Vinnie was eight or nine and watch perfectly groomed men save women who always wore heels and dresses when getting chased by knife-wielding psychos while trying to agree on which leading man was the cutest. She'd been one of the few stepmothers that he'd liked, although he wasn't actually sure she'd been a real stepmother. His father had learned early that prenuptial agreements had limits. If you married a woman, used your charm to emotionally eviscerate her, and then cheated, the prenup didn't hold up in court. His father had resorted to calling women Vinnie's stepmother and moving them in without actually marrying them. But Cynthia had been one of the few that Vinnie actually loved. When she'd left, her face streaked with mascara, Vinnie had hated his father, and he supposed that he'd never gotten over that.

So Vinnie still had his love of old movies and classic actors. Cary Grant had a lot of lust-worthy movies. Vinnie moved his hand down toward his cock, rubbing absent-mindedly as he imagined those dark eyes focused all on him. "There we go." Vinnie smiled and headed for his bedroom. His hand, his favorite vibrator, and he needed a little private time together. And if Charleston had touched his vibrator... well, he was going to try very hard to forget that little fact.

Pulling his blanket off, Vinnie settled in on his bed, his hand reaching down to undo his pants. Where was he? Cary Grant. The image of him in a wig for *I Was a Male War Bride* suddenly appeared, and Vinnie's lust scattered. "Fuck." Vinnie collapsed back on his pillows and stared at his stained ceiling. What had started as a small amoebae was quickly turning into a large brown blot that looked a little like a map of Russia. As much as he respected any man's right to dress up like a woman, that was not a kink that Vinnie had any interest in.

What he really wanted was to indulge in a fantasy of Charleston taking those police handcuffs and cuffing him to the bed. In seconds, his cock was hard again. He needed to come, but he was not going to keep indulging in these Charleston fantasies. As a fantasy, the man was hot as hell, but as a reality, he was terrifying and just a little strange. He'd gone through Vinnie's socks. Hell, Vinnie half expected the man to order him to refold everything to military specifications, and the sad part was that Vinnie would not have argued. There was just something in Charleston's gaze that truly did not allow for doubts or hesitation.

Okay, time for another fantasy. Vinnie smiled. Rudolph Valentino in *The Sheik*. Oh yes, that would do nicely. He squirmed out of his pants, kicking them to the floor as he leaned back against his pillows. His owner, a man with black eyes and a hook nose, had brought him to the sheik's tents, light filtering in through the flaps in the red, embroidered fabrics. Vinnie walked just behind him, respectful and silent. His owner had fallen in love with a dark-eyed girl he'd seen through the trees at the oasis, and now he would negotiate with her father.

He'd brought two horses, but the father leaned back against his gold and silver pillows and looked at his gathered men, laughing at the idea that he would trade his youngest daughter for such a paltry sum.

"I bring more." Vinnie's owner was desperate—a man in love. With a gesture, he ordered Vinnie forward, and Vinnie pulled out a bag of spices he carried for his owner. It was a symbol of how trustworthy he was as a slave that his owner allowed him to carry such valuable trade goods. He carefully laid the silk bag at the sheik's feet. Slowly the sheik's laugh faded, and he leaned forward. Vinnie's owner smiled and offered it all.

With a wave, the sheik summoned a man with a scale, and he set it up between the two groups. Vinnie's owner watched as the yellow spike spilled onto the scale, licking his lips as the dust rose, taking some finite amount away from the bride-price. It wouldn't be enough, and if it wasn't, there was just one thing he had left to barter. He looked over to where Vinnie knelt. Vinnie's hazel eyes and sun-bleached hair, his strong chin and his large hands... they would bring a good price in any slave auction. Vinnie was strong and obedient, and when he smiled, the rumor was that he could charm a Bedouin out of his last horse. He hated to part with such a loyal slave, but to win the girl of his dreams, he would surrender his boy.

Vinnie could feel himself sweat under his robes. He knew his owner understood the rules, and to be traded away would be... well, unthinkable would be too strong a term. Undesirable maybe. Vinnie held his breath as the sheik and his men discussed the offer. Finally, the older man answered with a slow shake of his head "no." It wasn't enough.

Vinnie's owner looked to him, and Vinnie could feel cold fear claw at him, even in the heat of the desert. He wanted to throw himself at his owner's feet and beg for mercy, but he couldn't. Instead he followed the silent order and moved forward to kneel carefully beside the scale. The men gathered in whispered talk again, huddled around the sheik. And then one figure stepped out.

His gray hair was covered by the traditional headcloth, but he was not a Bedouin. His blue eyes examined Vinnie, finding every hidden secret in one glance. Vinnie groaned. No, this wasn't the way it was supposed to go. But he couldn't deny the attraction as the stranger moved closer to him. He offered a single word, and the sheik raised his hand to accept the deal.

Vinnie's previous owner cried out in joy, and the sheik's man carefully gathered the spice in the scale. Vinnie was left kneeling at the feet of the stranger, suddenly afraid to look up into that sharp gaze. The man reached down and caught Vinnie under the chin, forcing his head up, and Vinnie held his breath. Slowly, the stranger gave a small smile and crouched down in front of Vinnie, running his hands over Vinnie's shoulders and wrapping his fingers around Vinnie's neck. Vinnie held very still and allowed the man to do as he liked. Was this man with the commanding personality his owner, or was the sheik?

"Storm Wolf?" the sheik asked. The man reached out and caught Vinnie's wrist with one hand and pulled a sash free from his waistband with the other. Vinnie sucked in his breath as the man the sheik had called Storm Wolf quickly tied his wrists together. Taking the end of the sash, Storm Wolf used it like a leash to pull Vinnie forward, but he pulled so hard and fast that Vinnie stumbled to his feet and crashed into Storm Wolf's solid form. The sheik and the others laughed, and Vinnie ducked his head in shame and fear. He'd displeased his masters.

Storm Wolf's arm came around his waist and pulled him in close. Before Vinnie could figure out what he was planning, Storm Wolf pulled the neck of Vinnie's robes back and bit him. He bit him hard enough that Vinnie cried out in surprise and pain. When Storm Wolf pulled back, he was smiling, and Vinnie was marked with a red bite, and his cock was hard with need.

The fantasy slipped through time, sliding past the wedding feast where Vinnie knelt at his new master's feet and took delicacies from his fingers. Vinnie's own hands were still tied and lying in his lap. Time didn't slow again until Storm Wolf led him to a private tent. Vinnie wanted to explain that he was a good and obedient slave who didn't need to be tied, but he couldn't seem to find the words. Storm Wolf would look at him, and Vinnie couldn't think past the raging need that made his cock swell and ache.

The inside of Storm Wolf's tent was thick with pillows and woven rugs, and he led Vinnie to the center. Normally Vinnie would prepare his master for bed, but with his hands tied, he didn't know what he was supposed to do. Storm Wolf pulled off his headdress and revealed gray hair still streaked with black. Moving so close that Vinnie would smell the coffee and mud that clung to his robes, Storm Wolf tangled his hands in Vinnie's robes, burrowing deeper and deeper until he touched bare flesh. Vinnie gasped, jerking his hands up, but Storm Wolf just pulled one of his own hands free and grabbed the bindings. Once again, Vinnie was utterly trapped and helpless. With a knowing smile, Storm Wolf tugged Vinnie into the center of the tent and then shoved him in the middle of the chest.

Vinnie fell back onto the pillows, his robes flying open because Storm Wolf had undone his sash at some point. He blushed, and his cock pressed up, only a single layer of white cloth hiding his interest. Bringing his hands up, Vinnie hid his eyes behind the bend of his elbow. He would have stayed like that except a hand firmly pulled his arm down, and Vinnie found himself looking into Storm Wolf's eyes. The man lay next to him, their bodies close. There were no words, only a warm palm resting against his cheek for a second, and then strong hands turned him, pulling his robes open and pulling at the fabric.

Vinnie gasped, clinging to the pillows and throwing his legs open. He didn't care if his new Master thought he was a whore, he needed his touch. Hands pulled his cheeks apart. Oil dripped over his back, his ass, down the crack where it heated and made Vinnie squirm until a sharp slap reminded him of his place. Reduced to helpless moans, Vinnie struggled to stay still as his master's cock pressed into him, claiming him.

The fantasy didn't get any farther before Vinnie cried out, coming all over his own hand. The vibrator he had pressed deep inside was still weakly humming, the batteries threatening to give out any second. Vinnie twisted the base to silence it, but for now he left it deep inside as he rolled to his side.

"Right... cast yourself as the sweet, obedient slave. I guess that's why they call it fantasy," Vinnie told himself with a derisive snort. Even when he wanted to be obedient, he hadn't been very good at it. Maybe that's why he had given it up. At least he had until that senior year when

Commander Charleston had come to the academy with his knowing eyes. And now.... Now what? Vinnie wished he had a clue. Either that, or he wished some tall, gray-haired Bedouin lord would walk in, tie his hands, and take control until Vinnie just learned to stop messing up.

Vinnie let his head fall back onto the pillow. God he was just screwed, and not in the good way.

Chapter
Eight

VINNIE dumped the wheelbarrow's contents to the floor, and he couldn't help but think that after this whole tiki beach night was over, he was going to have to sweep all this damn sand right back out again.

"I know that face." RJ sat on the edge of a table, one foot still on the ground, the other swinging loose. "You're about to do something really fucking stupid."

"Who, me?" Vinnie smiled and shook the wheelbarrow to make the sand slide out faster.

"You are trouble with a capital T."

"And that rhymes with P, and that stands for pool," Vinnie said cheerfully. She looked at him like he'd just lost his mind. "It's from *Music Man*," Vinnie explained.

She shook her head. "Distract all you want, babe. That does not change the fact that whatever bug crawled up your ass and died, the thing is rotting and threatening to give you gangrene."

"Such beautiful images you weave with your words." Vinnie turned to leave, but she stopped him by putting out a foot and putting all her weight on the edge of the wheelbarrow, forcing it back down to the ground. Vinnie looked at her.

"Stop bullshitting me. I may not be good with all this emotional crap," she waved an arm, "but I know when someone's on the verge of imploding."

"Maybe I just want to get back on stage. You fucking grounded me, RJ. You grounded me," Vinnie's voice threatened to crack. "I haven't been grounded in years."

"You haven't pulled a stunt like you did with that group of leathermen before. If you put yourself in the shit, you're going to come out stinking. Learn that rule now."

Vinnie took a step back and sank into a chair. "I just had a bad night, RJ. If you let me back up on stage, I won't pull a stunt like that again."

RJ studied him, and Vinnie squirmed under her gaze. Vinnie had heard stories about RJ. She had a big strap on cock, and more than one boy had been bent over a table for her, and they were all pretty unanimous in their admiration for her ability to give a man a hard fucking.

Sometimes he could almost imagine that she was a man, that she could push him down and make him suck her cock, and not one made out of silicone. He knew he really did want a biological man, someone whose cock would get dark and swollen, someone who would come with a shout, his juice sour in Vinnie's mouth. But as much as he really did want that, when RJ looked at him, he knew he'd go to his knees for her if she ordered it. The need for orders was growing like a wave that he couldn't seem to ride. It kept swallowing him whole.

She leaned forward. "I see you pull that again, and I'm going to do more than ground you."

Vinnie looked up. "RJ, I need this job." Fear crawled through his stomach. If he couldn't come up with money for rent and food, he would be too damn tempted to go back to his father and his trust fund and all the rules that came with those two things. He imagined his older sister's face when Vinnie came crawling home. Actually, he wouldn't even be Vinnie anymore. Pathetic little Troy Martello would crawl home to Daddy Martello. Vinnie would disappear. "I really need this job," Vinnie repeated for good measure.

"Then you follow my rules," she said firmly. Vinnie nodded, agreeing without even a comment. For a long time, she just looked at him, and Vinnie had to fight to avoid squirming like a bug caught under a glass.

"Does this mean I can go on stage tonight?" he finally asked.

She sighed and took her foot off the wheelbarrow, but Vinnie waited. She was still watching him with that hawk-like gaze of hers, the one that suggested he did not have permission to leave. "Fine, you can dance third on the lineup. I swear, sometimes I think I should just put a leash on you."

Vinnie blinked in surprise. For a second, he thought she was joking, but she looked deadly serious. "Wrong body parts here," he said with a laugh.

"I could take out a loan on the bar and buy you a sex change operation. You'd make a pretty little butch girl."

Vinnie just stared at her, not sure what the hell to say. He liked his cock. A lot. A whole lot. She gave a huge snort. "And the fucking terrifying thing is that you aren't even arguing." Shaking her head, she slid off the table, and stood right in front of Vinnie, her hand resting on his shoulder.

"Hey, I would not sign up for any castration or sex changes. I was just trying to find where all the brain cells had scattered to when the total and utter fear set in," Vinnie said, trying to pass it off as a joke. He took a long look at his boss. She was wearing leather pants and a frayed jean jacket over a T-shirt from an old rock concert. Her short hair stood up in graying spikes, and her face had hard angles normally found in a man. In the right light, she was handsome.

"You know I wouldn't object to the leash as long as you left all my body parts attached when you were done," he said slowly. Maybe Vinnie should look closer to home for a partner who could fuck him well enough to drive Charleston right out of his fantasies. He gave her his best coy look.

She rolled her eyes. "If cocks did it for me, you'd end up chained to the end of my bed every night, but as much fun as cocks can be to torture, they're a little like carousels—a hell of a lot of fun when you're in the mood, but not something you want sitting around in your living room."

"I think I should be offended."

"Get over it," she advised. "Listen, if you need help getting your head out of your ass, I am here. So, let's talk about what that means."

Leaning back in the chair, Vinnie closed his eyes. "This isn't going to be another safe subbing lecture is it? I mean, Dan already gave me that one. Actually, he told me to just start masturbating more, which is the ultimate in safe sex, even if it gets a little boring."

Vinnie opened his eyes and scooted back on the chair when RJ put her boot right between his legs and rested it on the edge of his chair. Her steel toes were entirely too close to his balls for comfort. "Well, I tried letting you subbie boys work it out. Clearly that didn't take because you're still crawling around here looking like someone kicked your puppy." She narrowed her eyes and studied him. "Or maybe it's that you look like the puppy that got kicked." Vinnie glared at her, but she just patted his cheek. "So, let me make this clear. You fuck up again, and you're going to have two choices: get out of my bar or take my punishment."

"Your punishment?" Vinnie had to work to keep his voice steady.

She shrugged. "I think you need a good whipping and some time in chains to get your head set back on straight. Danny over there thinks that you're a little too vanilla for that. He thinks you're still just a soft gray bandana—a little bondage, a little role-play, and then a quick orgasm. So we have a little bet, don't we, Danny?" RJ called to the bartender.

He didn't even pause as he counted bottles. "Yep," he agreed.

"If you fuck up again, I'm going to put you in chains and find out which of us is right. Got it?"

Vinnie swallowed and nodded. RJ patted his cheek again and walked toward the back, cursing when her boot slipped on the sand already scattered across the old wooden floor. Before Vinnie could gather his thoughts and get control over his shaking knees, Dan came over and dropped into the chair next to him, offering a bottle of water. Vinnie took it gratefully. Suddenly, his mouth was very dry.

"I couldn't hear the first part. She offered to get you a sex change, didn't she?" Dan asked.

Vinnie nodded. "How'd you know?"

Dan gave a little laugh. "Nothing makes a man go whiter than when a top he really admires asks him to do something he absolutely can't do. That and I know she made that threat with me ten years ago."

Vinnie looked over in surprise. Dan and RJ were best friends, but he just couldn't see that. Dan was physically twice RJ's size and about as masculine as a man could get. "No offense, but you'd make an ugly woman."

"Don't I know it? Besides, Evan would have someone's hide hanging from the wall if I came home with my equipment missing," Dan said, reaching down to adjust his crotch. Vinnie felt a familiar flash of jealousy. Oh, he didn't necessarily want the sort of forever relationship Evan and Dan had, but knowing that someone felt possessive of him, that would be nice. Dan looked towards the back. "She needs to find herself a woman who likes a hard whipping."

"If the alternative is her cutting my boys off, I'm all for more lesbian sex," Vinnie agreed, grabbing his own crotch.

Dan looked at him oddly for a second, and then his expression vanished as he cleared his throat. "So, are you planning on pushing her?"

"Pushing?"

"Doing anything that stupid ever again," Dan clarified.

"Me? No way. I am not suicidal, no matter how much my stupidity occasionally makes me seem like I am."

Dan's expression was still deliberately neutral. "You know if you do fuck up, she's only going to give you two choices. She is not the sort of person who goes back on her word."

"Yeah, I know." Vinnie knew he'd take her punishment before he'd walk away from this job. Yeah, it wasn't the best job in the world, but it was the first one where people knew him—where he was the submissive gay man with the adorable smile and not just one of the many masks he'd created for himself.

Most of his teachers had seen the "charming trouble" mask—the boy who just needed some help to stop screwing up. Headmasters and administrators typically got his "juvenile delinquent in training" mask. He'd managed to get kicked out of three military schools and probably would have been kicked out of Colyer Academy if Charleston hadn't shown up. Vinnie had made fun of the man the school had been named after, Wilbur Colyer, the very first time he'd met the headmaster. The man had turned red as a beet. Too many people saw him as his father's son, slotting him in as the poor little neglected boy with the father known throughout the country for his lack of morals. Others just assumed Vinnie would be a chip off the old block. They were all masks. Charleston had been the first to see past the masks, but RJ had been the first person to give him a place to be himself. He wouldn't give that up.

"If she punishes you, you won't like it," Dan warned. "RJ can make a whipping feel as good as any top in the state, but if she has to punish you, she's going to make it hurt."

Vinnie held up his hands. "You're preaching to the choir, because I don't want to end up with whip marks down my back. I promise to be a good little boy."

Dan's expression turned worried, but he didn't say anything. He stood up and headed back to the bar, leaving Vinnie to finish his work setting up the new theme before he finally got to go back on stage.

Chapter
Nine

VINNIE adjusted the padding in his G-string, listening to the heavy beat of the dance music. Michael was out there now, and the crowd was just starting to get rowdy.

Funny. Vinnie had a job that lots of gay men fantasized about, and yet the fantasy had become just one more job that had to get done. He had the third spot tonight, so the crowd would be a little drunk, a little grabby. He thought going out on stage would settle him, would give him a chance to get the attention that usually made him feel centered. When people were looking at him, it was like he could control how they saw him, what conclusions they drew. But now, faced with a chance to get back on stage for the first time in over a week, he just felt jittery.

RJ had the place set up like a tiki bar complete with sand an inch deep on the floor and bamboo rail around the dance stage, so there would be extra straight women and extra tip money. Theme nights always seemed to make them feel more welcome to come and ogle, and normally that was fine with Vinnie. He liked ogling. He worked hard to have a body worthy of serious-ass ogling. However, tonight he wished that he didn't have to perform for them. The straight women with their catcalls would get some of the men worked up enough to follow suit. Vinnie was definitely going to get a little extra lusting after along with the tips.

And instead of thinking about the audience or the exotic setup, all Vinnie could think about was the hours he was going to spend trying to sweep the sand out of corners come Monday when the bar closed. He might have begged off and let one of the other dancers take his slot, only

RJ would never let him hear the end of it after he'd practically begged to get back on stage. RJ was about out of patience, and Vinnie was not going to use up any more just because he couldn't get his head screwed on straight. He was going to do his job and do it well. Period.

The music ended and Michael came back, a grimace on his face. "There is sand everywhere. Everywhere, I tell you, including parts that are not fond of sand." Michael was pulling at his G-string and making an ugly face. "The next time RJ has a cute idea, I'm calling in sick."

"Bad?" Vinnie asked. The look Michael gave him made it pretty clear that the tiki bar had not been the best idea RJ ever had. Science fiction week had been fun with the strobes and the florescent body paint, but sand in cracks was not Vinnie's idea of good pain.

"Have fun," Michael said with a sarcastic tone and a generous wave of his arm toward the stage door. The sound system was pumping out the same low drumming that was used between each of the dances until Tom and his big finale. Think sexy thoughts. Think… Vinnie sighed. Face it, he had to think about Charleston. The man was hot. Terrifying but hot. Maybe he was hot because he was terrifying. God knows, back when he was still wallowing in denial, he had gone for girls who were scary enough to break him into little tiny pieces. At the time, he told himself that he picked scary girls because that was all he had to choose from. It took a scary girl to challenge the nearly all-boy system at the academy, but now, Vinnie was fairly sure he just liked scary. The leathermen had been hot, and in terms of females, RJ was about as hot as they came, and all of them were scary as hell.

The music shifted, and the familiar strains of INXS's "Need You Tonight" began. The singer started, "'All you got is this moment. Twenty-first century's yesterday'."

Vinnie opened the door and stalked out onto stage, his long toes digging into the sand. The lights had heated it so he could almost imagine he was on a beach instead of in Maryland. Two women right up against the stage laughed and beckoned him with gestures, but Vinnie played hard to get, choosing the other side of the stage to work first. The singer crooned, "So slide over here," and Vinnie slid his one leg so far out that he almost did the splits before leaning all his weight onto his right leg and then looking over his shoulder at the ladies. They'd be the real tippers. The singer mentioned raw moves, and Vinnie let his hand stroke down over his groin. Think sexy. Think sexy. Think Charleston standing on a beach with a gun in hand and a dangerous expression on his face.

"'I need you tonight....'" The sound warbled in Vinnie's ears as all his blood rushed to his head... or away from his head, maybe. Shock rocked him so badly that Vinnie lost his balance and fell forward onto his knees, his legs still spread. Charleston raised his beer in a sarcastic salute and for a half second, Vinnie thought he was imagining it. Maybe he'd done so much fantasizing about Charleston just randomly showing up that he was hallucinating. One of the waiters stopped at Charleston's table, checking with him, and Charleston waved him away without taking his eyes off Vinnie. Vinnie's cock started aching. With the stuffing in there, it definitely didn't have enough room in its tight prison.

The song was to the part where the singer claimed to be lonely before Vinnie's brain caught up with the fact that he was still on stage. He still had a job to get done. If he had still been Troy Martello, that pathetic boy who hid from his father's disapproval by courting it, channeling it, constantly giving his father and everyone else something to disapprove of... that boy would have curled up and died. But Vinnie Bernardi knew how to play with a Dom.

Since he was already on his knees, Vinnie arched his back and let his hands travel up to his chest. He'd worn his black harness with the black rip-away pants, but Vinnie definitely wasn't going to rush this strip. Instead he leaned back, resting his palms on the hot sand as he writhed in half-pleasure and half-pain. His cock definitely needed more room.

By the time the song got back around to "slide over here," Vinnie slid to the very edge of the stage, dragging sand with him so that it fell like a small waterfall. Holding the vertical bar, Vinnie reached out with a bare foot and rested it on the bench where the audience sat, right between two of the men. It was dangerous. If he touched a patron, he technically was breaking the law. God knows the morals police spent more time watching for that in the gay bars. Across the bar, RJ had a look of thunder on her face, but Vinnie arched his back and gave the room a hungry look before pulling himself back up toward the stage. Getting up, Vinnie twisted and slid down the stage, his eyes first caught by the sight of Charleston watching him and then moving away, denying Charleston the right to be the center of his attention.

Turning to face a small group of women who'd gathered near the stage, Vinnie danced for them. His muscles strained against his leather harness, and he was so horny that he would have let Charleston take him right there on stage, and Vinnie let all that flow through him. RJ sometimes joked that he looked like a dark god of gay with his nearly black hair and sultry expression, and he let that energy rush through him. He let his hands travel over his chest and his hips. He teased the women, running his finger over the tie that would undo his pants.

They screamed and held up bills, trying to tempt him to break the law and slide just close enough for them to touch. He threw his head back and let himself move to the music, striding down the stage and choosing a large man in a leather jacket to focus on for a second. Vinnie invited him in with a dark gaze, tilting his hips and undulating to the music. The man leaned forward.

"Strip, boy," he ordered loudly. Vinnie pulled the string and let the two halves of his pants peel away. His cock was pressing out, pushing against the padding so that Vinnie was obscenely large and dangerously close to breaking the law because his G-string was really pushed to the limit. Vinnie spun slowly, rolling his shoulders to the beat as he searched for Charleston. He had moved.

Vinnie lost the beat for a second, and his foot slipped on the sand. There. Near the backstage door. Oh yeah, Charleston planned to track him down after his performance. Vinnie moved to one of the vertical bars, holding it and leaning back so that his back arched and the bar pressed against his hard erection. Pain and pleasure in perfect proportion. He was sweating now, and his hand slid on the bar. "What do you think? Can't think at all." The music caught Vinnie, and he slowly went to his knees, sliding down the cool bar and feeling the hot sand under his knees. His cock hurt, and Vinnie pressed closer to the bar, groaning as his need to come and his need to not come on stage crashed into each other.

Reaching up, he ran his hand behind his neck, struggling with the lust that had wrapped around him. The song finally ended, faded out into the complex drums of the music RJ used between sets when the tip boys picked up the tips from the jars at the edge of the stage. For a second, Vinnie couldn't get up. His body was coiled so tightly that it refused to obey him. Finally he lifted his one leg up and around so that he could roll onto his stomach. The sand stuck to his sweat-slick body, but he ignored that, blowing the women at the edge a kiss and a wink before he got up, grabbed his pants and strolled back toward the prep area.

"Damn, trying for Tom's spot in the finale?" Brock asked him.

"Just feeling the groove," Vinnie said with a grin as he headed for the dressing area. Charleston had actually beaten him there. He was standing, leaning against the door with body language that told everyone he had a right to be here.

"Charleston," Vinnie offered, his grin widening.

"Problem, Bernardi?" Charleston glanced down at Vinnie's G-string.

"I can take care of it… unless you're interested in doing a little problem solving." Vinnie put his hands behind his back, rocked up on his toes, and waited. Shit. Where the hell was he getting all this cocky from? Yeah, he could play a good game, but this…. Vinnie was impressing himself.

"Don't let me stop you," Charleston said with a casual air, but Vinnie wasn't fooled. The man's body was tight—his arm muscles bulged as he strained to keep them crossed. Vinnie put an extra swing in his step as he headed for the back stall. The sand was gathering deep into uncomfortable cracks, but he kept his gait steady. There was something inherently erotic about enduring a little pain to give Charleston a better show, and Vinnie put on a show until he closed the stall door. How long should he play this out? He imagined giving himself a long, slow wank until Charleston was finally frustrated enough to slam the door to the stall open, grab Vinnie by the back of the neck and take him.

Stepping out of his G-string, Vinnie imaged that—his hands flat on the cold tile, Charleston pounding into him from behind. Taking his erection in hand, Vinnie gasped as he almost immediately began to come. Heat flooded his body, and embarrassment quickly followed. Damn. He hadn't had issues with premature ejaculation since he was fifteen. But something in Charleston's gaze just bored through all the cocky layers that Vinnie showed the world and got right down to his desperate need to have someone look at him with some approval. Maybe it was because Charleston knew his name. The Native Americans might have been onto something when they kept their real name secret from everyone for fear of giving their power away. By knowing Troy Martello, Charleston knew some secret part of Vinnie. The power was lying there, waiting for Charleston to take it, and Vinnie wanted him to.

Vinnie took time to calm down and let his body cool. He had to go back out there eventually, and either Charleston would be there waiting or he wouldn't. Vinnie couldn't control that because controlling or even predicting Charleston was like trying to control a winter storm. He went where he wanted. Vinnie sure as hell never expected him to show up at this place.

Flushing and picking up his G-string, Vinnie walked out into the dressing room naked as the day he was born. Charleston was still there, leaning against the door frame.

Vinnie just headed over to the chair next to his bag. "Can I help you?" He put one foot up on the chair and took a towel to all the cracks and crevasses where sand had gathered. He expected Charleston to look away in embarrassment, but the man watched, his gaze just as sharp and focused as when he had watched Cadet Martello perform pushups. One mistake in the form, and the pushup wouldn't count. But if he could do it perfectly, Charleston would count off one more number toward some impossible total. Charleston had a real talent at picking a number high enough that Vinnie never thought he'd make it but low enough that he always did just by the hair of his chin. Vinnie dropped his towel and squared off against Charleston, waiting.

"Are you through?"

Vinnie frowned, caught off guard. "Through with what? The night?" The tone had been a little sharp for that, but Vinnie couldn't figure out what else Charleston meant. "No, I help with clean up."

"I meant are you through attempting to manipulate some response out of me," Charleston asked.

Tom walked in the room at that moment, and he froze, looking from one of them to the other. No one moved. "Man, not to interrupt, but I have to get changed."

"No problem," Charleston said, his tone perfectly friendly, as if they were just three men who had run into each other at the basketball courts. "Vinnie, would you like to meet me outside in fifteen minutes?" That might have been a question, but Vinnie got the idea that he would need one hell of a good excuse to get out of it.

"I'll have to ask RJ."

"The man in the jean jacket who was glaring murder at you for your antics up there?" Charleston asked, and he still had that perfect calm going for him. Tom frowned in confusion, but he slid past Charleston to get into the room. He then stood fingering his bag, clearly unwilling to undress with this particular audience.

"Actually, she's the woman in the jean jacket who was glaring murder at me for my antics," Vinnie corrected Charleston. He was rewarded with a single flash of surprise. Then the emotion vanished, and Charleston was his stone-faced self. The man must be a real bastard to play poker against.

"I'll be waiting for you out back," Charleston said, and then he simply walked out of the room and toward the door to the alley.

Tom whistled. "Whoa. Are you okay, Vinnie? That guy does not look like someone to fuck with."

"I'm hoping that I'm more than okay, and I'm really, really hoping he is someone to fuck with or get fucked by." Vinnie smiled at Tom and pulled on his jeans as fast as he could. Shit. RJ. Vinnie had the feeling that if he went out there, she was going to rip him a new asshole, and he just needed a little more time to figure this all out. Obviously, his interest in Charleston was not as one-sided as he thought. Grabbing a pad of paper, he scrawled a quick note telling RJ that he was going to talk to someone and that he would be right back. Vinnie thought about adding a line about accepting whatever punishment she handed out, but he figured that was probably pushing things. Instead, he signed his name and folded it in half.

"Tom? When Brock gets off, can you have him run this out to RJ?" He held the note out. He didn't even wait to hear the answer before he headed out into the parking lot to see how much temptation Charleston could take.

Chapter
Ten

THERE were a few men drifting through the parking lot as Vinnie came out. RJ kicked people's asses if she found them hooking near her place, but that didn't mean they weren't doing it. It just meant they generally kept it just far enough away from her to avoid notice. There was a man under one of the perimeter trees, in the deep shadow. His hand was in his pants, and Vinnie recognized him as one of the regulars who propositioned the dancers as they left. Since Vinnie usually walked home late, he knew the guy, but he'd stopped making lewd offers just as soon as he'd figured out that Vinnie was more like competition for the big, strong men than he was a potential partner. When the leathermen left, Vinnie was guessing he was going to make a play for one of them.

Charleston was leaning on the hood of a fairly new car, his foot resting on the bumper. "With me," he ordered tersely before he turned and headed across the parking lot.

Vinnie smiled. Well, shit. How many times had he heard Charleston give him that same order in that same tone of voice? Once the other instructors figured out that Charleston knew how to handle their favorite problem child, they'd called Charleston in for every one of Vinnie's offenses, real or imagined. He couldn't count the number of times Charleston had shown up at the door to the math room, his eyes finding Vinnie right before he issued a curt, "With me."

Back then, those two words had promised worlds of pain and the slight glimmer of hope that he might get a "not bad, Martello." Of course, back then, Vinnie had still been underage, and Charleston was so very fond of his rules. Now, though, Vinnie was a full grown man, and if Charleston wanted to offer something more intimate than an order to do pushups, he would be more than happy to oblige.

Charleston stopped near an old truck parked at the very edge of the parking lot where the concrete edge crumbled into the grass. Vinnie smiled as he stopped inches from Charleston. "You called?" Vinnie asked with a cheeky grin.

For a long minute, Charleston stared at the truck, giving Vinnie a nice view of his wide back. Damn the man had muscles. Vinnie desperately wanted to reach out and run his hands up that strong body, but that wasn't how the game was played. Oh, Vinnie manipulated and topped from the bottom as often as he could get away with it. He was flat out naughty. However, Charleston had always demanded obedience, and Vinnie did prefer a partner who didn't let him get away with his games. So, he kept his hands to himself and waited for Charleston to make the first move. Or the second, actually. The first move had definitely been tracking Vinnie down to the club.

"What the hell is your problem, Martello?" Charleston demanded, emphasizing Vinnie's real name just to rub in that he knew it. Vinnie felt a frisson of lust roll through him at the dangerous game they were playing.

"I guess that depends. If you want me to get hard in the next hour or so, I'd say that's going to be a problem, but I'm young. I recover fast."

Charleston twisted around, and Vinnie sucked in a breath and took a fast step back. Even in the dim light that leaked through the dark from the distant streetlights, Charleston looked furious. In all the time he'd known Charleston, he'd never seen the man show any emotion, but now his whole body vibrated with a fury that scared the shit out of Vinnie. He didn't even breathe.

"What the hell do I have to do to get you to back off? Are you going to keep pushing until I hurt you?" Charleston took a step forward, and Vinnie tried to fall back, but Charleston's hand darted out and neatly caught him, yanking him forward.

"Hey, I am not normally into pain. I mean, if it takes some to help a partner get his end off, sure, but that is just not my kink," Vinnie hurried to say. Charleston flung him toward the end of the truck, where the tailgate was already down, and Vinnie didn't even try to fight. He'd seen Charleston take down four and five cadets at a time during combat training, and he sure as hell hadn't taught any of them the moves he used to do it. Catching himself on the edge of the tailgate, Vinnie just looked over his shoulder and waited to see what Charleston had in mind. The fact was, he was up for almost anything the guy had in mind. And if it was a little scary, Vinnie could handle that because he trusted Charleston more than he'd trusted anyone in his whole damn life. The man never pushed Vinnie harder than Vinnie was willing to be pushed. "Okay, this is your game, just let me know where we're going, okay?" Vinnie asked softly, ducking his head submissively. Yeah, he was mouthy, but he also knew how to play a good sub.

Charleston pulled something out of his pocket and threw it on the truck bed in front of Vinnie. Vinnie looked at the small bundle of crimped and bent wires.

"You want to explain this?"

Vinnie frowned. "No, not really."

Charleston pressed up behind him, his body trapping Vinnie against the back of the truck, and he sucked in a hard breath. "Think again, Bernardi. I really don't think you want to piss me off." He whispered the words into Vinnie's ear, but the power and anger still came through loud and clear.

"This much? No, I probably don't," Vinnie agreed. A little anger was an aphrodisiac, but this much was just too fucking terrifying. Vinnie's balls were trying to crawl back up into his body. "If you want to role play something, I'm up for it, but you need to give me a hint at the script."

"I don't role play, Bernardi."

"Why does that not surprise me?" Vinnie tried to put on a silly grin, but fear was still twisting his features, and he could feel his grin turn to a grimace. If he were as powerful as Charleston, he'd never role play, either. "Keeping in mind that you've pretty well intimidated me into stupidity, maybe you could explain what you want in very short sentences using very small words," Vinnie suggested.

"You aren't that easily intimidated," Charleston answered, but that emotionless mask was back. Vinnie was almost more afraid now because he didn't know what emotions were lurking behind it, and Charleston still had him very effectively pinned. "So explain to me why you bugged my phone after we had a very serious conversation about the inadvisability of invading my privacy."

"Bugging?" Vinnie's voice went unmanly high.

Charleston simply raised one eyebrow and waited. Vinnie felt about seventeen again as Charleston gave him the silent treatment. Unfortunately, the silent treatment clearly still worked.

"That was not me. All my kinks have to do with watching you, which explains the tree and the camera. I mean, yeah, you have a sexy voice, but face it: you're just this side of a functional mute. I could tape you for three months and get a dozen words—and most of those would be 'no'. I mean, I'm all kinds of stupid, but I do not do shit like that without at least a hope of a big payoff." Vinnie stopped when Charleston slapped a hand down on the bed of the truck, the slap seeming to echo against the sides.

Then Charleston put his hands on Vinnie's shoulders and flipped him around. "That wasn't you?"

With Charleston staring right at his face, Vinnie found he couldn't speak at all. He just shook his head. Slowly, the fingers that had been digging into his arms loosened, and Charleston stepped back.

Vinnie shifted uncomfortably, not really liking the way the mood had inexplicably shifted. "Did you enjoy the show?" he asked, twitching his body invitingly. Charleston didn't even look at him—he had his gaze focused off on the distant horizon. "I do private shows," Vinnie offered.

"Go back inside and stay there," Charleston ordered.

"What?" Vinnie frowned. This was not the direction he'd expected the conversation to take. If Charleston liked it rough, Vinnie was not wimping out on him. "Hey, you're nowhere near my limits. I can play rough if that's what you want," he offered, moving in on Charleston. He stopped an inch from the man, not sure he should initiate contact. Charleston struck him as the sort of man who liked to be the one to start things… and to finish them.

Charleston looked up at him, his eyes strangely gray in this low light. Vinnie was shocked to realize he'd gained an inch on the man at some point, either that or he'd been too intimidated by Charleston to notice that he was taller. But that didn't make sense because Vinnie was feeling pretty damn intimidated right now, and Charleston was just a little shorter. "Go inside and stay there. I'll call you if there's a problem."

"Problem?" Vinnie knew he sounded stupid, but he was not tracking this conversation. Instead of explaining anything, Charleston reached out and caught him by the arm, shoving him toward the club. "Get inside, now." The voice made Vinnie flinch. That was the voice that promised ultimate pain if it was disobeyed. Vinnie had disobeyed it exactly once, when Charleston had ordered him to peel about a million potatoes to make up for some prank that had ruined a batch of gravy. Vinnie had flat out refused. He'd even offered in a saccharine voice to call his father and have the old man send out a servant to do that sort of menial and worthless labor. The second Vinnie had seen the cook's face, he'd felt like a shit, and the look on Charleston's face had frozen him in place.

Adolescent pride had forced Vinnie to stick to his guns, and Charleston had walked away. He'd refused to even look at Vinnie, and all the little touches had vanished. The hands holding his feet during sit ups and the little punches on the arm as Charleston told him to shape up and even the way Charleston would flick his ear with a finger so hard that tears would come to his eyes or slap him upside the back of the head when Vinnie said something stupid—they'd all vanished. Vinnie had twisted in misery until he'd finally snuck out of the dorms and down into the kitchens. The pile of potatoes had grown by at least half, but Vinnie had sat there all night and peeled those stupid potatoes until his hands cramped.

Charleston never mentioned it, but at breakfast, he'd tossed Vinnie a banana loaded with potassium—good for sore muscles. And during pull ups, when Vinnie's hands had failed him, Charleston had been there with a firm grip around Vinnie's thighs to help lift him to the bar.

Right now, Charleston was using that "do not fuck with me" voice. Vinnie turned around and headed for the club, a jog covering the distance between the far edge of the parking lot and the door in no time. When he got to the door, he turned around, but Charleston and his truck were gone.

Chapter
Eleven

VINNIE moved through the crowd watching Tom dance. It really was
unfair that a straight man had moves as good as Tom, but it meant that
most of the customers were distracted. He almost made it to the dressing
room before RJ seemed to appear out of nowhere. "My office. Now."

Cringing, Vinnie headed for RJ's office, following her. Shit, shit,
shit. Okay, so the whole putting his foot near the customers was a little
borderline. That could have turned out badly, but it didn't. And Vinnie
hadn't tried that trick near any of the grabby women, so it wasn't like he
intended to break the law. Mentally, Vinnie practiced his defense until
they reached RJ's office.

It was a small room made even smaller by six file cabinets that took
up about a third of the floor space and stacks of supplies that took up
most of the rest. An old metal desk with RJ's laptop and a tiny space for
a visitor to perch on a stool were the only spaces not taken up by storage.
RJ had to turn sideways to squeeze between the desk and a towering
stack of paper towel boxes. "Sit," she ordered.

Vinnie dropped down onto the stool. RJ seemed to be ready to
break a tooth she was clenching her jaw so hard, and Vinnie hurried to
defend himself. "I was careful about who I got close to, RJ. You know I
would never break the law in your place." From the look on RJ's face,
that had been a mistake. Vinnie swallowed the rest of his argument and
just waited.

For a second, she stared at him so furiously that Vinnie was sure he
was about to get fired. Then, with a sigh, she started shaking her head.

"Easiest twenty dollars I ever won."

"What?"

She sagged back into her chair. "The bet I made with Dan. He thought you just needed a talking to. I said that you were a sub desperate for a good whipping and that if I put down the challenge, you would find a way to talk yourself into trouble. I just didn't expect you to put my whole bar at risk by doing something that fucking stupid. You do not touch customers on stage. I tattoo that rule into my dancers' brains, and I'm wondering what it's going to take for you to remember that. I understand that you need some punishment. I don't understand you taking a risk that could have pulled down fines big enough to close this place down."

"I didn't touch anyone," Vinnie said.

"You put yourself in a position to be touched."

"But I wasn't near the women who would have made a grab for me."

RJ glared at him, and Vinnie could taste the bile rise in his mouth, but he managed to just shut up. So far, it seemed like RJ planned to whip him and not fire him, so he wasn't going to push it with her. She scrubbed a hand through her spiked hair and then leaned back in the chair. "Do you trust drunk men, Vinnie?" she asked slowly.

"What? No way."

RJ nodded. "Okay, then were you out front to see how many drinks each of those men had consumed?"

Vinnie groaned as he saw the trap. "No, but…." He started to point out that they hadn't been acting drunk, but RJ held up her hand to stop him.

"So, you put yourself in a position where you couldn't protect yourself with two men when you had no idea whether or not they were drunk. If one of them had reached out or shifted or even leaned to the side, you would have made physical contact with a customer from the stage."

"Which would have been bad—"

"Which would have been illegal," RJ snapped. "You would have been in a jail cell in a pair of tear-away pants and a harness. I would have been fined enough money to strip this place of all the profit for the next three weeks, and if we were really unlucky, they would have slapped a sign on the front door and everyone would have been out of work."

"They didn't touch me." Vinnie wasn't as confident now. At the time, he'd been focused on Charleston, and all those other realities hadn't quite sunk in.

"Luckily," she snapped. "Don't fucking depend on luck, Vinnie. She's a bitch, and she'll shove a knife in your back the second she can. You fucking take care of yourself. Got it?" RJ leaned forward and slapped her hands on the desk so hard that her half-open laptop flopped closed.

Vinnie nodded.

"Now, I'm honestly too pissed off to whip you tonight. You fucking well need to learn how to ask for punishment instead of acting out."

Opening his mouth, Vinnie tried to answer, but he really didn't have one. He'd wanted Charleston to pay attention to him, but he really didn't want to bring that up. After the leatherman incident, RJ had been more than clear about the fact that he was supposed to keep irresponsible and stupid flirting out of her bar. "I want to keep working here," he finally said.

RJ nodded. "Monday morning I plan to tie you to that stage and then take a whip to your back until you finally open up about whatever is eating you from the inside. We are then going to spend a little time getting your head back on straight, so you bring a few changes of clothes because you will be at my place until Wednesday or Thursday, understand?"

Vinnie nodded. Part of him shivered in anticipation at the idea of being under someone's control for that long, but no matter how much that part wanted to submit, there was still a little part of Vinnie that didn't want it to be RJ. He wanted to be controlled by a man, and he knew that RJ would rather have a woman under her thumb. Vinnie nearly laughed; this situation was fucked up in so many ways. However, she was right that he had put himself in this position, and he was going to suck it up and deal. "Am I working this weekend?" Vinnie asked.

For a second, she could only look at him with shock in her face that he'd found the balls to ask something like that. Vinnie cringed, wishing he could just erase his words. Fuck. She sighed and rubbed her hand over her head again. "Staff off stage. If you want to work, you do dishes in back. You stay away from customers. If you don't want to do that, then you spend the next couple of nights at home thinking about just how badly you've managed to get yourself twisted around. I swear, if you weren't so cute and sweetly submissive, I would have kicked your ass right out my door already."

RJ got up and came out from behind the desk. "Sweetly submissive?" Vinnie asked, disbelieving. He was a hell of a lot of things—argumentative, naughty, manipulative, and screwed up were all near the top of the list, but submissive was a distant fifth or sixth and sweet wasn't even on the list. RJ stopped and put a hand against his cheek. RJ wasn't normally one for tender gestures, and the hand seemed to hold Vinnie in place.

"You're the most fucking submissive man I've met since Danny out there. And if you keep looking at me with those big eyes of yours, I'm going to start calling around and getting prices on that sex change operation for you. Go home." With that, RJ gave his face a little slap before she turned around and headed back out to the bar.

Sitting on the stool, Vinnie listened to the music end for Tom's first set. The customers were yelling… or the women were, anyway. Their high voices carried through the thin walls. Fuck. Vinnie pressed the heels of his hands into his eyes as he struggled with feelings that he couldn't define or control. Fuck. He'd never meant to screw up, and part of him still didn't think he had, but RJ's look…. Oh, she'd thought he'd fucked up big time, and he hated seeing that expression in her eyes.

God, what was wrong with him? When he got off the stool, Vinnie felt like an old man with a body stiff and slow to react. By the time he'd gotten his stuff out of his locker, at least half the staff had managed to look at him with pity. He was surprised Dan hadn't tracked him down, but he slipped out the back door without seeing the bartender.

Chapter
Twelve

THE street was quiet when Vinnie went out. A few cars drifted past, but for the most part, the night was silent except for the chirping of bugs. Vinnie felt like one more bug out wandering through the dark. Shit. What the hell was he doing pissing off Charleston and RJ in the same night? Clearly he had a death wish, and he'd chosen the two tops who really might be willing to kill him.

Vinnie cracked his neck first one way and then the other. As he was reaching the corner of the bar, a man stepped out from the shadows. Vinnie's hands curled into fists, because that first flash impression was of size and danger. He took a step back, and that's when his rational mind finally started seeing the details. Yes, the man was large, but he was starting to go soft in the middle, and he wore tailored pants that were clearly from some suit—not exactly the standard gay-bashing sort. However, the man's eyes tracked Vinnie, so he wasn't some lost tourist trying to find LaQuinta Inn, either.

Vinnie kept walking, but he slowed down. If RJ were out here, she would kick his ass for doing this, but Vinnie smiled.

The guy had been nervously checking the shadows like a cop was about to bust him for solicitation, but at that smile, he seemed to relax. Yep, this one was fishing. And he was going to land someone. He was nicely groomed, and the gold watch on his wrist didn't look like a Kmart knock-off. "Evening," he said. His voice was low and sent a shock of desire right through Vinnie.

As Vinnie walked closer, he looked the guy up and down. He had the body language of a dominant. When he saw Vinnie looking him over, he took an aggressive step forward, crowding into Vinnie's personal space. However, the moves weren't polished. This was a guy who wanted to be dominant but didn't really have the experience to pull it off. So instead he was like a Ferrari driven by someone who couldn't drive a manual… starts and fits and sudden acceleration followed by almost panicked braking. Vinnie ducked his head and smiled.

"Hi," Vinnie answered. He twitched his body and watched the man's hands curl into fists. An experienced Dom would have recognized the invitation and moved in, but this guy was struggling to not overstep his permission.

"Are you looking for company tonight?" He inched closer.

Vinnie almost said no. The man had a passing resemblance to Charleston—he was the right age and he had hard-earned muscle under that layer of middle class fat, but his moves were all wrong. However, when Vinnie opened his mouth to tell the guy to take a hike, "sure" slipped out instead. The man smiled. That smile was so genuine and relieved that Vinnie could feel himself respond with his own smile. Shit, he knew more than most what it felt like to be totally terrified of taking the first step. Besides, this guy was pretty good looking. He was a little more into appearance than Charleston with his designer suit pants and expensive haircut, but he had a certain charm.

"Good," he said. Now that Vinnie had given him permission, the man moved forward, holding out a large hand. "I was planning on introducing myself as Wordsworth or Kipling, but now that I'm here, it occurs to me that might be a little silly. I'm Rudy Thompson."

"I'm Vinnie." Vinnie shook the man's hand. His grip was strong, and Vinnie actually liked the fact that the guy hadn't given him a fake name… especially not one as fake as those. He smiled. "Wordsworth?" he asked.

Thompson shrugged. "I will admit that I am a fan of the great poets. You?"

Vinnie shook his head no. "I only learned as much as my English teacher could shove into my brain with a crowbar."

"Ah. English teachers never know the right poems. 'East is East and West is West and never the twain shall meet 'til Earth and Sky stand presently at God's great judgment seat. But there be neither East nor West, Border nor Breed nor Birth, when two strong men stand face to face, though they come from the ends of the Earth.' Every young man can understand that—the desire to find one's equal and challenge him, the need to test oneself and prove oneself the better man." The man had a dreamy sound as he described the poem, and Vinnie was guessing he was an English teacher… one who hated how other English teachers did their jobs.

"Is that your favorite?" Vinnie asked. He moved closer in invitation, and Thompson took him up on it, draping a strong arm across Vinnie's shoulders. He was a large man, and this close, Vinnie could feel his heat and his hard strength. Tonight might not be so bad after all. While Vinnie didn't normally look for the inexperienced Doms, he'd found one or two that were new enough he had to guide them around a few corners. He'd still enjoy the night.

"Not at all," Thompson said with a smile. "Kipling was a bit of a racist, I'm afraid, and that makes it a little harder to enjoy."

"But you considered using his name," Vinnie pointed out. He started toward home, and Thompson fell in next to him, matching his stride.

"Yes, well, I thought better of it, now didn't I? You can't hold a passing bit of stupidity against me, can you?"

"Nope not at all," Vinnie immediately agreed. He leaned into Thompson's strength as they reached a crosswalk with its red "no walk" sign. Thompson tightened his arm around Vinnie's shoulder and smiled. The light turned, and Thompson hesitated for a second. Vinnie took the initiative and started toward his place. After just a split second of indecision, Thompson followed.

Walking through the dark, they passed yards with giant trees singing with bugs. "So, which is your favorite poem?" Vinnie didn't actually care, but the man had a beautiful voice. Once, in a fit of stupidity and weakness, a boy called Isaac had admitted that the thing he missed the most at military school was his mother's voice as she read stories to him in the evening. Oh, the pain and suffering Isaac had suffered for that bit of honesty, but Vinnie could almost understand it. Thompson was nice to listen to.

Thompson's voice fell into a lilting sing-song. "A traveler on the skirt of Sarum's Plain pursued his vagrant way, with feet half bare, stooping his gait, but not as if to gain help from the staff he bore, for mien and air were hardy, though his cheek seemed worn with care both of the time to come, and time long fled. Down fell in straggling locks his think gray hair; a coat he wore of military red, but faded, and struck o'er with many a patch and shred." Thompson paused in his recitation and glanced at Vinnie. Unlike Charleston, he was an inch or so taller, and somehow that felt right. "I do like reading to you. I like my toys attentive."

Vinnie got a little shiver. Oh yes, stroke this one right and he would be nicely dominant. "You have a nice voice," Vinnie offered.

"Yes, I do. I had thought as a young man to go into the theater, but I lack the acting skills."

"Acting I can do," Vinnie said. "However, my voice seems to annoy anyone who listens to it for too long."

"Does it, now?"

"Oh yeah."

Thompson stopped Vinnie and turned him around. Raising his hand, Thompson stroked the side of Vinnie's face before sliding his fingers around to the back of his neck. With his thumb, he stroked the pulse point, making Vinnie's heart race along. "Perhaps you should charm them with other gifts." The streetlight shone behind Thompson, giving him a weak yellow halo.

"Maybe," Vinnie agreed. This guy had definitely found the dominance accelerator, and he was giving that puppy full gas. Just as Vinnie thought that, he could see the doubt suddenly derail Thompson. His hand fell away, and he took a step back.

"I shouldn't bore you with poetry," he blurted. "After all, I'm sure it wasn't my poetical nature that drew us together." He looked around as if suddenly panicked and expecting an ambush from every side. "So, how far is this place we're going?"

"My apartment." Vinnie pointed. His corner of the converted

house was just visible behind a magnolia tree. "We're almost there."

"So less chance for me to make a fool of myself?" Thompson asked. "I really am not good at charming the young boys, I'm afraid."

"You seem to be doing fine," Vinnie disagreed. True, if he had a choice, he'd pick a stronger top, someone who didn't seem to be so unsure, but beggars weren't choosers, and tonight, Vinnie was begging for it.

"You are not as good at acting as you think," Thompson said. He draped his arm over Vinnie's shoulders again. "But I can forgive you since it seems words have never actually been my strong suit."

"So, I should look forward to other talents?" Vinnie asked with a little wiggle.

"Oh yes." Thompson's voice was husky with lust. They reached the house where Vinnie rented the apartment, and suddenly Thompson grabbed him and pushed him up against the wall. Strong hands pinned him in place. "I have many talents. I assume that you won't mind if I push you down and take exactly what I want?"

Vinnie's dick twitched. "Oh, I think I'd be fine with that," Vinnie agreed. His own voice was rough and breathy. "I don't bareback, but other than that, I'm remarkably flexible in all kinds of ways."

"Are you now?" Thompson pulled Vinnie away from the wall only to turn him and push his stomach against the wall. The siding pressed lines into Vinnie's chest and stomach and he stood silent, his dick growing as Thompson manhandled him. "I like a flexible partner."

"That's me."

The game was just getting interesting when Thompson suddenly stepped back, his face a mask of insecurities and uncertainties. Vinnie watched Thompson over his shoulder. Letting his gaze drop to the ground, he then looked up at the man from under lowered lashes. A better top would take a strap to him for being manipulative, but Vinnie didn't think Thompson would mind. The guy seemed to need a little prompting.

"Do you want to go upstairs?" Vinnie finally asked. Thompson was wringing his hands like he wasn't sure what to do with them. For one second, Thompson stared at him all wide-eyed, and Vinnie was almost sure that he was going to run for it. Considering that Vinnie already managed to piss off two tops in one day, driving a third one away almost seemed inevitable. Maybe that would be best. Vinnie wasn't sure he had the energy to prompt an insecure top. Sure, he could. Hell, he was a fucking expert on topping from the bottom. Oh please, big, bad top… don't tie me to the bed. Oh, don't make the knots a little tighter. Yeah, Vinnie could play that game, and if a little game playing got him what he wanted, he could do that.

"If we go upstairs, you can show me all the talents you have." Vinnie inched away from the siding and towards Thompson. Thompson looked at him for a second, and then the man seemed to find his dominant side again.

"You need it bad, boy, don't you?" Stepping forward, Thompson caught Vinnie by the back of the neck.

"Oh yeah," Vinnie agreed. He did. He needed to be held down and nailed to the bed. He needed to be filled and know that some man wanted him. He wanted to have some man's weight on his back, pinning him down and making him feel real. He craved a perfect moment of lust where he didn't feel like such a monumental fuck up.

Chapter
Thirteen

VINNIE groaned into consciousness, aware that his body felt stretched and used and very happy. After getting jerked around by Charleston and threatened by RJ, it had felt good to do a little of the manipulating last night. Thompson had been nicely dominant at times, but he had also been nicely led by Vinnie into doing exactly what Vinnie wanted—a little bondage, a little dirty talk and a lot of stuffing cock in places that made Vinnie so very, very happy. Yeah, he was feeling good.

The sun was darting in through a crack in the curtains, and Vinnie could see the dust swimming in the light, each mote with its own halo. Watching the particles slowly swirl as the air lazily moved, he drifted toward consciousness. He had nowhere to be. Monday would be soon enough to face RJ, and he'd just have to eat a little extra peanut butter to make up for the wages he was losing. He arched his back and enjoyed the stretched feeling in his ass. Maybe he could hit the bars on Larkspur and pick up a few extra dollars.

That thought made Vinnie cringe. He hated having to do that. Yeah, he didn't really have a moral problem with selling himself. Hell, he gave himself away on a fairly regular basis, so getting a little money for doing something he really loved doing… that was like getting paid for a very pleasant hobby. However, every time he did it, Vinnie worried about getting caught. If his fingerprints went into the system, his father, a flock of reporters, and some guy with commitment papers, a syringe full of tranquilizers, and a funny white jacket weren't going to be far behind.

Vinnie suspected that stepmother number two had gone that way. That had been the only mother Vinnie had cried over, and his father seemed to take it as a personal insult that Vinnie had wanted her back. Then again, maybe Rose really had gone a little nutty after living with Martello, Senior for three years. God knows Vinnie came out of his father's house with a few loose screws. However, if his father found out that Vinnie's idea of independence included not only gay sex, but gay sex with men who could show a little monetary appreciation, his father would hide him in the deepest darkest hole he could find. Considering who his father was, Vinnie had no doubt that some judge would sign off on it.

So peanut butter and poverty were probably the safer route. Too bad, because money really was sexy. For a man to give up hard earned cash for the privilege of fucking him… that really pushed more than a few of Vinnie's buttons. Vinnie reached up and scratched his ass. A warm hand ran up his back, and Vinnie shivered at the contact.

"Hi." Vinnie opened his eyes and smiled at Thompson. Most men vanished with the sun, and Vinnie did like the morning after. He liked to be tired and well-used and sleepy while some man's hands explored his body. That was definitely his kink. Right up there with having some Dom look at him like he was the last piece of chocolate, having a Dom tie him down and totally control him, and having a Dom pay for the honor of touching him. Actually, Vinnie had a whole lot of kinks. Yeah, if his father ever found him, the old man would drop Vinnie into a loony bin, but at least Vinnie would have the great pleasure of giving him a heart attack first.

"My boy, you were absolutely wonderful," a low voice praised him. Vinnie smiled and arched up into that touch.

"Oh, that was just the start. I'm all sorts of wonderful," Vinnie promised. Fingers threaded through his hair and then tightened into a fist. Vinnie moaned. It was too early for him to really get seriously interested, but he didn't want Thompson feeling neglected. The man had been sweetly considerate the night before. He'd varied wildly between being as dominant as Charleston to suddenly backing off and requiring reassurance.

Overall, though, Vinnie was giving the guy a solid B+. His cock certainly got the job done, and if he had an odd fetish for trailing his fingers over Vinnie's back and reciting poetry, well, at least he'd waited until after Vinnie had come and lay sated and happy. The hand tightened more, and Vinnie opened his eyes wide, the lethargy of sleep fleeing.

"What?" he asked, surprised at the reappearance of the uber-toppy Thompson.

"There are those beautiful green eyes. Such a rare thing, green eyes." The hand went back to stroking him, and Vinnie lay still, watching Thompson. In the morning light, he looked a little older and a lot more dominant. His cock gave a twitch. Maybe this one would even be the one to make him forget about the great, straight Charleston. Either Charleston was heterosexual or he just didn't like Vinnie, so Vinnie was going to assume he was straight enough to use as a ruler.

Or maybe Vinnie was using a really sweet guy to try and pretend he had Charleston in bed. Vinnie was messed up, but he wasn't too messed up to realize that he was using Thompson. The guy had the same broad shoulders and hair just starting to turn gray. However, Charleston had the most god-awful butchered haircut, and Thompson had neatly trimmed wavy hair that was tapered back and contoured. Hell, he had clearly been up for a while because his hair was already magazine-perfect, and Vinnie had definitely made a mess of it last night. Still, they were the same age with similar bodies, although this guy's muscles were hidden under a soft layer of fat.

Reaching out, Vinnie ran his fingers along the guy's leg, keeping his touch tentative.

"Such a good boy you are," the man said with a sigh. "To look at you, one would expect a junk-yard dog—all muscle and teeth, but you're really just a puppy. Rub your tummy and you'll roll over and wiggle." Vinnie pushed himself up on one elbow, not sure he liked that particular comparison.

"A puppy?"

"A helpless, worthless little puppy," Thompson agreed. Vinnie's guts knotted. Okay, some guys were into humiliation, and Vinnie could respect that, but no fucking way did he need a lover to take shots at him.

"If you don't like how I look, feel free to leave," Vinnie said seriously.

Thompson frowned. Reaching out, he caught Vinnie by the back of the neck and pulled him so close that Vinnie's cheek was pressed into his thigh, about an inch from a cock that was starting to take interest in the proceedings. Enough was enough. Vinnie started to shove Thompson away. Clearly, sweet-Thompson had vanished this morning, and Vinnie did not feel like playing with someone into humiliation.

Vinnie shoved, and Thompson grabbed for his wrist. Vinnie cursed and fought back. Yeah, from his physique, Thompson was some sort of bad-ass twenty years ago, but he couldn't win a fight with Vinnie. Vinnie worked out every day, and he'd been in his share of scrapes. He punched Thompson in the side, feeling a brief flare of victory before Thompson caught Vinnie's thumb and twisted.

Vinnie gave a strangled cry and tried to jerk his thumb away, but the angle was wrong, and Thompson still had his neck. Desperate now, Vinnie brought his knee up and bone cracked against bone. He'd hit something, and he was guessing from the reaction that he'd caught Thompson's shin. Vinnie didn't have much time to enjoy his victory, though. The guy twisted around, and Vinnie tried to attack, only to have his thumb almost torn from his body. He screamed.

Before the pain had cleared, Vinnie was on his stomach with Thompson sitting on his back, still holding Vinnie's thumb. With a sharp yank, he forced Vinnie's hand up to the headboard and then cold steel closed around Vinnie's wrist as Thompson cuffed him to the bed. Unfortunately, Vinnie had spent way too much money on this bed frame specifically because it was solid wrought iron set into thick wood beams in a mission style headboard. Vinnie hadn't cared about the style nearly as much as he'd cared about the fact that he would never be able to get free if cuffed to it.

"You're frisky this morning," Vinnie purred, hoping to bring back nice-guy Thompson. The cold expression on Thompson's face suggested it wasn't working. Vinnie's heart pounded heavily, but he didn't use his safeword. If he did and Thompson ignored it, he'd have a heart attack, and he was far too young to die.

"I do like watching a young thing struggle," Thompson said. His voice had the same sort of dreamy quality it did when he was quoting poetry, and a cold shiver went through Vinnie. Now that he had Vinnie cuffed, he returned to stroking over his captive body.

"Maybe we could pick up from here after I pee." Vinnie gave the guy a winning smile.

"If you need to pee that much, I'll get you a pitcher, but you aren't leaving this bed until I give you permission. You're mine, and you don't do anything that doesn't please me." Leaning over, he put his teeth on Vinnie's side and slowly bit down. Yelling, Vinnie tried to twist away, but the guy's weight on his legs was too much for him to move. When the guy finally stopped, Vinnie sagged into the bed and panted from the pain.

"I guess you don't like pain that much. Pity." He went back to stroking Vinnie. "That man I saw you with in the parking lot last night, is he into pain? Does he make you suffer prettily?"

"Who?" Vinnie's stomach was tightening in fear. What the hell was going on here?

"Middle-aged guy, marine-toned body, and really bad hair."

"Charleston?" Vinnie blurted the name out the second he realized who Thompson was asking for. Vinnie liked to please his tops, but he'd never felt this panicky, desperate need to keep one happy before.

"Ah, yes. Commander Joshua Sawyer Charleston, the great teacher of rich men's children—the ignominious employee of a capitalistic world." Thompson laughed at that. Vinnie could only watch in faint horror as he finally realized that RJ's prediction had come true and he'd just landed himself in a whole lot of trouble. "After all the time that Kalb spent preaching against greed, now he's just one more tool of it. You have no idea how amusing that fact is. So, if he wasn't hiring your rather mediocre services," Thompson said with a slap on Vinnie's undefended ass, "then what were you doing meeting him? He certainly seemed to get some pleasure out of pushing you around."

Vinnie couldn't answer because anger and horror were silencing him pretty damn effectively. Mediocre? The word burned, and the realization that he'd brought a psycho home burned even more.

"Hey, I tell you what," Vinnie finally said, nearly choking on his friendliness, "let me up, and I'll introduce you two."

Thompson's face twisted into something dark. "Answer my question, boy, understand?" He slapped Vinnie's ass even harder.

"I used to go to school at the academy. Someone pulled some prank and I guess it was so good he only thought I could have done it." Vinnie went for a casual smile, one that suggested that he was just a pretty face. The reality was far less comforting.

When he'd been up on that hill spying, Charleston had told him to expect counter-surveillance. At the time, that had just seemed like part of Charleston's mystique, but now Vinnie was thinking that he had been waiting for someone to spy on him—someone like Thompson. Put that together with the fact that Charleston had battle-trained skills but he was working in a backwoods little academy, and it added up to some pretty damn scary sums. Even the wire tap that had brought Charleston to the club last night made sense now. And then there's the fact that he'd spotted Vinnie sitting in that tree—that he always seemed obsessed with knowing everything in his surroundings. And now... now some scary-ass guy was asking very pointed questions. Maybe Vinnie had watched too many movies, but this was not adding up to a pretty picture.

Thompson laughed. "You were at the military academy? Tell me, did your precious Charleston teach you to be the worthless little fuck toy you are now?"

"Hey!" Vinnie objected, but Thompson seemed too amused to take offense.

"My little puppy is the son of some rich man who sent his naughty little boy away for Charleston to straighten him out. Well, 'straighten' might be the wrong word. I am going to enjoy this." Leaning down, he put his teeth to Vinnie's shoulder and started biting down again. Vinnie started to cry out, but Thompson pressed a thumb into a spot on Vinnie's neck, and suddenly Vinnie had the sensation of gagging and choking. He opened his mouth just to try and gulp down enough air to stay conscious. Suddenly the fiery pain in his shoulder was much less important. Thompson finished and pulled back. Vinnie blinked, aware of a red streak across his fair skin. Vinnie had spent his life trying to avoid AIDS, and right now, he wished like hell he had the shit. He had the uncomfortable feeling he was going to die, but if he could give this asshole some deadly disease on his way down, that would make it just a little better. "Now you be a good little puppy while I go make a call."

With a cheerful smile and lips stained red with Vinnie's blood,

Thompson stood up and headed for the kitchen where Vinnie had his phone. Vinnie waited until the guy was out of line of sight before he started pulling on his cuff, testing the tightness. The metal pressed against his wrist. This could be an issue. They were clearly too tight to slip out of.

Well, Vinnie did not plan to go down without a fight. He looked around his bedroom. Unfortunately, Vinnie also had very little with which to fight, and Vinnie needed to stop thinking about himself in third person before he totally lost it. His heavy shoes were next to the bed. As weapons, they left something to be desired, but they might attract a little attention. Using a foot to snag one, Vinnie pulled it up to the bed and grabbed it with his left hand. If deaf Mrs. Williams downstairs was out with her roses, this was going to really piss her off. Hopefully it'd piss her off enough to call the cops. Aiming carefully, Vinnie lobbed his shoe at the window. It hit with a crash and tumbled out, tinkling glass following in a light rain.

Vinnie had his toes on his second shoe, ready to bring it up to the bed and repeat his performance when Thompson appeared at the door, gun in hand. Vinnie froze as he looked down the barrel of a gun for the first time.

"Well, well. Puppy has teeth. I'll have to remember that." Sliding across the room, Thompson kept the gun trained on Vinnie as he looked out the window to check the damage. Vinnie held his breath and prayed for a little luck. From the smile on the guy's face, Vinnie was all out of that. So he was down to bluffing. Even a long shot was better than no shot.

"Hey, I'm all for fun and games." He gave a wicked smile, "but this is too intense for me. Nemesis. I'm safewording out here." Vinnie gave Thompson his best blank expression and prayed that he looked stupid enough to mistake all this for a sex game. For a split second, Vinnie thought that it was going to work. Thompson blinked and studied Vinnie like he was trying to decide just how low Vinnie's IQ might be.

"Don't play stupid." Thompson eventually said. "Don't play more stupid than you actually are, anyway. You did bring me back here, so I would believe some level of stupidity out of you. On your stomach. Now."

Vinnie swallowed. Fuck. Not really seeing many choices, Vinnie shifted around so that he could lie on his stomach. His skin crawled as the guy ran a hand over his calf. "If Kalb makes the wrong choice, you and I might get to spend a lot of time together, boy." Vinnie clenched his teeth while he wrapped Vinnie's own robe tie around his ankles and tied them tightly. Walking around to the side of the bed, he clicked a second pair of handcuffs around Vinnie's left wrist and then attached that to the headboard.

"Be a good boy." With a slap on Vinnie's bare ass, he stepped back out of the room, and Vinnie was left totally tied up. And he still needed to pee. Shit.

Chapter
Fourteen

THE guy wandered back in with Vinnie's cordless phone in one hand and a bulky suitcase in the other. Vinnie was trying hard to not think about what might be in that case, but he had seen one too many gangster movies to make that easy, especially when the guy put the case on the edge of the bed. He dialed and then wedged the phone between his shoulder and ear and started digging in the suitcase.

"Why, if it isn't a voice from the past," he said in a delighted voice as someone answered the phone. He listened with his smile fading. "Now, Kalb. Let's not play games."

Vinnie hated only being able to hear one side of the conversation, but unless he was missing something, Charleston was Kalb. Kalb. Short, snappy, powerful—the name fit him better than Charleston.

"I found something you lost. He really is a sweet piece."

Vinnie glared at the man, but since he was handcuffed to his own headboard with his feet tied, he didn't think he made much of an impression. Whatever Charleston said, the guy laughed again, and it was not a nice sound.

"'This is the year the old ones, the old great ones, leave us alone on the road.' Do you remember that poem? Do you remember how much I love my poetry?" The guy leaned over and ran a finger up the back of Vinnie's thigh. "Do you remember how much I love carving poems into the bleeding bodies of my young friends?"

Vinnie's skin crawled as he remembered the way Thompson's

fingers had traced over his back. For a second, Vinnie thought he was going to throw up. The only thing that kept him from doing it was the realization that Thompson would let him lay in it. Every gesture and every touch from the night before twisted until Vinnie couldn't hold back the shiver of revulsion. Thompson just patted him on the ass.

"I have the perfect poem picked for young Vinnie. I will either get the enjoyment of seeing you face to face or I will start carving such pretty, pretty words into Vinnie's pretty, pretty flesh."

Vinnie trembled as Thompson traced figures across his vulnerable back. "'The darkness twists itself in the wind, the stars are small, the horizon ringed with confused urban light-haze,'" Thompson told Charleston. His languid movements across Vinnie's body were a violation Vinnie couldn't escape. Then Thompson froze, his hand hovering somewhere near the back of Vinnie's knee.

"Oh, Kalb, you always were about the threats," Thompson said, but his laugh was strained. Vinnie pressed his forehead to the pillow and prayed that Charleston got here before the bleeding started. No matter what this asshole said, Charleston wasn't one for threats. If Charleston was threatening this psychopath, that meant he was going to follow up on every single word of it, Vinnie knew that in his heart. He just hoped that some of the wilder rumors about Charleston being a black ops trained killer were true. He really hoped that Charleston was just as dangerous as the guys in the dorms liked to imagine as they told each other wilder and wilder tales about their newest teacher.

"Do you know why I picked that poem? He's such a pathetic little puppy that he really can't imagine life without you. That will be such a perfect poem to carve into his back."

"Fuck you," Vinnie snapped. The only answer he got was a sharp slap on his ass.

"Oh, Kalb. You sound unhappy," Thompson said, immediately distracted by the phone. "You know what you need to do if you want your boy back. You'll find directions at his house. You see, the poor trusting boy brought me home last night, and he did show me quite a good time. Well, a mediocre time anyway. I really do hope you've sampled what he offers others so freely. I will admit that I managed to come without even making the boy bleed. Of course, this morning we spilled a little blood—not much, but you know I can't deny my urges forever, and I've been waiting so long for a new toy. That's your fault too. So either you show up or I start working on Vinnie's back—it's a win-win situation for me." Taking the phone away from his ear, Thompson pushed the off button.

"So, I suppose we must get moving fast. It'll take him a few minutes to gather his weapons, but he's definitely going to break a few speeding laws to get here. He has a real complex when it comes to saving others." The last bit clearly disgusted Thompson.

"So, what's the agenda, Berkowitz?" Vinnie asked with as much bravado he could muster. He was afraid it wasn't that much.

The guy stopped. "Berkowitz? Do you really think I'm anything like the Son of Sam?" Thompson laughed. "First, I don't generally kill my partners, not unless they twitch when I'm working a particularly sensitive area. I had one bleed out once when I nicked the femoral artery, but I prefer to see the bloody and scarred results of my work." Sitting on the side of the bed, he ran his hands up and down Vinnie's legs. "You will be a beautiful canvas. I always hate it when I have to work around tattoos."

"Give me a few hours, I'll go out and get an entire back full of them," Vinnie mouthed off. Thompson narrowed his eyes.

"I'm going to teach you some manners with the point of a knife. You'll beg for ways to please me before we're done." Thompson drew a sharp fingernail down the length of Vinnie's back.

"Fucking freak. If you're going to play these games with Charleston, he's going to eat you alive."

"Oh, don't bet on that. I won last time, and I'll win this time too."

Vinnie looked at Thompson with contempt. A little rabbit part of his brain screamed at him to shut up, but Vinnie had trouble shutting his mouth, even when he knew he had to. It was like his brain just lost all common sense and everything he thought fell out of his mouth. "If you won, it's because he let you. You don't have half the power he does."

"You will shut up." Thompson pulled a muzzle style gag out of the bag. Unlike most gags, the rubber was flesh toned and the mouthpiece was too large for comfort. "Open up."

Vinnie locked his teeth and glared. Thompson raised one eyebrow and then took a large knife out of the case. Putting the gag down, he pulled the sharp blade out of the sheath. The second Thompson looked at the edge, he was lost in his own desire. Vinnie could practically smell the lust. Bringing the knife down to Vinnie's shoulder, Thompson stroked the cold metal over Vinnie's skin. Goosebumps broke out all over Vinnie's body and he couldn't even breathe. Cutting wasn't a threat to get Charleston to come, or at least it wasn't only a threat. Thompson wanted to do it. He wanted so badly that he was having trouble controlling the need. Fuck. How the hell had Vinnie missed these signals?

"Either open your mouth, or I'm going to take what enjoyment I can and leave you here for Kalb to find. That should successfully put him off his game."

"Charleston isn't going to care that much. You really have it wrong there," Vinnie warned, but he then opened his mouth obediently.

"No, you have it wrong. He thought you bugged his phone, and he didn't break your bones. That says something. He is a small-minded man who lashes out at anyone he can when he thinks he's been crossed." That didn't sound like Charleston at all, but Vinnie never had a chance to say that. Thompson pushed the gag in, and Vinnie could feel the pressure in his whole head because the gag was dangerously large. If he wore it too long, his head was going to start getting stuffy and then he'd be in real trouble. Reaching around, Thompson pulled the buckle so tight that Vinnie could feel the corners of his mouth ache before Thompson finished fastening it.

Then Thompson gave Vinnie a friendly pat on the cheek. "You'll get used to it. I prefer to work in silence, and this is particularly good at ensuring it." Vinnie glared, but couldn't do much else as Thompson brought out a wide range of bondage equipment. Heavy leather cuffs around his wrists locked to a chain that he threaded through Vinnie's legs before making him kneel up. Vinnie grunted as the guy threaded a loop around his cock and balls. Clearly he would not be trying to wiggle free, not unless he wanted to castrate himself.

"Since you're going to be walking, we need to hobble you without making it too obvious," the guy said with a cheerfulness that made it clear he was enjoying the hell out of this. Vinnie would have loved the guy to be this dominant last night, but now he felt like he might throw up. Unfortunately, he was positive that if he did, psycho-dude would let him choke on his own vomit.

Vinnie tried to squirm, but Thompson caught his calf and held it down as he wrapped an X-shaped strap around Vinnie's foot and ankle. The straps kept a small metal ball just at the juncture of Vinnie's foot's arch and the heel. If Vinnie put his weight on that, it was going to hurt like hell, and walking on his toes was going to get old fast. Thompson whistled as he did the same on the other side. Vinnie had never seen any sort of hobble like these, but they were going to be effective. Vinnie already had a nagging urge to scratch and stretch his foot, and when he tried to walk, it was going to be painful as hell.

"Now let's get you dressed." Thompson smiled, and Vinnie had an almost irrational urge to head-butt the bastard even if that would lead inevitably to his own death. Thompson pulled out an oversized sweatshirt and pulled it over Vinnie's head. An even thicker hoodie followed, with sleeves that had been stuffed to look like arms were in them. The jeans were Vinnie's own, and the guy fastened the hoodie's sleeves to it so that it would look like Vinnie had his hands in his pockets. Pulling the hood up, he fussed with it some and then pulled out an odd collar.

The front was skinny, but the back had a wicked curved spike. Thompson pressed the curve to the back of Vinnie's head, and Vinnie looked down to keep from getting poked in the head. Thompson then wrapped the leather around Vinnie's neck and buckled it. These weren't cheap restraints—and they weren't the play toys of a middle class couple trying to spice up their sex lives. Vinnie had browsed enough kinky websites to know that. This guy was inventing and making his own restraints, and that suggested that he was not only telling the truth but more experienced than Vinnie wanted to think about.

He imagined his father getting a call that the police had found Vinnie dead in some back alley, his back carved and the marks from cuffs pressed deep into his flesh. Maybe Charleston would show up, and they could compare notes about how shocked they were that Vinnie had ended up so badly. Or maybe they'd compare notes about how Vinnie had ended up exactly where he deserved for inviting a fucking psychopath into his fucking house like a fucking moron.

Thompson puttered around the room, but Vinnie just closed his eyes and waited since he couldn't do anything else. To be fair, Vinnie didn't think Charleston would ever have that conversation—not with Vinnie's father, anyway. He probably talked to the other teachers about what a fuck up Vinnie was, but the teachers had always presented some sort of united front against Martello, Sr. Maybe they were just afraid to bring the man's wrath down on them by suggesting that his heir was anything other than perfect. Maybe they just hated him as much as Vinnie did. It was funny; facing certain death was supposed to make you a better person as you faced your guilt and thought back on all the people you'd make up with if you could. Not so much.

Now, Charleston? Yep, Vinnie had guilt there. The man had practically waved a neon sign telling Vinnie he was in danger, and Vinnie had not only ignored him, but he'd gone home with the first person to come out of the shadows. And now Charleston was getting blackmailed because of it. Vinnie wished he could apologize to Charleston, because Vinnie had just reached whole new levels of total and complete stupidity.

"I'm about ready. How about you?" Thompson laid a hand on Vinnie's shoulder, and Vinnie was too tired and too tightly restrained to even try to shake it off. "Just one more thing." He pulled the stuffed fake arms out of Vinnie's jean pockets and threaded them through the straps of a backpack. After he fastened the strap across Vinnie's chest and tightened it, the backpack was firmly attached. With a little hummed tune, Thompson tucked the ends of the stuffed arms back into Vinnie's front pockets so that once again, it looked like his hands were tucked into his jeans. The backpack hid the bulge made by Vinnie's arms behind his back. Oh yeah, this asshole had done this before. He was too smooth and too calm about this whole thing.

Grabbing Vinnie's own sneakers out of the closet, Thompson put them on over the hobble straps. The shoes pushed the attached metal ball farther into the soft spot on Vinnie's foot, and he cringed helplessly. Within ten minutes of starting, the guy had his arm around Vinnie's waist, leading him to the door. On the back of the door, Vinnie had hung a mirror so he could check himself before heading out the door. Out of the corner of his eye, he could see himself. With his head down, the gag was hidden and the hoodie gave him the slumping impression of a man with a hangover, a common enough sight in this neighborhood.

"I wonder if Kalb will come, or if he'll try to stage some rescue. I almost hope he's stupid. I would so love to mark that skin of yours." Thompson reached up and ran a hand along Vinnie's cheek. With the collar restraint, Vinnie couldn't even move away from it. He shifted, his toes already starting to cramp from the hobbles. Thompson chuckled and then tugged on the sides of the hood, bringing it up higher so that Vinnie's face would be lost in the shadow of the hoodie. "Let's get you down to the car. I bet you'd love to get off those feet."

Vinnie grunted, but the gag was so thick he doubted that the sound even penetrated. With nothing else to do, he followed as Thompson led him out onto the street with a familiar arm around his waist. A dirty van waited near the corner, and he unlocked the back and urged Vinnie up into the dark. Fuck. From the start, this had been a set up.

Vinnie wondered if Thompson had been planning to pull him off the street and into the van. Well, clearly Vinnie had made it easy on him. If he had seen someone, anyone, on the street, Vinnie might have fought. However, he didn't see how he could free himself, so he was going to have to rely on Charleston to save him. He climbed awkwardly into the van and listened as Psycho slammed the door.

"Keep being a good boy, and you'll come out of this alive," Thompson promised. Vinnie noticed that the guy didn't promise that Vinnie would come out unscarred, just alive. He obeyed when the psycho put him on his knees at the edge of a gym mat. A quick loop of rope, and Vinnie's feet were tied to the bottom of the van, and he had no way to free himself.

"Such a very pretty boy, submissive, head bowed, silent. If you were bleeding, you'd be the picture of perfection, Vinnie." Psycho sounded positively romantic about that. "'I was a child beneath her touch, a man, When breast to breast we clung, even I and she, A spirit when her spirit looked through me, A god when all our life-breath met to fan, Our life-blood, till love's emulous ardours ran, Fire within fire, desire in deity.'" He sounded breathless. "I can make you a deity, Vinnie, a beautiful, perfect deity." He unzipped his pants. With the collar forcing his head down, Vinnie could only see out of peripheral vision and even that was partially blocked by the hoodie, but the sounds were familiar enough. Thompson came with a little sigh, and Vinnie cringed as the warm come splattered onto his face. "I will make you a perfect deity." Psycho knelt down next to Vinnie, running his fingers over Vinnie's eyes, forcing him to shut them. "I will make you absolutely perfect."

Then Thompson was gone, and the van started. As they pulled away from the curb, Vinnie prayed to hear a siren or the sound of screeching tires as Charleston pulled up. He heard only silence and the heavy purr of the van's well-tuned engine.

Chapter
Fifteen

THE light that filtered in through the front window darkened, and Vinnie could hear the echoing of the engine, so clearly they were inside somewhere. Shit. He had always prided himself on playing safe, but this was not safe. Vinnie couldn't believe he'd let this guy into his home, into his bed… into his body. As much as Vinnie hated to admit it, RJ had been right. He'd been looking for trouble, but after this, he was going avoid trouble for the next century or so.

Vinnie still felt faintly ill about the idea that this creep had actually been inside his body, and Vinnie had invited him right in, but there wasn't much he could do about that now. Hell, he couldn't do anything if Psycho decided to come back and push him to the floor and do it again. All his hopes were riding on Charleston, and Vinnie was suddenly feeling so very, very unsure that Charleston would even show. From the sounds of the conversation, he'd known Thompson before, and that meant he knew just how dangerous the guy was. The smart move was to run straight to the cops. That's what Vinnie would do. The problem was that if Charleston did that, Vinnie would pay in blood. He didn't doubt that.

"How is my boy?" Thompson asked cheerfully as he stuck his head into the back area. Turning the van off, he knelt down in front of Vinnie and stroked his hands over Vinnie's cheeks. The sensation was odd because the touch vanished each time Thompson's fingers trailed from the overheated skin to the gag. The van was too hot for the layers of clothing Vinnie had on, but he couldn't do anything except pant through his nose and hope this psychopath cared whether or not Vinnie passed out from heat stroke. Then again, maybe he should hope he did pass out. He really didn't want to be conscious when this guy figured out that Charleston had gone to the police.

"Up, boy." Reaching back, he pulled the rope loose from Vinnie's feet. However, between the fear and the lack of circulation, Vinnie couldn't actually get to his feet. He stumbled, and the metal ball from the hobbles wrapped around his feet dug into the soft spot right in front of his heel. Screaming behind the gag, Vinnie fell back onto the mat, jarring his backbone so hard that passing out seemed like a really good idea.

"Submissives are all the same: weak." Thompson spit the words at Vinnie and then hauled him up. Vinnie screamed again, feeling like his foot was being torn in half. "If you subs weren't so beautiful, you really would be quite worthless. I find it simply amazing that Charleston has given up so much just because of some pathological need to take care of subs. A sub exists to serve a Dominant. Don't you, boy?"

Vinnie figured his participation in the conversation wasn't really required since he was both gagged and restrained tightly enough that he couldn't nod. He could feel a cold trail of slime where his spit was slowly leaking out the bottom of the gag, and his neck was screaming in pain. Even rolling his head slightly to the side couldn't really ease the pain of being unable to straighten it.

When Psycho shoved him, Vinnie fell to one knee in the middle of the warehouse's main floor. Before Thompson could tie him, he shifted onto his ass and pulled his legs in front of him Indian-style. His neck and head were aching enough, he didn't need for his knees to hurt too. Vinnie snorted his disgust. Trying to save himself some pain seemed like a pretty pointless gesture right now. Unless Charleston showed up, Thompson would carve on his skin, and Charleston would have to be an idiot to show up.

"He had a career, you know." Thompson kept on with the friendly chatter as he pulled the jacket's hood down and clipped a chain from the floor onto the collar. "He was a military man. 'Boldly they rode and well, Into the jaws of Death, Into the mouth of Hell.' Kalb rode into hell, and I was right there with him. I was his commanding officer, but he got too cocky, and he lost his job." Thompson's hands paused in the middle of randomly patting Vinnie in uncomfortable places. "Worse, he lost me the place I had earned," Thompson said, his voice dark with anger. "I trusted him. I trusted him, and he screwed me over." Thompson wasn't sounding as romantic now. He jerked the hood back up to hide most of Vinnie's face. As he paced, his shoes slapped the concrete floor. "But I won. 'Cannon to the right of them, Cannon to the left of them, Cannon behind them.' That's from Lord Tennyson's 'Charge of the Light Brigade'. They all died, you know. Kalb hasn't died yet, but he was outmaneuvered, and he fled from the field of battle. I fucking won. But he was like some sort of suicide bomber—blowing my reputation to hell on his way out. He'll pay for that."

Thompson stopped right in front of him, and Vinnie couldn't breathe. He wasn't sure if the gag or just fear had stopped him, but the world was graying around the edges. "He has to come. I'm going to look him in the eye before he dies. I'm going to make him watch you bleed, and then I'm going to kill him."

Vinnie snorted again, and snot dribbled out. Considering that he had always put more than a little effort into his appearance, he was oddly bothered by the fact that he was going to die all sweaty and snotty. He should probably be a little more upset by the potential for a bloody and painful death. He had a brief flash of his father coming to the coroner's office to identifying his body and explaining to everyone how his son normally looked so much better than that. He could just hear good old dad now, explaining in his grave voice how Troy, Junior was normally such a charming young man, and he couldn't imagine how the boy ended up sweaty and slobbery and covered in bondage marks and knife scars. Vinnie figured he was in danger of turning hysterical.

Psycho went back to pacing, and Vinnie just focused on trying to roll his head far enough to one side that he could ease the strained muscles. If this guy didn't loosen something up, Vinnie was running the danger of muscles cramping, and if that happened, he wasn't giving himself good odds. Too much screaming behind a gag this tight, and he figured he had equal odds of suffocating or choking.

"Sit still." A strong hand slapped him upside the back of the head, and Vinnie could feel his impotent rage building. He normally thought of himself as a pretty happy, laid back person, but he'd never wanted to commit murder so much in his life. He could not only kill this guy, but feel good about it as he pulled the trigger.

"Trouble?" a familiar voice asked. Vinnie's mind blanked for a second, hope and horror denying him the ability to identify the speaker even though some part of him knew exactly who had just walked in the room. The sharp sound of boots against the concrete stopped. "You never did know how to get the best out of your partners."

Thompson didn't answer immediately. When he did, his voice had an edge of panic, and Vinnie seriously hoped that meant Charleston had shown up with a SWAT team and a fully-automatic weapon. The damn restraints kept him from raising his head to look, and Thompson had pulled the hoodie's hood down so that all Vinnie could see was six inches of concrete floor and his own legs.

"Don't start with me," Thompson shouted. "I'm in control here. I'm in control."

"You're in control, Thompson," Charleston agreed calmly. "So, you called me. How do you see this ending?"

"Get rid of the gun."

"No." Charleston had that tone of voice that meant he was not going to debate this. Vinnie'd heard that tone often enough to recognize it.

"If you don't, he's dead."

"He's dead if I do."

There was an awkward silence that followed that, and Vinnie struggled to stay perfectly still. Whatever happened, he really didn't want to make it worse by distracting Charleston, not now. Just the man's presence oddly reassured Vinnie. Yeah, the situation still sucked just as much, but some little part of Vinnie's brain insisted on believing that Charleston could handle anything. The man had handled Vinnie. Hell, the man had even handled Vinnie's father when he'd show up all full of charm and vodka. That had been an interesting evening, to say the least. Surely Charleston could handle one little psychopath with a poetry obsession.

Charleston's next words had an edge to them. "So I assume you have more than just a switch."

"The bomb is in the backpack."

Vinnie's world went black for a second as panic robbed him of all thoughts. All he could feel was the weight of the backpack against his spine. A bomb. He had a fucking bomb strapped to his back.

"No offense, but I don't believe you."

"Check for yourself." Thompson had that disturbingly friendly tone in his voice—the one that convinced Vinnie to take the man home for the night. He was guessing that Charleston was going to be a little smarter than he had been. Actually, pretty much anyone would have been smarter. Vinnie tried to imagine Dan making a mistake like this—trusting some totally unknown Dom and letting them tie him up. Yeah, that wouldn't happen. Vinnie clearly had a few screws loose, because he fell for an act so over-the-top sweet that it should have rung huge alarms.

The sharp clicks of Charleston's boots against the concrete were oddly mirrored by Thompson's footsteps. Vinnie felt something brush against his arm, and he flinched back.

"It's only me," Charleston said, his hand falling on Vinnie's shoulder. Vinnie took a deep breath through his nose and sagged a bit. A rapid clicking, and Vinnie was guessing Charleston had opened the backpack. If Vinnie was really, really lucky, it was all a bluff and Charleston would put a bullet between Thompson's eyes. After a second, Vinnie realized that he was never going to be lucky.

"Put the gun on the floor and kick it over here," Thompson ordered.

When Charleston bent down, Vinnie got his first look at the man; it made him suck in a fast breath. He thought that he'd managed to piss Charleston off a few times during senior year, but the look on Charleston's face now was absolutely murderous. If Vinnie had seen someone with this particular expression on his face, he would have run the other way. Charleston carefully put a good-sized handgun on the floor and then shoved it toward Thompson. The clattering of the metal against the concrete sounded entirely too final.

"Now your backup piece."

Charleston repeated the process with a smaller, silver gun from an ankle holster, and then, after another order, a huge knife. As Charleston turned over each weapon, Vinnie could feel his own panic rise. This was feeling less and less like a rescue and more like a trap.

"Any more weapons?" Thompson demanded.

"You have everything," Charleston said, his voice mild.

"Move, move to the wall, hands against it. If I find so much as a pocket knife, I'm going to trigger this just so you have the pleasure of watching young Vincent there explode. I'll do it."

Charleston's even footsteps walked away from Vinnie, stopping twenty or thirty yards away. "I know you would. You're still just as crazy as ever, aren't you?"

"I'm not the one who denies himself. You're so caught up on your precious rules and regulations that you ruined your life. But I could forgive you that, Kalb. If you want to flush twenty years of service down the drain, that's your choice, but you had no right to take everything away from me, and now you're going to pay."

"Is that why you took Vinnie?" Charleston asked. "You can't actually think I'd have a relationship with a kid I taught."

"What? Does that violate your precious sense of ethics?" Thompson laughed. "I almost hope that's true. It would be entirely too perfect to watch you die for a sub you haven't even taken yet. Vinnie has a nice tight ass. He's a little mouthy, but I find a gag has cured him of that." Feet wandered through Vinnie's limited field of vision—Thompson walking backwards. "Subs exist to serve, but you never understood that. You had to turn it into something more complicated to ease your conscience. You denied yourself until you couldn't even see the truth."

Charleston didn't answer, but his boots clicked across the concrete as he returned to Vinnie's side. Vinnie felt a cool breeze across his neck as Charleston pulled the hood down. For a second, Charleston smoothed Vinnie's hair back from his face, his fingers sliding over the sweat-slicked skin.

"You still have to force them into submission, don't you?" The derision in Charleston's voice would have made Vinnie wither, but Thompson just laughed. Strong fingers pulled at the buckle, loosening it, but Vinnie's jaw hurt so much that he couldn't even push it out.

Charleston pulled it out for him. Standing at Vinnie's back, he rubbed his thumbs into Vinnie's sore jaw, and Vinnie blushed as he felt himself drool a bit.

"You haven't changed," Thompson practically spit.

"Don't see a good reason to change." Charleston undid the collar and tossed it to the ground.

Vinnie had to bite back a groan as he tried to straighten his neck. The muscles bunched painfully, and Charleston's calloused thumbs rubbed small circles on either side of his neck. "Thanks," Vinnie said softly. Now if Charleston would only take the fucking bomb off his back, life would be perfect. A hand stroked over his face, and Vinnie shivered. It probably made him a shitty person, but he couldn't help being happy he had someone on his side in this little bit of hell.

"He's too hot. I should take off the jacket," Charleston commented.

Thompson was pacing the middle of the warehouse, holding up his hand with a small black box in it. Vinnie had seen enough Bond movies to recognize a trigger for a bomb. "Take off the bomb, you mean? No, I think we'll leave it right where it is. In fact, zip it back up." The smile that had looked sweet last night now had a sarcastic twist to it. Without comment, Charleston zipped it back up.

When he finished, he stood and held his hands out from his sides in an exaggerated shrug. "This is your game, Thompson. How are you playing it?"

Thompson stopped pacing and glared at Charleston. "Are you trying to manipulate me? Do you think I'm one of your little submissives that follows you around with big eyes?" Thompson screamed the words. Charleston held his hands up in surrender, but his body was tense. He might play at surrender, but Vinnie could see the danger in every line.

"Nope. I just think you need to decide how to end this. You let go of that switch, and you're going to have a lot of questions to answer."

"Or everyone will just assume that the kinky Cap died with the pretty little boy he'd picked up on the street." Thompson laughed and looked at Vinnie with such hatred that Vinnie felt a cold shiver. "That one is an alley cat—following any cock that promises to push him down and take him hard. I did, too, you know. I took him. He tried so hard to not beg, but he made these desperate little cries when he needed to be taken harder."

Vinnie could feel himself blush, but he couldn't deny it. It had been a long time since he'd been humiliated by his sexual preferences, but he could feel that self-hatred growing. Charleston's fingers tightened on his shoulder. "That's why you came out of the woodwork now, isn't it?" Charleston asked. "You still can't get a submissive to follow you, and here I am trying to fend off Vinnie and his big, green eyes. I haven't stepped into a bedroom or playroom for three years, but I can still get a submissive to chase me. You still can't figure that out, can you?" Charleston kept a neutral tone of voice, but the words hit their mark. Vinnie watched as Thompson withdrew, his fury simmering impotently beneath his skin.

"My toys know how to submit." Thompson's eyes flicked between Vinnie and Charleston.

"Your toys need to be tied in place," Charleston commented. He moved his hand and stroked Vinnie's cheek. "You can't get them to go to their knees without a weapon."

"They've crawled to my side, bleeding and trembling for my touch."

Charleston shrugged. "After you've broken them, sure. They're desperate by the time you've finished your fun, desperate enough to crawl after any hope you dangle in front of them. But they don't pursue you. You have to make them bleed. But Vinnie here, he's pursuing me, and you just can't understand that." Charleston ran a finger over Vinnie's cheek, and Vinnie instinctively leaned into Charleston's leg. The more he heard, the more convinced he was that he was totally and completely fucked and Charleston was his only hope of getting out of this.

"We'll see." Thompson looked nearly white with fury. "We'll see who Vinnie ends up following. He can follow you to the grave if he wants, but I don't think he will. Now get up and move." Thompson gestured with his gun toward the far end of the warehouse. Charleston got a hand under Vinnie's elbow and pulled him up, guiding him in the direction Thompson had indicated.

Chapter Sixteen

VINNIE'S feet ached by the time they reached the far side of the warehouse and entered a short hall. The metal ball pressing into the bottom of his foot had nearly crippled him, but he gritted his teeth and just kept as much of his weight on his toes as he could. Thompson ordered them into a room to the right, and the second Charleston ushered him into the room, Vinnie froze. It took Charleston's hand on his back to get him moving again.

The freak had set up his own prison cell, with two walls lined in cinderblock and steel bars on the other two. Inside, a single army cot was the only furniture. Vinnie didn't know why the sight of that scared him spitless, especially considering he already had a bomb strapped to his back and should have already maxed out on the fear, but it did. If they went into that, they weren't getting out. He knew it. A heavy door stood open, and Charleston urged him toward it. Allowing himself to be herded into that cage was the hardest thing Vinnie had ever done. His whole body screamed at him to run… to get as far away from this psycho as he could. Only Charleston's hand on his back kept that panic from overwhelming him.

Charleston stepped into the cell behind him and turned to watch, his gaze as impassive as ever while Thompson pushed the door closed with a heavy clang. Thompson braced the bottom with his foot and held the bomb trigger up high before pulling out a monster key. Vinnie held his breath, waiting for Charleston to storm the door and shove it open so fast that he broke Thompson's fucking knee. Instead, Charleston crossed his arms and watched as Thompson locked the door.

"'Oft have I brooded on defeat and pain, The pathos of the stupid, stumbling throng.'" Thompson quoted his stupid poetry again, glee in his face. "Time to pay the piper, Kalb. And what a bill you have managed to rack up." With an honest-to-God giggle, he backed out of the room, still holding up one hand with the trigger. He stepped out, closing the door, and Vinnie waited, prepared for the bomb on his back to go off and blow him into a million pieces.

"Sit," Charleston ordered, giving Vinnie a nudge toward the cot. Vinnie's breath left him in a massive sigh, and he collapsed onto the cot. "I assume he used ball hobbles." Charleston started unlacing Vinnie's tennis shoes.

"Straps around my heel and ankle that hold a metal ball right at the place where the arch and heel meet so that if I put my weight down I feel like my foot is being ripped off? Oh yeah, that's a pretty safe assumption. You know, if Thompson ever wants to give up the torture and killing gig he has going, he could make a good living as an S&M designer."

"He didn't design them," Charleston said as he pulled Vinnie's shoe off to get to the straps. "I did."

"You?" Vinnie stared at Charleston; he was pretty sure that hell had just frozen and a few pigs had flow by. Watching while Charleston unbuckled the straps and rubbed his thumbs into the bottoms of Vinnie's feet to get the circulation going, Vinnie softly said, "That's some hard core equipment."

Charleston shrugged. "I like to play hard." He put Vinnie's foot back down and rocked back on his heels, and Vinnie was suddenly struck by the whole wrongness of the scene. Charleston was on his knees taking Vinnie's shoes off. "Or I did. I haven't played for a while, but my guess is that Thompson is amusing himself by using my old equipment. Either that or the man doesn't have the imagination to make his own."

"So that…." Vinnie looked at the complicated tangle of leather strap and buckle and the metal ball that looked so small and harmless now that it wasn't crippling him. "That's yours?"

Charleston stood up and took one of the two hobbles, turning the strap around to show Vinnie the underside of the worked leather. A simple JK was carved into it.

Vinnie didn't try to hide his confusion "Just kidding?" he guessed.

Charleston sighed. "Jeff Kalb. Captain Jeff Kalb."

"Oh."

"Okay, I need you to stand up." Without giving Vinnie a chance to protest, Charleston got a hand under his elbow and pulled him up. "What did he do after putting the backpack on you?"

"Um... I don't know, dragged me out into the street, shoved me into a van, and then came all over me? Is that what you mean?" Vinnie bit his tongue as he tried to cut off his own vitriol. He could hear the anger in his voice, and Charleston wasn't the one to get angry with, but he just couldn't seem to get hold of the emotion.

Charleston's voice got softer. "Did he wrap anything around it, use wire or work on any part of the backpack once it was on?" Charleston asked without even commenting on Vinnie's pissiness.

"Oh." Vinnie blushed as he realized that Charleston was just trying to figure out if the backpack had any booby traps. Yeah, nice job, Bernardi. He was really being helpful. "He put the pack on and then we left."

"That's good." Charleston was slowly running his hand over the hoodie, stopping to explore each seam and bump with his fingers. In other circumstances, Vinnie would enjoy being so thoroughly felt up, but now he was just drained. He wanted to climb into bed, pull the covers over his head and then pretend the world didn't exist. Instead, he stood silent while Charleston walked around, feeling the edges of the pack and peering at the bomb.

"So, how do you go from Jeff Kalb to Joshua Sawyer Charleston?" Vinnie finally asked. If he didn't change the subject, he was going to start panicking and flailing and saying really inappropriate things that Charleston was not going to appreciate. Things like, "what kind of a fucking moron walks into a fucking trap with a fucking psycho?"

"By making fun of someone else's name. When people have power over you or your potential false identity, it pays to not piss them off. Unfortunately, I seem to piss a lot of people off."

"Like Thompson?" Vinnie guessed. Charleston's hand paused in their task, warm palms pressing into the small of Vinnie's back just under the backpack.

"Yeah," Charleston agreed, and his fingers went back to work, slowly inching up between Vinnie and the backpack. For several minutes, Vinnie waited for some sort of explanation, but Charleston seemed pretty content with leaving things right there.

"Hey, I respect your right to secrets, but if I'm going to die for this, I think I have a right to know what type of 'this' is getting me dead."

Charleston walked around to the front and looked at Vinnie. He had that expression, the one that meant Vinnie had missed something obvious and Charleston was waiting for him to figure it out. This time, though, Vinnie really didn't see what he was missing. They were locked in a tiny cell by a madman who had all of Charleston's weapons. Oh, he figured Charleston probably had a pocket knife or something, but psycho had three guns and a bomb on his side. That definitely trumped anything Charleston might have hidden.

With a sigh, Charleston reached up and tapped Vinnie on the cheek. "The very first time I ever put you on the ground and made you do pushups, you think about that. I'm going to try to get the bomb off you."

At first, Vinnie opened his mouth to protest. He'd had a bad fucking day, and he didn't feel like playing games. However, protesting had never worked well with Charleston. The more Vinnie protested, the more pushups Charleston would make him do until Vinnie just caved and went along with Charleston's plans, and the thing that really sucked was that Charleston usually seemed to be right in the end. The first time Charleston had made him do pushups was that time he'd found Vinnie taking the headmaster's car apart. Vinnie had turned around to find Charleston leaning against the brick wall in this old green Army jacket. It was like he'd appeared out of nowhere, and Vinnie dropped his wrench right in the middle of taking out one of the bolts that held the car door to the frame.

One of Charleston's eyebrows had gone up in that expression Vinnie had learned to both love and hate. "Problem, Martello?" he'd asked. He hadn't even tried to hide his amusement.

"Um. I was just...." He'd stopped there. He really didn't have excuses, and he was smart enough to know when he'd been caught red-handed and just shut up.

"Putting the car back together?" Charleston suggested mildly.

Vinnie had flashed the man his biggest smile. Maybe Charleston would be easier to manipulate than he'd thought. That hope had carried Vinnie through the next fifteen minutes as Vinnie replaced all the bolts he'd just taken out and then tried to scoot past Charleston on his way for the garage door.

Charleston had put out a hand to block the doorway. "We aren't done, Martello. Drop and give me fifty."

"Fifty?" Vinnie remembered he'd practically squeaked with indignation. No one ordered him to do that many pushups. At worst, he had to do twenty and then listen to his father rant and rave after the headmaster put him on speakerphone.

"Fifty." Charleston still hadn't moved, and Vinnie eyed his escape routes. If he ran down the side of the garage, the barking dogs would bring everyone out in time to see Vinnie fleeing, and witnesses were never good. The garage door was the safe route, but Vinnie was pretty sure that Charleston would physically grab him.

"Hey, how'd you get back here, anyway?" Vinnie demanded, going for a little obfuscation and misdirection instead.

Charleston had just looked at him. Leaving the wall, he stepped into Vinnie's personal space, and Vinnie could feel the cold sweat start. This man wasn't like any of his other teachers; Vinnie had realized right there that he was so far out of his league that he didn't have a chance. Vinnie had never felt that way before. Hell, he could manipulate his father by the time he was four. He probably still could except it was more fun to wind the old man up and watch him splutter. For nearly a minute, Charleston just stared at Vinnie, studying him until Vinnie was nearly shaking just from the effort of standing still and not retreating—or even better, running for his life.

With a slow and honeyed smile, Charleston stepped back and leaned against the wall again. "Start your pushups and I'll share a few truths."

With a sigh, he got down on the dew-soaked ground and started doing pushups. His hands sank into the damp earth, and his knees were cold and wet the second they touched the grass.

"Shape up, ass down. I won't count a sloppy push-up, Martello," Charleston warned, but before Vinnie could defend himself, Charleston kept talking. "If you're going to continue this war with the headmaster, you need to consider a few realities. First, I will be keeping an eye on you. If you want me as an enemy, you can have that."

Charleston's words had sent shivers through Vinnie. He stopped his pushups, but Charleston strolled over and put a boot in the middle of Vinnie's back, pushing him toward the ground. Vinnie flinched when his whole front was pressed into the damp earth. When he went back to the dorms, everyone was going to be whispering about exactly what Vinnie might have been doing to get so dirty. If the stains had been on his back, he could have made up all sorts of great stories, but not with the stains on his front.

"Second, your tactics need work. You have only one way in and one way out of here. The dogs block your secondary retreat, and the one access point is used irregularly, meaning you took too big of a risk coming out here."

"No risk, no fun," Vinnie countered. He grunted as Charleston's boot landed on his back again. This time, instead of forcing him down, the boot just added some weight so that every pushup was even harder. Vinnie gritted his teeth and focused on not showing any emotion other than a happy sort of disdain for all rules. That was Vinnie's persona, and Charleston wasn't going to get to see past it.

"Never engage an enemy without multiple escape strategies. Not unless that is a battle worth dying for. Never engage unless you have a clear objective that benefits your side. I can see your objective, Martello, but there is no benefit to it. Tonight, after an evening run, you will write me a three page paper applying military tactics to this little outing and defining the flaws in both your objectives and your tactics. Clear?"

Vinnie gave a gasping laugh. "The headmaster tends to prefer detention."

"I didn't plan to ask for his opinion."

Vinnie had fallen to the ground again when he realized that Charleston wasn't going to pull the headmaster and his father into this.

"Count off," Charleston ordered.

"Um." Vinnie cringed as he realized that he had no idea how many pushups he'd done. Enough to make his arms start to ache was probably not a good answer.

"Twelve, Martello. The first twenty-five are for touching other people's property and the last twenty-five are for being stupid while doing it. Those are the ones that are going to hurt. Get moving before I get more creative."

Vinnie had pushed himself up and started counting off the pushups. Charleston's foot had disappeared around pushup twenty, but the last half of the set had still been slow and painful, and Vinnie had collapsed to the damp ground more than once. He hurt even more as he tried to write that damn paper on tactics with arms that felt like they were going to fall off.

Vinnie watched as Charleston carefully pulled the backpack off and set it to one side. That little trip down memory lane hadn't made a whole lot of sense, but at least it had distracted him from Charleston's careful work getting the bomb off him.

"I don't suppose you were bomb squad in the service?" Vinnie asked hopefully.

Charleston shook his head. "Special forces. Infiltration and counter-insurgency."

"Professional bad ass, then," Vinnie translated.

Charleston looked up at Vinnie and gave him a small smile. "I suppose you could say that."

"So, then you're Superman or MacGyver or something, and you can disarm the bomb?" Vinnie flashed Charleston his best smile, as though he was trying to charm the man into buying him some expensive gift.

"It's not as easy as they make it look on television," Charleston explained, "and I'm no Superman. Hell, I met Thompson because I was reassigned to desk duty after taking shrapnel in the leg."

"What, like throwing yourself on a grenade to save an entire unit from unavoidable death?" Right now, Vinnie just wanted Charleston to be larger than life and heroic and perfect. He needed his illusions. However, Charleston was definitely not cooperating.

"Nope. Roadside bomb went off when I was patrolling an area."

Vinnie leaned back into the cold brick wall. "Feel free to start lying to me at any point," he suggested.

"Nah. I don't have to. You're keeping your head, Bernardi."

Looking at the bomb, Vinnie wondered just how long he was going to keep it attached to the rest of him. They couldn't protect themselves from the bomb if it went off. Yeah, he felt better for having it off his back, but he wasn't exactly feeling good.

"Hot?" Charleston asked.

For a second, Vinnie's brain blanked as it tried to fit the idea of sexually hot with their current situation. The fact was that he'd never been so *not* turned on by bondage. When Charleston raised an eyebrow, Vinnie realized that Charleston had been asking about the temperature. "Um, yeah."

"Come on, let's get the sweater off you," he suggested.

"Hoodie," Vinnie corrected him.

Charleston gave him a dirty look before grabbing the stuffed sleeve and pulling the entire hoodie up and over Vinnie's head. He casually tossed it to the side, but it landed right on top of the backpack, hiding it. Lifting up the back of the shirt, he tugged and pulled at the restraints around Vinnie's wrists. "These are locked. You'll just have to live with it."

"So, we just sit here?" Vinnie asked when Charleston just turned to lean against the bars.

For several minutes, Charleston ignored him. "I could try to disarm the bomb, but I could blow us up."

"Correct me if I'm wrong, but we're going to blow up if you don't try. So, faced with possible death or certain death, possible is sounding pretty damn good."

"Let's leave that for a last resort," Charleston finally answered with a glance over toward the bomb.

Vinnie stopped breathing. Last resort. If that was their last resort, that implied that there were other resorts that weren't last. What had Charleston told him to remember? The first time Charleston had put Vinnie on the ground, he'd been pissed because Vinnie didn't have a backup plan. Something dark and ugly that had been sitting on his chest shifted, and Vinnie found he could breathe easier.

"You okay?" Charleston glanced over.

"I've been tied tighter for longer," Vinnie said with an awkward shrug. "So, I don't have anything to do other than listen to a long story about how you know our local poet-babbling psycho."

Charleston looked around the room, either checking exits or searching for a way to not tell this story. The man had never let anything about his past slip out, making it a subject of great interest during high school; however, Vinnie was starting to put together a few clues.

"Were you in the military together?" he asked.

Charleston took a long time to answer. He stepped over to the cot, sitting down and resting his elbows on his knees. "We were in Iraq. I was recovering from a wound and temporarily assigned to his unit as logistical backup until I got full clearance to go back into the field."

Vinnie snorted. "Logistical backup as in doing paperwork? They had you on paperwork? No offense, but you couldn't get your attendance done on a regular basis."

"Sure I could, Martello. It was just more fun making you run down to the office." Charleston's smile twisted into a sarcastic grin. "I was helping Thompson with background checks on Iraqis who were requesting political asylum. A lot of the time, I called around and made informal checks with soldiers in the refugees' home towns, looking for any sort of red flag."

"And there was one, only the red flag was Thompson," Vinnie concluded.

Charleston shook his head. "Nope. If anything, the man was overly cautious about granting visas. One sniff of anything, and he rejected the application. I thought he was a good officer."

Vinnie didn't even comment on that. From the sour expression on

Charleston's face, he didn't like thinking about just how wrong he'd been.

"It was a few months before we ran into each other in a certain type of club some of the soldiers set up informally."

Vinnie raised an eyebrow.

"Yes, Bernardi, that kind of club." Reaching over, he slapped Vinnie upside the head.

Damn. Charleston had been a Dom. While Vinnie had always thought the man would make a hot Dom, he'd never guessed that Charleston actually was one already. Clearly, he was an idiot. "Sorry, sir," Vinnie said with a playful version of contrition and a smirk. He didn't care how many head-slaps he got, it was worth it to get this kind of dirt on Charleston.

The glee evaporated. "Wait. You're actually a Dom and...." Vinnie stopped and swallowed. Okay. He could handle this. Charleston liked playing hard, but he just didn't want to play with Vinnie.

"You were a student, Bernardi." Charleston said.

"What?"

Charleston caught Vinnie's arm and tugged at him, forcing Vinnie to look at him. "You were a student," Charleston repeated. "I never dominated a man in my command, Bernardi. Never."

That might have comforted Vinnie except for one thing. "I haven't been a student for two years."

"And I've known that Thompson was somewhere in the background." Charleston ran his hand over his head, scrubbing his military-short hair. "He was convinced that we were the same—that I would cover for him when I found out about his scheme. He was so convinced of it that I knew he would come after me for betraying him, and I didn't want you in the middle."

"And you were not going to cover?" Vinnie guessed.

The dark laugh that came out of Charleston made it pretty clear that he hadn't even considered it an option. "His side business was human trafficking. Some of the families who applied, the ones who were most desperate, most in danger, and had the prettiest daughters—well he gave them an ultimatum. They handed over one child—one girl—or he would reject their application and they would most likely all die."

"And they went along with that?" Vinnie asked. Any incipient wisps of interest vanished under the horror.

"All of them? No. Plenty refused. They were sent back to the combat zone where insurgents executed them for cooperating with Americans." The muscle in the side of Charleston's jaw bulged.

Horror washed over Vinnie as he thought of families facing that choice—of families dying because Thompson sent them back into a war zone. It was almost worse to think of families escaping because they handed over a daughter. The thought made his stomach turn unhappily. As much as he hated his father, and he did, the man wouldn't have sold Vinnie in return for a ticket out of hell. Probably. "Didn't they complain?" Vinnie demanded.

Charleston looked over at Vinnie with the expression that suggested he couldn't quite believe the stupidity that was coming out of Vinnie's mouth, but it was a valid question. If someone tried blackmailing Vinnie, he would scream bloody murder until everyone within a five-hundred mile radius was as miserable as he was.

"Vinnie, every person who is turned down for a visa complains. Every single fucking one, and somewhere, all of their complaints are sitting in a pile that will only be uncovered after the documents are declassified and some egghead is writing a doctoral dissertation on the stupidity of the armed forces." Charleston's quiet laugh sent a shiver down Vinnie's back because he could hear the contained fury in it. "Maybe some geek will write about how many people Thompson indirectly killed, but as long as he was doing his job and keeping visas out of the hands of terrorists, his commanders were just too busy to worry about locals with a few complaints."

Vinnie slumped back against the wall; now he had more than one reason to hate psycho-boy. Whatever backup plan Charleston had, Vinnie was really hoping it included Thompson getting really, really dead. "Wait." Vinnie sat up. "He thought you would go along with that? Did he really think you'd go along with blackmail and slavery? Okay, the crazy guy is crazier than I thought."

"He never could tell the difference between a strong Dom and an abusive one. If I convinced a boy to kneel on the ground until he was so crippled he couldn't walk—all because he wanted to please me—then Thompson thought he should take a girl and cripple her to prove he was just as good."

"And he's not in jail because…."

"Because he covered his ass."

"That must have been a hell of a lot of covering."

"Well, he didn't cover as well as he thought. He had the whole alphabet soup sniffing around, but none of them had fingered him until he laid his whole plan out for me and tried to convince me to pick the boy of my choice from one of the cooperating families." Charleston's face twisted with disgust. "When I turned him in… well, it was a mess, but it put the feds on the right path."

"Go feds," Vinnie said. He'd be happy to have a few break down the door right now. "Which feds?"

Charleston snorted. "Most of them. The CIA caught wind of some overseas buyers getting slaves from an American. The FBI intercepted two slaves stateside and started an investigation. When I came forward, CID opened an investigation." Charleston's tone shifted when he mentioned CID, and Vinnie wondered about that.

"CID?"

"United States Army Criminal Investigation Command," Charleston said without explaining why he sounded constipated when he said it. For a long time, Charleston stared out the bars, and Vinnie wished he could read minds. Or maybe he didn't…. He wasn't sure he wanted to know what Charleston had rattling around up there. "The paperwork disappeared along with the last of the girls, slowing down the investigation, and then Thompson himself just vanished."

"If he was a killer, or even accused of being a killer, shouldn't someone have been keeping track of him?" Vinnie didn't have much experience with killers, but logic said that you should probably lock them up before they vanished.

"You'd think." Charleston ran his hand over his head again. "The

CID turned up a few badly scarred women who wouldn't testify and paperwork that implicated me, so they weren't too quick to throw him in a cell."

"Oh shit. He blamed you." Vinnie could just imagine how that went over. Charleston was not exactly warm and cuddly under the best of circumstances, but if someone accused him of human slavery and murder, Vinnie didn't even want to consider how scary the man would have been.

"I was the one who turned him. He always loved the symbolism of things, and getting me sent to prison would have made a certain justice in his twisted world."

"And you ran?" Vinnie couldn't keep the shock out of his voice. Charleston gave him a withering look.

"I stayed until the investigation stalled, but after a few attempts on my life, CID decided that I was more likely to be a target than a suspect... probably. Unfortunately, that didn't really solve my real problem. I couldn't go back into my unit knowing that someone was gunning for me. I was putting my entire unit at risk because Thompson would have killed them all just to get his revenge on me."

"So you went into hiding."

"So I temporarily retired from the engagement," Charleston corrected him.

Vinnie looked around at the cell and gave a weak laugh. "We seem to be engaging, again."

"Yeah, Martello, I noticed."

"Bernardi," Vinnie automatically corrected him. Charleston reached over and put a hand on Vinnie's knee. "Charleston, I'm really sorry I put you in this spot," Vinnie apologized. "I know I complicated this mess pretty badly."

Charleston gave a weak smile. "I knew you'd never follow the order. I just thought I had a twenty-four hour window before you'd go out and deliberately do the exact opposite of what I'd told you. I should have remembered that you always were ahead of the curve—in more ways than one."

Vinnie cringed. If he hadn't been such an easy target, if he hadn't spread his legs for this guy, then maybe Charleston would be on the outside of this cage trying to find a way to bring this guy down.

"Don't worry about it. I didn't plan to live in hiding forever, Vinnie. You did what I couldn't; you flushed him out."

"By spreading my legs."

"There's nothing wrong with sex, Bernardi. Now your taste in men? That could use a little work." Charleston gave his leg a pat and then leaned back against the cinderblock wall and closed his eyes. Vinnie realized that Charleston had ended the conversation, and he really didn't have anything to do except settle back against the wall and try to not think about the potential for a horrible, painful death in his near future. Charleston would have a plan. Vinnie was just going to hold onto that belief with everything in his soul.

Chapter
Seventeen

"Isn't that cute?" Vinnie opened his eyes, startled to find he'd dozed off. In his sleep, he'd slipped to the side so that his cheek rested against Charleston's shoulder. Thompson was standing in front of the cell with a sneer on his face. "Aw. I woke the wide-eyed boy. He's just like a bunny rabbit about to get shot by the big, bad hunter." He looked Vinnie up and down, the sneer deepening.

"Funny enough, he's still leaning on me, Thompson. Maybe one day you'll finally learn how to get a sub to truly submit, but not today." Charleston sounded supremely self-assured. With one heel resting against the edge of the cot and an arm resting casually on the knee that stuck up, he looked like a model posing for a camera—all dominance and calm confidence. Vinnie certainly didn't feel like moving, especially since his bound hands would require him to squirm and wiggle awkwardly. While he liked the idea of squirming and struggling under Charleston's gaze, he was not about to give Thompson that privilege.

"Is that so?" Thompson's smile widened. "'Grave men, near death, who see with blinding sight. Rage, rage against the dying of the light.' So tell me, Vinnie, will you rage? Will you fight against the dying of the light, or are you going to sit in that cell and die with Kalb?" Thompson moved closer to the cell, his eyes on Charleston even though he was talking to Vinnie. "Come with me, boy, and I promise you'll be safe even as crime scene technicians are trying to find all the pieces of Charleston for the coffin."

Vinnie arched his back and tried to gracefully sit up. He failed. Charleston had to reach over and push him upright, his large hand resting against Vinnie's shoulder, bracing him.

"You have got to be kidding me. Do you really think I'm stupid enough to go anywhere with you?" Thompson's mouth came open, and the smug grin told Vinnie exactly what he was about to say. Yeah, he'd been an idiot, but Vinnie hurried to cut Thompson off before the man could point that out. "Well, would I ever go with you if I weren't so fucking desperate? It took two Doms turning me down before I decided to take the first pathetic poser who wandered along. Seriously, if I had to pick between you and a dyke with a big old strap-on, I'd pick the dyke every time, and women don't really do it for me. Actually, if I had to pick between you and a bomb, I'm picking the bomb." Vinnie gave Thompson the same arrogant smile that always drove his father past the point of rage. This was the smile that had first gotten him exiled to military school, and it seemed to work just as well on Thompson.

With a glare, Thompson turned toward Charleston. "You made him some sort of promise, didn't you? I know you, Kalb. You wouldn't walk in here without a plan. Did you tell him that you had a plan? That you had contacted someone before coming here? That you texted someone?"

"Charleston texting?" Vinnie almost laughed. "Honestly, I'm not sure he knows how to turn a computer on, much less text."

"Is that true, Kalb?" Thompson sounded overly friendly again. When he sounded friendly, Vinnie started to worry.

Charleston put his foot down on the ground. "I do what needs to be done."

"You always did, Cap." A new voice came from the hallway just outside the door, and a new man walked in. He was a tall man with wide shoulders and a crew cut. He was older, but he had the look of someone who still worked out on a regular basis. Vinnie looked from Charleston to this new man, but Charleston's face had gone utterly blank. "I never wanted this, Cap. I told Thompson to leave you out of the middle."

"He's weak. I watched him in those clubs. He knows what it means to want to take control over someone—to own them, but he'll never give himself permission to follow his true nature," Thompson sneered at Charleston. "I could practically smell the need every time he tied one of his boys and put them over his lap, but then he goes and plays sanctimonious."

"I don't play," Charleston said coldly. He stood, each movement deliberate and slow, and Vinnie held his breath, aware that some storm front was moving through. "Thompson is just a crazy son of a bitch. What's your excuse?" he asked the new man.

"Same one as always, Cap. Money. If those people want to rip their country apart and put my life and the lives of my men in danger, the least they can do is pay for the privilege."

"You took money to enslave young girls that had nothing to do with any of that."

The new guy gave a soft laugh and shook his head. "God, Jeff, you haven't changed. You're still the arrogant son of a bitch who thinks he has the right answer for everyone."

"No," Charleston moved to the bars, wrapping his fingers around one of the bars. "I know what's right for me, and I know that I don't have a right to hurt other people."

Thompson interrupted. "You enjoy hurting other people. I've seen the expression on your boys' faces as they struggle to please you, suffering to stay still or do some pointless task. You watch them with this hunger.... You eat their pain."

Charleston slowly shifted his gaze, looking at Thompson for one second before he turned back to the new man. "I enjoy their submission, their willingness to try and please me no matter what. But I would never carve on a woman's back until she was so scarred that her shoulders couldn't fully rotate without the damaged skin pulling tight and splitting. I would never torture someone, enslave them, and tell them that their families would die if they complained. I never left a sub lying in a pool of her own blood. Until today, I would have said the same about you, Steger."

"Torture isn't my thing, Cap. Murder isn't either."

"But you plan to kill me. If you didn't, you wouldn't have come in here," Charleston said. Vinnie was amazed at how calm he sounded. The pit of Vinnie's stomach was starting to churn with acid, and the idea that this might have been Charleston's backup—this might have been the person Charleston called before coming—that fear was eating a hole in his stomach lining.

Steger's expression turned sad, and his voice got soft. "I thought I owed you an apology, face to face."

"For murdering me?" Charleston's eyebrow twitched.

"I tried to get you out of the way. If you hadn't found that wire...." The man looked down, and for a half second, Vinnie almost believed he was sorry to be doing this. However, since the man was talking about murdering Charleston in order to cover up selling girls into slavery, he clearly wasn't the sort that actually had all that many human emotions or morals.

"He's a loose end. We should have killed him three years ago," Thompson said.

Steger looked over at him. "All you had to do was fucking stay away from him."

"He found the wire." Thompson sounded defensive. "You said he wouldn't find it if we put it on the outside line, but he did. Was I just supposed to wait until he tracked me down?"

Steger glanced over toward Vinnie. "He was motivated to look at potential surveillance a little more closely. I suppose we have you to thank for that, Bernardi." Steger focused on Charleston again. "You always did attract the pretty young recruits, Cap. If I had a gay man in the command, I could always spot him by seeing who went sniffing after you. I could never understand that."

"They trust me," Charleston pointed out.

"No doubt they do. Maybe that's why Thompson thought he could trust you. I certainly told him often enough that you weren't going to go along with this scheme. Not for money and certainly not just to get first pick of the toys, but he insisted on trusting you. You shouldn't have been so inflexible, though. You lost a lot, and for someone who always preached about having clear objectives and making sure that you gained more than you lost in any engagement, you have lost a lot and gained very little. I'm just sorry that we're having to end our friendship this way."

"I'm not friends with slavers."

"I knew you'd say that." Steger nodded as if he was agreeing. "Thompson, you make it quick. I don't want him suffering."

Vinnie half stood and half rolled off the cot and eased closer to Charleston. "Please tell me this isn't your backup," Vinnie whispered. His stomach couldn't take any more uncertainty. Charleston looked over his shoulder at Vinnie, his eyes blank.

"Ah, young Vinnie has just realized that his great mentor failed," Thompson said with great glee. "There's no rescue coming for you. You had your clever plan, and it has totally fallen through. The all-powerful Kalb has feet of clay. *Horse and hero fell*, Kalb. Your glory fades."

Charleston looked at him. "I've always wondered, how many scars do you have? Even in Iraq, you always kept your arms covered, so did the person who tortured you use knives or cigarettes? Was it your mother—is that why you prefer to torture women? Did she recite her poetry while she tortured you, or were those two separate events that you connected later in life? Maybe she read you poetry when she put you in your bed at night, and then later she'd come in, drunk or angry or maybe just mentally ill, and she'd start hurting you, watching you cry and beg for her to stop."

While Charleston normally had a terse speaking style, his voice got a sing-song lull to it, something that reminded Vinnie of the third therapist that his father had dragged him to. However, the therapist never managed to cut as deeply as Charleston clearly had. Thompson staggered back, his left hand clutching at his right arm and his eyes wide like an owl's.

"You never give up, do you, Cap?" Steger stepped forward, right between Charleston and Thompson. "It won't work this time, Jeff. The more miserable you make Thompson, the more he's going to take it out on that boy of yours. Think about him."

Vinnie sucked in a breath, and Charleston took a small step back so his back pressed right up against Vinnie. "He's a sadist. He's insane and a sadist. If you help him get away, every girl he kills will be on your conscience. You were a good man, Steger. Think about this."

"Malayeen was a mistake." Steger said calmly. "Thompson isn't a killer. Hell, Cap, you and I have both killed a lot more than he ever dreamed of. Malayeen was just an unfortunate accident."

However, Thompson was already shaking his head, clearly not happy about the way the other two were talking about him. "She begged. She said that she wanted my words carved into her flesh. It's no different from what you did when you tied your boys down and took the whip to their backs."

"My boys always walked away," Charleston said. "I never left a permanent mark on them. They got up the next morning and lived their lives."

"She wanted—" Thompson started yelling, but Steger reached back and rested a hand on Thompson's shoulder and the man quieted.

"Cap, I give you my word that I will check on your boy. Thompson will not mark him up like he did Malayeen, but he needs a toy to keep him occupied, and the only other alternative is to eliminate Vinnie as a witness."

"Nice choice," Vinnie whispered. Leaning forward, he let his weight rest against Charleston's back. This was so very bad. So very, very bad.

"'Grave men, near death', and you are so very, very near to death," Thompson sounded happy again. "Vinnie, you can choose to live. Rage against death. Walk away from him and live."

Vinnie looked at Charleston, but the man had absolutely no expression on his face. Clearly, he wasn't going to get an answer there. Gathering up what courage he could, Vinnie swallowed and tried to work up enough spit to actually talk without his tongue sticking to his mouth. Rolling his head to the side, he moved away from Charleston with a languid roll of the hips and a long gaze at Thompson.

"I have another poem," Vinnie said. He spoke slowly, but that was as much about fear as seduction. "Roses are red, violets are blue. Bite me." Deliberately turning toward Charleston, Vinnie looked at the man, reveling in the respect he could see in Charleston's face. Yep, he was going to die, but at least he could say he'd done one thing right in his life first. That was one thing more than a lot of people could claim. Walking over to the cot, Vinnie dropped down. He'd picked his side, and he wasn't going to change now. "Some things are worth dying for."

Charleston stared at Thompson with the same cold, emotionless expression. "It looks like you still can't get a sub to follow you." Thompson had turned absolutely white, and Vinnie sneered at him. If he had to die, he'd do whatever damage he could on the way down. He sure as hell wasn't going to kneel at Thompson's feet.

Steger stepped close to the bars. "Talk to him, Kalb. You don't want the kid dying."

"I don't tell my partners what to do; I give them choices. You know that, Steger. What, is your conscience bothering you on this one, or are you afraid that killing Martello, Junior is going to bring down a little more heat than you're willing to deal with? Thompson might have walked into this blind, but I know you. You did enough digging to know exactly who Thompson was using as bait."

Thompson's face was slowly pinking, and now he frowned. "Martello?"

With a small smile, Charleston looked at Thompson. "You always had a talent for finding souls that no one would care about, but if the forensics people dig deep enough, they're going to find out that you killed Troy Martello Jr., the wayward and footloose son of a rather influential man. This isn't some faceless and helpless family you're fucking with. Martello, Senior is going to make more noise than you're willing to deal with."

Steger answered. "There's not going be enough of either one of you left for anyone to make that connection. Come on, Thompson." Steger opened the door out into the warehouse area. "Cap, I am sorry. You're a good man, but business is business." With that, Steger pulled Thompson from the room. As the door closed, it occurred to Vinnie that they were so very, very screwed.

Chapter
Eighteen

"DUMB move, Martello." Charleston sighed.

"Bernardi," Vinnie corrected him. He got the briefest glare before Charleston shook his head.

"You could call them back. It's not too late to get yourself out of this."

"And ruin my perfect parting shot?" Vinnie gave a snort to let Charleston know how much he didn't like that idea. "Now that was a perfect insult. Usually I run my mouth too much and ruin the moment."

This time the look Charleston gave him was almost amused. Vinnie shrugged and grinned. He knew his faults well enough. He looked damn pretty in bondage, but his mouth had absolutely no off-button, which might explain his fondness for gags.

Vinnie shifted on the bed and tried to stretch his shoulders. The cuffs were tight enough that his shoulders were starting to really ache. "So, what's the plan, sir?"

"Sir?" Charleston's eyebrow went up.

"Master?" Vinnie said. If he was going to die for submitting to Charleston and not idiot-poetry guy, he might as well make the most of it. True, his cock wasn't feeling all that interested in having sex with the bomb in the room, but damn it, Vinnie was going to indulge in his submission as much as he could, all the way up to the point where they blew up.

"Stick with sir," Charleston said. Turning around, he looked at the backpack with the hoodie still thrown over it.

"Right, sir. So, what's the plan?" Vinnie could see the calculating look in Charleston's eye. Vinnie might be down and out, but Charleston still had a trick or three to play.

"We stop the bomb from going off." Charleston walked over and tossed the hoodie to one side before unzipping the backpack.

"Can you do that?" Vinnie edged closer, his stomach rolling at the sight of all the wires. He was expecting some sort of big countdown, an electronic clock with the digits inexorably rolling toward zero when the bomb would go off. Instead, there was only a shoebox sized grey box with a lot of duct tape and two little wires attached to a thingy. It was a little disappointing.

Without answering, Charleston pulled a tiny knife out of the back of his boot and started prodding at the edges of the box. Shifting around until he was hunched up over the bomb, Charleston carefully sliced through the layers of tape.

"Um, sir, what are the odds that we're about to get very blown up?" Vinnie asked.

"Higher if you don't stop talking, Bernardi."

"Shutting up, sir." Vinnie sat on the edge of the cot and watched Charleston work. Charleston shifted and bent down farther, studying the box as he worked the knife up under the tape and carefully peeled back the layers. Sweat started soaking through Charleston's shirt, but then Vinnie was feeling the stress, and he wasn't even the one with their lives in his hands. When the world started going gray around the edges, Vinnie figured out he was holding his breath, and he let it out with an explosive sigh. Charleston turned and looked over his shoulder, his displeasure pretty fucking clear. "Sorry," Vinnie offered, cringing the minute the apology slipped out.

Charleston always told the class that apologies were worthless. Words never made up for any action which required an apology. If someone's actions, like distracting the guy disarming the bomb, were offensive, the offender had to commit an action that would remediate that situation. Vinnie smiled as he remembered Charleston explaining that rule in painful detail after ordering Vinnie to the ground for a hundred pushups. So instead of being worthless, Vinnie just needed to find some way to help. Yeah. Not really much chance there. He strained against the cuffs more to stretch the muscles than out of any hope of freeing himself.

"Damn it." Charleston cursed as the small knife slipped out of his hands and clattered across the concrete.

"Sir, do you want to put the box up here so you can see it better?" Vinnie offered.

"I need to hold it steady, Vinnie." Charleston had the box braced between his outstretched legs, but that made working on it even more awkward as he hunched over. Reaching for his knife, Charleston bent back over his work.

"Sir, bring it over here. I'll hold it with my legs," Vinnie offered. That made Charleston look up at him.

"Do you really want this between your legs if it goes off?" Charleston raised an eyebrow at him, and Vinnie could feel himself blush under the scrutiny. Charleston had always done that to him—made him feel like squirming out of his skin with just one look. However, Vinnie wasn't little Troy Martello anymore.

Vinnie gave a wicked smile. "Trust me, if that thing goes off between my legs, you are going to hate yourself because you have no idea just how much talent you would be wasting." Vinnie shocked himself by giving Charleston a wink. Imminent death obviously did good things for him, and the impertinence amused Charleston because he almost smiled; Vinnie could see it in the way the corners of his eyes sort of crinkled a little. He was the only man Vinnie knew who could smile without his lips moving—or maybe Vinnie had just spent more time studying Charleston than he had most people.

Shaking his head, Charleston lifted the box. "Don't let this move as I'm peeling the tape. There may be wires."

"Got it, sir," Vinnie promised. Shifting around, he put his back to one of the concrete walls and stretched his legs. Charleston lifted the box and put it between Vinnie's knees. With one knee bent, Vinnie could hold the box steady, and Charleston gave a short nod of approval that made Vinnie glad he'd thought to offer.

With a sigh, Charleston sat on the ground next to the cot so that he was eye level with the box. "I'm getting too old for this shit," he muttered. However, he went right to work, his strong fingers feeling each millimeter of tape for any wires right before he pulled it back bit by bit. The silence hung heavily in the air, and Vinnie rested his head back against the cold concrete and tried to not feel utterly helpless. He loved submitting—he loved letting someone else work his body like it was an instrument—but this utter helplessness left him feeling like he was sitting on the edge of panic. Charleston was down to the last strip of tape when he sighed and stretched his arms over his head to work out the kinks.

"So, how much bang could you get out of a box this big?" Vinnie asked before Charleston could get to work again. The silence was really getting to him.

Charleston glanced up before shifting on the floor and leaning over Vinnie's one leg to work on the taped edge again. "Depends on the explosive. RDX, PETN, mercury fulminate, CL-20, Nitroglycerine-triacetine, C4, primacord, TNT... they're all different."

"But poetry freak couldn't get the really good stuff, could he?" Vinnie tried not to hold his breath as he waited for the answer.

Charleston kept working on the tape, carefully separating the layers as he tried to get the box open without disturbing wires. "Thompson? Nope. He's been a desk jockey for most of his military career."

Vinnie breathed a sigh of relief.

"But Steger? He was the compliance officer. He had access to any number of munitions since he had to sign off that we were handling all ordinances in compliance with UN law and military procedures."

Letting his head thunk back against the cinderblock, Vinnie swore. "Well fuck. Nothing like putting the psycho in charge of the big bombs. That's the military for you." Vinnie knew he hated the military for some reason other than his father's bad habit of shoving him in military school.

Charleston shook his head. "Steger's not psycho—just greedy."

"Psychotically greedy."

The room went silent, and both of them stopped breathing as Charleston carefully lifted the top off, and they finally got to look inside the guts of the bomb. Vinnie could see wires and colorful coils and shiny, copper squares that reflected the light. If the damn thing wasn't set to blow them both up, he'd be tempted to call it pretty. Charleston just stared down into the bomb guts.

"Is that a good blank expression or a bad one, sir?" Vinnie finally asked.

Charleston didn't immediately answer, but he did start moving again. Using the tip of his knife, he traced the path of each wire and coil. "Primaline 85." His knife circled around the light apple-green coil. "C4." He pointed at the four gray squares. "Copper plated shrapnel." With his knife, he pushed the copper, watching it wiggle.

"You do know that none of that answers my question, right?"

"Yep," Charleston answered. Then he went to work pulling out the copper strips, dropping them to the ground with little tinny ringing sounds. Since Vinnie couldn't really do anything else, he just stared at the ceiling and tried to not think about Charleston's weight against his leg holding him down or the bomb between his knees. Yeah, he'd had plenty of fantasies about serving some Dom, but serving as the bomb-disarming table hadn't been high on his list. Hell, he might have taken a runner, only serving as psycho-boy's carving board sounded even less fun. If he blew up in here, at least it'd be quick.

The last of the copper came out, and Charleston rocked back on his heels and looked at the guts of the bomb.

"Prayer time?" Vinnie guessed.

"Never quit on me, Bernardi."

"I never would, sir," Vinnie promised. "I'm just wondering exactly where you're leading."

Arching his back so that it gave an audible crack, Charleston looked around the small room. "We might be able to get the explosives out and slide them across the floor."

"Would this be life saving or just death delaying? Honestly, if we're going to end up dying of smoke and third degree burns anyway, I'd rather just be sitting on top of the damn thing."

Charleston patted his leg. "A lot of the damage is done by shrapnel." Charleston stood up and used his toe to shove some of the copper strips. "Those would have fragmented and cut through us like hot bullets."

"So, if we get the bomb outside the cage?"

Charleston shrugged. It wasn't the most comforting gesture, but then, Vinnie knew that Charleston defined emotional constipation before he'd went and fallen madly in unrequited lust with the guy.

"What do you want me to do, sir?"

"Sit there." Charleston picked up the box and headed over toward the bars before carefully angling the box to the side. He put his hand over the various components to hold them in place and crumpled the very edges of the box to get it to fit through the bars.

"On it, sir," Vinnie whispered. Unless Charleston was going to pull something truly spectacular out of his very nicely shaped ass, this was it. This was the end of the line for Vinnie Bernardi. When Vinnie'd picked out that name, he'd had such high hopes for it. Vinnie was going to be a confident man, someone who didn't hide his sexual preferences or his emotions or his very nicely formed biceps. He was going to be successful without ever turning into an asshole like one Troy Martello, Sr. He was going to be fucking awesome.

Instead, he was a half-time stripper, half-time janitor with a crappy apartment, lousy taste in one-night stands, and a stupid crush on an old high school teacher. Vinnie watched Charleston. His forearms were slick with sweat, and his graying hair lay dark against his neck where more sweat had made it stick to the skin. Those streaks of black hair still staining the gray really stood out this close up, and Vinnie wished he could run his fingers through it. Did Charleston have coarse hair or fine? How would he react if Vinnie did that? His eyes always seemed to have some perfect storm behind them, like there was all this passion dammed up waiting for it all to break loose, and Vinnie sighed.

The doorknob started to turn, and Vinnie's stomach lurched and felt like it had gotten lodged half-way up his throat.

"Fuck," Charleston cursed. Pushing the bomb to the corner, he stepped back and put himself right in front of Vinnie.

"Kalb?" a soft voice called. A new voice. Vinnie was starting to think he needed to keep a scorecard.

"About damn time you got here," Charleston said, and that was the voice that would have sent Vinnie running if he wasn't tied up and locked in a cell with the man. He was pissed.

"Temper, temper. Someone told me to keep my damn distance."

"Whoever did that is a moron," Charleston said. Vinnie could tell from the tone Charleston was talking about himself.

The new man walked in, a gun drawn and a smile on his face. "Yeah, I can't imagine who would have said that. Probably some other bastard who wanted Steger so much he put his neck on the line. It's good to see that your neck didn't actually get cut off when you did that." The man was so average he almost vanished. His hair was starting to gray, but unlike Charleston, he was losing it. He was totally average height and average looks and even had on an average brown suit with an unremarkable tie. Vinnie still noticed the guy for some reason. Maybe it was because Charleston's whole body relaxed the second this new man walked in.

Charleston reached down and rested a hand on Vinnie's shoulder. Average guy's eyebrows went up. "Yeah, or some other idiot who thought Steger was honest and expected this whole thing to prove it... you mean that idiot?"

In the past, Vinnie had always thought Charleston was too tough on people. He pushed the cadets harder than any of the other instructors had ever dreamed of, yet from his tone and the self-hatred on his face, Charleston pushed himself even more. And he was even harder on himself when he fucked up.

"You had faith in a fellow officer—that's not a bad thing, Kalb." The new guy walked over and looked into the box with the bomb. "Um... is this a problem, and were you planning on mentioning it eventually?"

"Primaline 85 with C4."

"That would be a problem," the new guy agreed. "I don't suppose they were stupid enough to leave the keys hanging around here?"

Charleston didn't even answer. The new guy pulled a radio off his belt and started quietly calling for a bomb squad and some tactical team. Charleston leaned forward so that he looked like he was trying to push down the cell bars. "Keep your surveillance team back until we're out of here, or Steger is going to send us all to hell," Charleston warned.

"Speak for yourself, Kalb. I plan to head up."

"Kaplan, you're going to hell with all the other bastards, and you know it."

Kaplan didn't have time to answer before three men in body armor came into the room. Immediately, Kaplan—the all-average guy—became the center of the room. He directed two men in armor over to the bomb and directed the third to the cell door. He stood at the open doorway with the radio held up near his ear, clearly listening to every word as teams coordinated through a dizzying flurry of numbers and code words that made no sense to Vinnie. Charleston must have understood, though, because he would hear something through Kaplan's radio and tense up, his fingers curling around the bars until the knuckles turned white, and then he would hear something else and let out a sigh and hang his head. Overall, if Vinnie had to guess based on Charleston's body language, the good guys were not coming out on top.

Vinnie jumped when a little popping sound echoed against the cinderblock, and then the cell door swung open with a puff of smoke.

"Oh thank God," Vinnie breathed reverently. After today, he was ready to take up religion again.

Charleston pulled on Vinnie's elbow, rushing him out of the room so fast that Vinnie nearly got tangled in his own feet. "I need bolt cutters, and I need to go after that bastard." Charleston strode toward the now-open cell door, and the explosives guys at the door seemed to scatter out of his way just as quickly as the cadets always had at school.

"Kalb." Kaplan was left to chase after Vinnie in an odd sort of parade. "Kalb!"

Charleston stopped in the warehouse hall, and Vinnie flattened himself against the wall so he wasn't in Charleston's way as he turned to face Kaplan.

"What?"

For a second, Kaplan just stared at Charleston like he couldn't believe what he was hearing. "I have Steger. You're a witness in this—hell, you're supposed to be a protected witness, not that the protected status worked all that well, but you can't go after the main suspects."

"The hell I can't."

Vinnie held his breath as Charleston's eyes turned as cold as Vinnie had ever seen them. He wanted to kill…. Vinnie could see that in every line of Charleston's body.

"Jeff, you have other responsibilities here. You've gone above and beyond the call of duty here, so let me take care of this." Kaplan turned to look at Vinnie, and slowly Charleston turned to look as well. Between the two men's gazes, Vinnie felt pretty well pinned in place. Like water draining from a tub, the tension seemed to leave Charleston. Reaching out, he rested a hand on Vinnie's shoulder before looking back over at Kaplan.

"Steger is going to get away if you don't move fast."

"Then let me do my job. You have done more for this investigation than anyone who's officially assigned to it, but this part is my job, Jeff. You take care of things here."

Charleston hesitated. Usually Charleston made decisions so fast that it was hard to even keep up, but he looked from Kaplan to Vinnie and then back. Eventually he turned to Kaplan with an evil glare. "You nail that bastard, or I will never let you forget that you fucked up," Charleston warned. Vinnie knew just how much motivation that kind of fear could be. He'd actually aced his last semester just out of his utter terror of Charleston.

"I wouldn't expect less from an old bastard like you." Kaplan smiled at Charleston fondly right before two men in suits came up. Then his expression turned emotionless. "Let the agents get you somewhere safe. I'm going after Steger and Thompson." Kaplan trotted past them both.

"We need to clear the area immediately," one of the new suits suggested, holding his arm out to invite Charleston to head down the hall.

Charleston didn't even bother to answer. He put his hand on the small of Vinnie's back and hurried him down the hallway. Vinnie tried very hard to not read too much into it when Charleston's hand continued to rest against his back as the two suits finally herded them into the backseat of a car. Even better, neither one of the agents batted an eye at Vinnie being tied up or barefoot or even about the fact that he was glued to Charleston's side.

Chapter
Nineteen

CHARLESTON put one hand over the back of Vinnie's head and the other on his shoulder as he helped him into the car. Vinnie might have protested that he didn't need the coddling, only his legs were shaky and he was afraid he might fall on his face if he tried to do it on his own. One agent got behind the wheel, and the other walked around the car while Charleston got in.

Vinnie stared out at the gray sky and the dirty warehouses that surrounded a parking lot with huge cracks that allowed a paper-thin jungle of weeds to grow up in the middle of it. Charleston sat so close that Vinnie could feel the heat of his body.

"You did good, Bernardi." Charleston offered the rare praise, and Vinnie could see the agent glance in the rearview mirror. Vinnie wondered how much they knew—for example, did they know he got himself captured by spreading his legs for the biggest psycho this side of a Stephen King novel? "You kept your cool, kept the enemy off guard with your verbal attacks, and followed my lead. I know battle-tested soldiers who would have struggled to do as much." Charleston fell silent, and Vinnie bit his tongue to avoid begging Charleston for more. Charleston wasn't an easy one for giving praise. Actually, Vinnie had never heard him give so much praise at once, and Vinnie clung to that as he replayed the words in his head over and over. After all, Charleston wouldn't have said them if they weren't true.

The door opened, and the second agent got in on the passenger side. Leaning into the car, he offered Charleston the red handled end of a very large tool. "The bolt cutters you asked for, sir."

Charleston took them, and Vinnie twisted around to give him room to get to the cuffs. One sharp snap and then another echoed in the car while the agent started the engine. "How are your shoulders?" Charleston asked.

"Better than my ego," Vinnie answered. He brought his hands around to the front and studied the cuffs that were still locked around his wrist. The lock was embedded in the leather. Charleston reached out and captured his hand, running his fingers over the leather and lock.

"I can't get the cutters under this. Either we're going to need a rotary cutter and some place much safer than a moving car, or I'm going to have to find a good lock pick." He put the bolt cutters on the floor of the backseat.

Vinnie nodded. When Charleston gave him his hand back, he let it fall to his knee. He'd let Thompson cuff him. Oh, he'd let Thompson use the padded handcuffs back at his house and not these monsters, but he'd allowed it to happen. How many times had RJ told him that he was headed for a fall? How many times, and he still just went tripping merrily down the path.

"Agent Kaplan would like a report as soon as we get to the safe house," one of the agents said in the silence.

Charleston just nodded.

They were in the middle of city traffic before the agent spoke again. "They managed to contain the bomb."

"Disarmed?" Charleston asked.

The agent shook his head. "Bomb squad wouldn't even try. They did a controlled detonation." He glanced over his shoulder. "Apparently, that was one seriously large explosion."

Charleston studied the man for a second. "Jordan, right?"

"Yes, sir."

"You were there when I was being questioned."

Jordan nodded without looking particularly bothered by the accusation. Vinnie would have curled up and died if he'd ever done anything as stupid as accuse Charleston of being involved in slavery. Charleston however, just gave an amiable nod. "Steger was always efficient," Charleston said. "I wouldn't have expected any less from him."

"Efficient or not, Kaplan is going to take him down." The driver nodded without actually adding anything to the conversation.

"He is a stubborn bastard," Charleston agreed. "If anyone can go toe to toe with Steger, good old Dwayne is the man to do it."

"Dwayne?" Vinnie couldn't keep the horror out of his voice.

The agent turned all the way around in his seat. "You might want to avoid commenting on his name. He's a little cranky when people do," he advised Vinnie.

"Yeah, look at the false identity he saddled me with for the last three years," Charleston said. "I sound like a minor character from *Gone with the Wind*. Dwayne is not only stubborn but mean as hell."

"Yes, sir, he is," Jordan agreed before he turned back around to face front.

"Stop it," Charleston said out of nowhere.

Vinnie jumped and looked over, not sure who Charleston was ordering to stop.

"The cuffs." Charleston gestured, and Vinnie looked down where he was slowly rotating the one around his left wrist. "You're going to chafe the skin, so stop."

"Oh." Vinnie did stop, laying his hands in his lap. They'd left the decaying city, and now the old storefronts and chain link fence topped with barbed wire had given way to apartments and cramped little houses. Watching the streets go by, Vinnie still couldn't quite get his head wrapped around the sudden twists and turns his life had taken. Clearly all the rumors about Charleston and his shady past hadn't even come close to living up to the man's reality, and he was just as badass as every story Vinnie and the others had made up at night after lights out. It was funny. He did seem to fall for the guys with something to hide.

There were Charleston and Thompson, although with Thompson it was more of a stumble than a fall. He hadn't even liked Thompson as well as the faceless fucks he'd picked up in a dozen bars. It was only Charleston who really caught not only his lust but his imagination. About the only other Dom to seriously catch his eye was this middle-aged man with a shock of white hair in the middle of his mop of red curls. He had a square jaw, and when he had come into RJ's place, he had a commanding authority that pulled Vinnie into his orbit. He'd certainly enjoyed Vinnie's attention, and one night Vinnie had followed the guy home to spy on him in the suburbs as the guy watered his lawn. And yes, Vinnie did see the irony in that. He got all suspicious of the harmless guy, and he had no worries at all when he took a psychopathic killer to his bed. He sucked. He sucked in more ways than one.

But the red-haired top with the commanding attitude turned out to be just a city worker. Vinnie's fantasies had died as he watched the man smile and nod at the complaints of people who didn't like their driver's license picture or the length of the line. Seeing the real man had ruined the fantasy, something he had complained about to RJ as he washed beer glasses. RJ had called him an idiot. While he hadn't been willing to admit it out loud, he'd sort of agreed because he'd lost his chance at some really hot sex with a red-haired Dom with these huge hands. But Vinnie just couldn't get past the idea that the guy was faking it.

Vinnie could totally understand not liking yourself and wanting to create a new identity. RJ had done it. He'd caught a glimpse of a picture in her wallet once… her in a little dress dancing with her father. But now she was all man… or mannish maybe. At least she talked and dressed like a man, and the last guy who'd called her Rebecca had gone running out of the bar screaming in fear. And Vinnie was fairly sure RJ still hadn't done her census.

In his own life, he'd hated Troy Martello. Troy was a sad little twerp who tried so hard to fit in that he had this mask that he wore so that people would like him. His father had started dumping him on nannies and stepmothers and just about anyone he could by the time Troy was five, and Troy had learned to either entertain his father or watch his father go off with the first pretty woman to cross his path. Of course, even when Troy played the fool, his father had still left, so Troy had developed a whole new set of behaviors, one that included police reports and courtrooms. It was harder to ignore court-ordered family therapy than it was to ignore some little snot-nosed kid who wanted you to stay with him instead of chasing the leggy blonde who'd just walked into the restaurant.

So Vinnie could admire someone who had the strength to just throw one life away and start another. He admired Charleston. He admired RJ. He just couldn't understand or forgive Mr. Red-haired Authority for holding onto a life he hated while he played at being dominant at RJ's place. Vinnie figured he probably wasn't a good person, because that sounded cold and judgmental, even in the privacy of his own brain, but it was true. He'd prided himself on not having masks and living the life he wanted, and then he turned around and fell for the biggest mask of all. His damn internal alarm had warned him that red-haired guy was a poser, but it didn't even chirp when a psycho killer chatted him up.

Vinnie suspected that his brain was melting down. His thoughts shifted from topic to topic. He had been so rude to the red-haired Dom when the guy had tried to get friendly after Vinnie made his little covert mission. And RJ had been quietly pissed at him for being pissed at the guy. And Charleston had to think he was an idiot for falling for Thompson, even if he had done well by not falling apart afterwards. Troy would have fallen apart. Silly, stupid little Troy Martello would have taken one look at that bomb and screamed like a little girl.

But Troy Martello was dead now. Troy was as dead as if he'd been shot in the head. He didn't write his father or any of the random stepmothers who still tried to keep in touch. He didn't feel any need to chase his father's money or put up with his father's shit. He'd stopped being some twerp with masks.

And now Vinnie's thoughts returned to Charleston. The man was still staring straight ahead with a murderous expression on his face. Apparently he'd been wearing a mask for three years, but his mask seemed pretty much exactly like the person beneath the mask. Rip off the Charleston bad ass persona and you got the Kalb bad ass persona. Both men had an edge of danger and all this control and a sense of bottled up emotions that you really didn't want to explode in your face.

"Problem, Bernardi?" Charleston asked.

"No, sir," Vinnie said with a smile. Instead of placating Charleston, that just seemed to make him frown more. For long minutes, Charleston just looked at Vinnie with this expression that made Vinnie think that Charleston was about to order him to do a hundred pushups.

"What?" he finally asked.

This time Charleston didn't bother saying anything; he just kept looking at Vinnie. Hell. Vinnie was clearly not firing on all cylinders today. Either that or it'd been so long since he was in Charleston's class that he'd forgotten that the man just didn't take glib answers.

He sighed. "Just wondering when you were going to tell me you had a backup plan for the backup plan," Vinnie admitted.

"Don't count on other people to save your ass, Bernardi."

Vinnie snorted. "Yeah, that's a good rule for you. Personally, I was just planning to wait for you to save me from the psychopathic poet." Vinnie fingered the cuffs with the little flat lock that Charleston couldn't use the bolt cutters on. They were lined and probably cost more than all Vinnie's bondage equipment put together, and he still hated the things.

"You held your own, Bernardi." Charleston's voice was soft, and Vinnie hated it. Vinnie wanted to be tough; he wanted to know that Charleston admired him, but Vinnie sure as hell didn't admire any of his actions today... or last night. He flinched as he thought about last night. He'd taunted Thompson, urging him to go faster and harder when the man seemed to hesitate. Looking back, Vinnie realized the guy was probably imagining Vinnie all cut up, even then.

"Did it get bad in there?" Jordan asked from the front seat. Vinnie was starting to think the other guy was a mute or something. He made Charleston look absolutely talkative.

"Bad enough," Charleston agreed. After a slight pause, he kept going. "Thompson captured Vinnie, strapped the bomb to him, and then put us in a cell. Using his legs, Vinnie held the bomb so I could expose the wiring, and when given an opportunity to go with Thompson, he royally pissed that bastard off by not only turning him down but making fun of him while he did it."

Vinnie smiled at that description. "Roses are red, violets are blue, bite me," Vinnie told Jordan with a little smirk.

"Good for you, kid." Jordan smiled at him, and Charleston patted him on the leg. As much as Vinnie knew, he was being manipulated by two seasoned warriors who were probably just afraid that he was going to break down and cry. It still felt good. Vinnie was okay being manipulated every now and again.

"I did do pretty good, huh?" he asked. "I mean, I really stung him when I refused to go with him. He really thought that he'd found a way to get me to crawl to him, and...." Vinnie stopped as Charleston whacked him on the back of the head instead of just telling him to stop babbling. Vinnie smiled. "Sorry, sir."

"Any time, Bernardi," Charleston answered, but he was smiling, so Vinnie couldn't keep himself from smiling back.

Chapter
Twenty

THEY jumped on a freeway and then off again, and this time they were in one of the middle class neighborhoods far from the warehouse or RJ's place. In those neighborhoods, the buildings were old and drafty and peeling.

This neighborhood, though, had shining white colonials and cottages, all with their cute gardens, green lawns, and flowers. Every once in a while, a house would have a sagging porch or a patchy old dog lying in the shade of some tree, but for the most part, these were the people who cared about appearance. Vinnie was guessing these neighborhoods would rise up in revolt if someone tried to get a zoning permit for a gay bar down here. Vinnie was already starting to itch just from being in close proximity to so many "proper" folk.

"Agents have found a possible location on Steger," Jordan offered. He reached up and touched his ear, and Vinnie spotted the cord leading around his ear and then down to his collar. Of course he had a radio. Vinnie wasn't sure why that hadn't occurred to him before, but his brain was clearly not firing on all cylinders.

"So, Steger was the target the whole time, not Thompson?" Vinnie asked. Maybe his brain really was only half-functional, but he was not sure he understood exactly what was going on.

Charleston didn't answer immediately. He seemed to be searching the side window for the meaning of life or something. Finally he gave an odd sort of sour expression. "The feds were all fighting over the case; however, every agency seemed to have a different theory. As far as I can tell, some of them still think I'm involved. Personally, I thought Thompson had organized it and just threw the blame onto me and Steger when he got caught."

"Wait. What? Even now they think it's you? You've been stuck ordering rich brats to do pushups for three years, why would they blame you?"

Jordan answered for Charleston. "That's the CIA for you. They see conspiracies everywhere."

"Because they run conspiracies everywhere," Charleston pointed out.

Jordan turned his head toward them and smiled. "Good point, sir. However, I tend to believe my boss that you're just a mean son of a bitch and not an abusive one."

Vinnie crossed his arms. "If they think Charleston would abuse people, they're idiots. No fucking way would Charleston ever abuse someone. No fucking way. They have brain damage if they really believe that." Charleston looked amused at Vinnie's verbal flailing.

"Kaplan made that suggestion," Charleston agreed. "Then again, he seems to enjoy calling the CIA idiots in general. But before you throw too many stones, remember that these two tricked me too. I was certain Steger just needed a chance to clear his name—I thought that if I could help flush Thompson out in to the open, he would have a chance to lay all these rumors to rest and get back on track for promotion. Three years is a long time to have a career derailed by rumors. When I called Steger for help, I thought for sure he'd come in there with guns blazing and take Thompson down. And then, when Kaplan came in, he'd have his proof that Jack Steger was a good officer and lay those rumors to rest."

"Only they weren't rumors," Jordan pointed out. Charleston didn't answer.

"Maybe I'm just slow," Vinnie said slowly, "but if Charleston came forward with information, why would anyone still suspect him? Even if the CIA is as stupid as everyone thinks—"

"They are," Jordan offered.

"Even so, shouldn't the fact that Charleston offered to help mean he's not the bad guy?"

"That's not the way it works." Charleston stared out the side window, and Vinnie was bothered by the fact that he couldn't see his face except in the distorted reflection on the window. "After Thompson confessed to me and invited me into the slavery business, I told my superiors about his offer, but some members of the CIA and CID, and even some people in the FBI, seemed to think that it was a ruse. The feds were already getting close. Apparently, they thought I was clever enough to turn on my co-conspirators just before the whole operation went down. After all, if I like tying up young Marines and watching them strain and sweat, that must mean I would support slavery."

"Okay, that's the same argument that the totally insane guy made. I don't think that really says much about their logic. In general, anything crazy guys believe, I try to avoid believing." Vinnie stopped, not sure what to say. The tires made a little thump every time they hit a seam in the road, and that was the only sound in the car. Vinnie squirmed. He did many things well, but silence was not one of them. "So, Kaplan—is he really on our side?" he finally asked when he just couldn't take it anymore.

Charleston glanced at him with amusement. "He's a pain in the ass, but he did just get you out of a room with a ticking bomb."

"Which would usually win a lot of loyalty points from me," Vinnie admitted, "but it seems like there are games in games here, and I'm a little more for just a direct line from A to B."

"He's a good guy," Charleston said. "He's the one who offered to set me up here as bait when the Army was ready to boot me. Don't ask, don't tell means that your superior officers really don't want to hear about your deviant and homosexual lifestyle." He pursed his lips. "And they're nearly as unhappy with an officer who can't recognize an enemy from two feet away."

"Hey," Vinnie said with a little laugh, "you believed Steger, who is clearly skilled at looking rational. I fell for the truly crazy half of that little partnership. I mean, I really fell for a guy who read me poetry, and seriously, who quotes poetry? Now if he'd been quoting a Dirty Harry movie, then maybe I would have been justified in trusting him, but no red-blooded American male reads poetry without a teacher standing over him. Mrs. Everson will testify to that, and since she's about a hundred, I figure she must have taught most of the men on the east coast, and in every single case, she had to stand over them with that ruler of hers and threaten them."

"Or call me to threaten them for her after some little shit intentionally misreads organ as orgasm a few dozen times?" Charleston asked. He almost sounded cranky, but he had that expression again, the one that said he was trying to not be amused.

Vinnie ducked his head. "At least it was interesting when it was an orgasm blower. Trust me, that poem needed some spicing up, but you see, I am clearly a trustworthy male because I hate poetry. Thompson—not so much." Charleston could say whatever he wanted; Vinnie could already see the way his shoulders were loosening up. "I really think I shouldn't be allowed out by myself. After all, that's twice now that I've fallen for guys that were hiding something. I clearly need some guidance." Vinnie could feel himself slip back into his own skin. This was territory he knew. Oh, playing with Charleston was new and terrifying, but this sort of verbal teasing with a Dom was familiar ground for him.

For a half second, Vinnie thought that Charleston's façade was going to crack. A hint of emotion slid just under the surface, but then his expression cleared, and once again, Vinnie was left looking at the world's best poker face.

"You're good, kid, but you're up against a pro with this one," Jordan said. Vinnie felt his stomach clench for a half-second as he realized he was hitting on a guy in a car full of cop-types. However, the driver just kept driving, and Jordan looked amused. Vinnie gave a wry smile and shrug.

"So, what now?" Vinnie asked.

"Kaplan arrests them, or I'll make him the sorriest man in the known universe."

Vinnie nodded and turned his attention back to the scenery, not sure what to say from here. His mind was stuck on the image of Charleston tying up some Marine and watching him sweat and strain. That was more interesting than any arrest.

A sudden thought hit Vinnie. "So, are you going to stick around as Charleston or go back to being Kalb?"

"Are you always this full of questions?" Charleston asked. Vinnie supposed that in school he had been more interested in telling everyone else what he thought instead of asking questions.

"Yep." Vinnie gave Charleston his most charming smile.

This time, Charleston didn't look amused at all. He leaned forward, focusing on the two agents in the front seats. "How long?"

"About five minutes to the safe house," the driver answered. He was clearly trying to compete with Charleston on the curt and laconic front, but he didn't have the attitude for it, Vinnie thought. He considered pointing out that the guy sounded a little too nasally and whiny to pull it off.

"The second Kaplan has those two in custody, I want to hear from him," Charleston said, his foot tapping impatiently against the back of the front seat. Jordan glanced back toward them, but he didn't answer. He just gave a short little nod.

Vinnie opened his mouth to keep asking questions, but a single look from Charleston made him close his mouth. Okay, he could wait. Vinnie started pulling at the cuffs as his wrists sweated uncomfortably. Reaching over, Charleston put his hand over both of Vinnie's wrists, pressing them down into Vinnie's thighs and stopping him from pulling at the cuffs. When Vinnie opened his mouth, he got another Charleston glare, so he closed his mouth and decided to just wait.

The driver pulled up into the driveway of a two-story white house with blue shutters, and the garage door started sliding up. The outside might look pretty normal, but the inside was way too clean to look real. "Is there a shower I can use?" Vinnie asked before the garage door was even closed. He reached for the car door, but Charleston caught his arm and kept him inside until the last sliver vanished under the door.

"Inside. I'll show you in a second," Jordan said. He got out of the car, but then he waited by the side as the driver got out and moved toward the door. Charleston kept his hand on Vinnie, pinning him in place.

"Charleston?" Vinnie asked in a whisper. The way all three men moved—their bodies tight and their eyes wary—made his guts twist.

"Give them a chance to clear the area. We aren't armed," Charleston explained. Both agents went into the house, their hands near their belts as they disappeared inside.

"Can I just say that I'd be a lot more comfortable if you were," Vinnie muttered unhappily.

"Me, too, Bernardi."

"All clear," the driver called out in his nasal voice. Vinnie darted out of the door and had nearly gotten in the house when Charleston's hand caught him and pulled him back.

"What?" Vinnie looked at him in confusion.

"Just let me go first."

Staring at Charleston, Vinnie tried to decide if the man was serious. "Are you really that suspicious?"

"Yes," Charleston simply answered before he went into the house. Vinnie moved behind him, but maybe Charleston's paranoia was contagious because he found himself half expecting Freddy Krueger to jump out at him. Instead, they walked into a normal-looking living room. An arch led through into a dining room, and Vinnie was guessing the door at the far end was the kitchen. It was all pretty boring. Jordan and his nasally partner were standing near one of the windows talking.

"Bathroom?" Vinnie asked. He hated that he didn't have a change of clothes, because he was feeling pretty gross; however, he'd settle for having a chance to wash Thompson's come out of his hair.

Jordan looked over. "We should probably have the crime scene techs come over first."

Vinnie's brain shut down in total panic as he imagined what they'd find. Thompson had spilled the contents of his condom over the small of Vinnie's back, which, at the time, had been sexy and possessive and more toppy than Vinnie had expected from a man who seemed more like a grade school teacher than an experienced top. He'd come again in the van, splattering the side of Vinnie's face, and Vinnie's hand came up as he realized that Jordan had seen the white specks drying against his skin. Oh shit. No fucking way did he want to talk about what was consensual and what hadn't been. Fuck. Vinnie suddenly wished he had just been raped, because he could feel shame clawing at him, and the worst of it was knowing that he had gone along with it. He'd chosen Thompson.

Vinnie was on the verge of a full-out panic when Charleston caught him by the arm and steered him away from the kitchen and toward a short hall that probably led to bathrooms. "Check that door," Charleston ordered him, giving him a little shove toward one while he turned to another.

"Sir," Jordan said, stepping forward. "You should wait."

Charleston's door turned out to be the right one. With a quick grab, Charleston caught Vinnie's arm and hauled him into the bathroom. "No," he said, and then he followed Vinnie into the bathroom and shut the door.

Vinnie backed himself up into a corner of the bathroom, his heart pounding even faster than it had in the damn cell—which was just stupid.

"Breathe, Bernardi," Charleston ordered.

A weak laugh slipped out, and Charleston raised an eyebrow at him.

"You can't order me to not panic."

"Nope. But I can order you to keep breathing so you don't pass out on the floor."

"I'm not going to pass out." Vinnie could feel anger curling in his guts, but getting angry at Charleston in a small space really didn't seem all that clever.

"Good." Charleston leaned back against the door and just waited.

Vinnie pressed himself into the corner until the metal handle of the shower poked him painfully in the back. Charleston still just stood there. "Are you leaving?" Vinnie finally asked.

"Nope." Charleston didn't show even a hint of emotion.

"Seriously, you can leave now," Vinnie said. He went to take a step forward, but he stopped before he actually moved more than a single toe. "I'm fine."

Charleston looked him up and down. At another time, Vinnie would have been more than happy to put on a show; right now, he just wanted to climb in the shower. "Enjoying the view?" Vinnie asked when Charleston didn't stop.

"Anger—good."

Vinnie glared. "Get out."

"Fair enough," Charleston said, and for one second Vinnie was shocked into silence. However, Charleston didn't actually move away from the door. "Just tell me one thing. How are you feeling?"

"Are you— Seriously? Are you asking me that seriously?"

"Yep." Charleston stared at him, and Vinnie had to fight to stay still.

"Well, let's see. I want to take a shower and this guy won't get out of the bathroom, which is kinda creepy. Or hey, maybe you just want a show. I can do that, you know." Vinnie looked Charleston up and down. The man was still seriously fine, even dusty and dirty and sweating. Actually, he was hotter when he sweated, and that was not true of everyone.

"And we're back to flirting."

"Hey, feel free to save yourself from listening by just leaving." Vinnie crossed his arms, and then he realized that made him look like he was mimicking Charleston so he just dropped his hands to his side again.

"Bernardi, I asking because I'm worried about you."

"Hey, I held my own back there. You said that." Once, when Vinnie had been about six, his father had given him this really cool mini-racecar and then taken it back two hours later when Vinnie had started crying over something totally unimportant, like getting told that his father wasn't going to stick around for Christmas. Vinnie had the same feeling now. Charleston had given him this really incredible compliment, and now he was taking it back.

"You did, Vinnie. I've led soldiers who didn't hold their own that well under fire. However, I'm worried about you now. You're angry one second, quiet the next, and ready to jump my bones two seconds after that."

"Kinda stressed here," Vinnie pointed out.

Charleston's expression softened. "I know. If you were one of my men, I would order you to head over for some post-mission work with the doctor."

"You mean therapy."

"Yes, Bernardi, I mean therapy. However, you aren't in the Army, and I can't order you to go talk to the unit chaplain or the base doctor. So instead I'm asking you to talk to me."

"I'm fine."

Charleston didn't even bother to answer that one. He just stood and stared.

"Okay, so I'm not fine," Vinnie said after about three seconds of trying to hold out. "My feet are sore," he said.

Charleston's eyebrows rose.

"And I'm freaking out. I let that fruitcake handcuff me to the bed before I came with his dick up my ass, is that what you wanted to hear?"

"I have a few skeletons in my sexual closet, Bernardi. You aren't alone there."

"Really? And did any of them ever end up being psychos?"

"One was later convicted of arson, conspiracy to obstruct justice, wrongfully touching a corpse, conspiracy to commit rape and murder… and drinking. He wasn't my finest choice."

Vinnie's mouth fell open. "Oh shit. Really?"

Charleston's wince was enough to answer that.

"Well, shit. We really do suck."

"Choosing a shitty sexual partner is not the end of the world."

Vinnie studied his own face in the large mirror. The come was visible as tiny speckles in his hair and along his face. Reaching up he brushed it away, flinching when he saw the cuff still locked around his wrist.

"So, how are you feeling?" Charleston asked again.

"Do you really want to know?" Vinnie avoided looking at Charleston or even catching a glimpse out of the corner of his eye by studying the yellow birds on the world's ugliest bath towels.

Charleston sighed, and Vinnie immediately braced himself. He'd asked, so if Charleston wanted to completely end this little fantasy by telling him to fuck off, that was Vinnie's own fault for asking. He'd take his emotional lumps like a man and cry like a little girl later, when no one was around to see it.

"I won't pretend that I'm good with this stuff." Charleston stopped. Turning so his back was to the mirror, he leaned against the counter and looked at those same horrible yellow birds. "The Army kept pushing officers to reach out to the soldiers in the unit as part of suicide prevention, but my problem is that I will always see the world in terms of tops and bottoms. I'm pretty sure the rest of the world doesn't exist as either submissive or dominant, but that is how I interpret their behavior. So, yes, I do want to know how you feel, because I don't want you quietly self-destructing on your own, Bernardi. However, I am just as likely to misunderstand what you're saying as understand it. Like right now, I see you as a submissive who was betrayed and now has a lot of justifiable anger toward the top and a significant amount of guilt because a submissive gives part of himself to his Dominant, and Thompson tricked you into giving something away that he never would have been able to take by force, not even if he had all the rope in the world."

Vinnie stared at Charleston, his mouth open and all the words shocked right out of him. "But I could be wrong," Charleston said with a shrug.

"Not so much," Vinnie confessed. Three years ago when he was still in school, he would have cut off an arm before admitting that, but he figured he'd grown up enough to admit it. "The worst part is that I thought he wasn't dominant enough, and I kept trying to prod him into taking charge more."

"I'm glad he didn't. His idea of dominating someone is leaving scars and then screwing with their heads until they thank him for it."

Vinnie pressed his hand to his stomach as nausea hit him like a wave. "I'm an idiot."

Charleston shifted slightly, and his leg brushed against Vinnie's in the tight quarters. "If you are, then so is the FBI and CIA and CID, and for that matter, so am I. You knew him for a few hours, and you trusted him. After I went to work in his office, I respected how tough he was with the regulations and the way he didn't back down from the pressure. I worked there for a lot longer than a few hours, and I trusted him all the way up until the end."

"I thought I was better at seeing through bullshit," Vinnie said sadly.

Charleston shrugged. Vinnie didn't know what he was supposed to be saying, so he just chewed on his lip and shifted uncomfortably. His feet were still a little sore, although they weren't as bad as he'd expected. He sneaked a look at Charleston and thought about the fact that Charleston had designed them. That was a little hot, even if Vinnie's stomach was still rolling over just how close he'd come to death. Charleston had his eyes half closed and his arms crossed—like he was halfway asleep. Great. Part of Vinnie just wanted Charleston to give him some privacy, but there was no way the man was going to back off until he got what he wanted. He'd asked about feelings, and Vinnie wasn't getting any privacy until he talked about them.

"I just don't feel really good about myself right now," Vinnie admitted, "and my cock is shrinking from having to talk about feelings, sir."

Charleston's lips twitched. "You're not the first soldier to say that. But just…. Give yourself permission to not feel good, okay?"

Vinnie nodded, watching as Charleston straightened up and reached for the door.

"And don't think you have to put on a show for me, Vinnie. If you feel like shit, I'm not going to think less of you for saying it. But these mood swings of yours are going to get you shipped off to therapy as fast as Kaplan can pick up a phone. He likes to pretend to be a bastard, but when he sees a victim hurting, he turns into a fucking mother hen."

"Got it," Vinnie agreed.

Charleston started out into the hallway, and Vinnie could see Jordan and his freakishly mute partner waiting with cranky expressions. However, Charleston closed the door before Jordan could even say a word, and Vinnie turned on the shower to drown out any chance of overhearing the conversation. Right now, he just wanted to pretend that he was alone and not an idiot. It was a sad little illusion, but he really just needed to hold onto it for a bit.

Chapter
Twenty-One

"WELL this is fun." Vinnie poked at a pile of old magazines. After nearly two hours, he was starting to wonder if he should call the ACLU and accuse Kaplan and the FBI of torturing them.

"Sit," Charleston ordered. He was settled in a chair with a three-year-old magazine in his lap.

Even though he wasn't happy about it, Vinnie dropped onto the end of the couch and glared at the room. Jordan and his partner sat at a table playing cards while still glancing up suspiciously from time to time. On the other hand, Charleston kept his eyes on the magazine, slowly turning the pages, and yet Vinnie had the odd feeling that Charleston was far more aware of his surroundings than the two agents.

"How much longer are we going to be here?" Vinnie asked.

The mute agent ignored him, but Jordan gave a vague shrug. "However long it takes. You really can't time an operation like this."

Vinnie gave a big sigh.

"What? You have something better to do?" The normally silent agent gave Vinnie a cold look. Charleston looked up from his magazine.

"Maybe I do. There's a gay bar with a dance pole that's calling my name," Vinnie shot right back.

Jordan's blush was slow, and from the way his eyes went big, Vinnie was guessing the man was dealing more with shock than any actual phobias or prejudices. However, his partner turned a particularly vivid purple around his neck and his stiff body, and the way he pulled his arms in close made it pretty damn clear that he didn't like Vinnie. Actually, hate might come closer. Vinnie knew this sort. This guy liked to pretend that he was better than Vinnie—he was like Vinnie's dad who always had this mental "status" ladder and put people on one of those rungs and then treated them accordingly. Whether it was the gay thing or the stripper thing, for one reason or another, he thought he was better.

However, Vinnie didn't need this guy's permission to be exactly who he wanted to be—Vinnie Bernardi, a man who was quite happy to have lots and lots of gay sex and kneel at the feet of some really hot top. "Oh, I have lots of better things to do." Vinnie leaned forward and tilted his body as he openly evaluated the asshole and then made a sour face to make it very clear that he found it lacking. The guy blushed. Even if he wasn't gay, this guy did not want to be told he was unattractive. Truthfully, the guy was more average than actually unattractive, but Vinnie made sure to throw a little extra disgust into his expression. "Much better things to do," he repeated.

"Like what?" Jordan without looking up from the cards he had decided to study very carefully. Okay, Vinnie hadn't thought Jordan was an idiot, but the alternative was that he was providing Vinnie a chance to torture his partner. Confused, Vinnie glanced over, but Charleston didn't look up from his magazine. Vinnie hesitated a half second to see if Charleston would make him stop torturing Agent Asshole.

"Oh, I find all sort of things to amuse myself," Vinnie said. "Watching a DVD, reading a book, having a little cock al dente." Jordan flinched at that one. Straight guys were so fun to fuck with… especially when they couldn't beat the shit out of you for having some fun.

"It's Friday night, and I haven't had a Friday night and Saturday off together in nearly a year. There are so many things I could be doing." Vinnie kept a straight face as Jordan's mouth came open. Yep, he might have been willing to give Vinnie a little leeway to torture his idiot partner, but he hadn't expected Vinnie to take it this far. Agent Asshole was slowly turning red, and his mouth was open, but he hadn't said anything yet. It was probably killing him to not call Vinnie a faggot or white trash or something equally unimaginative.

"Honestly, there is nothing I like better than ass play. Fingers, tongues, cocks, it's all good. Maybe if I'm lucky, I might get fisted, and I have until Monday to recover from a really good fisting." Vinnie leaned back and watched the facial gymnastics both agents went through. Horror... shock.... From Jordan there was a deer in the headlights look while his partner had the classic "stepped in dog shit" disgust going. Charleston turned a page a little louder, and Vinnie grinned. This was fun.

Neither agent seemed to have any comeback, so Vinnie turned his grin on them. "I don't suppose either one of you would be interested in using my very fine ass, would you? I really feel like getting stuffed full tonight, and sometimes straight boys are the very best stuffers. After all, their girlfriends don't often let them put their cocks in that nice, tight asshole."

"I..." Jordan just stopped.

"This is inappropriate," the first agent said, all prim and proper.

"Appropriate is boring. Hey, this is your chance to go walking on the gay side of the street, and you could not find a better tour guide than me. Anyone want to go for a ride? If you don't want to go for the full menu, you could just sign up for a little cock sucking. I'm very good at cock sucking."

Both agents were staring at him with unmitigated horror, and Vinnie could feel his cheeks ache from his effort to not smile. A little part of him felt guilty about including Jordan in the torture, but then the guy had wanted to bring crime scene techs in. He'd argued for it so loudly that Vinnie had heard him over the sound of the shower washing all the evidence away. So, if he got his little straight feelings a little tarnished, Vinnie refused to feel guilty about it.

"Kalb, I thought you were going to keep an eye on him." Kaplan appeared at the archway between the living room and the dining room. The door that led to the kitchen was still swinging. Surprised, Vinnie sucked in a breath.

Charleston glanced up from his magazine. "I am keeping an eye on him. He's having fun torturing your agents."

"I noticed." Kaplan walked in and sat on the opposite end of the couch from Vinnie. He looked tired. He'd pulled his tie loose so that it hung low around his neck, and his jacket was missing.

"So, does this mean I can go home now?" Vinnie asked. He really needed out of this room.

Charleston carefully closed his magazine and set it on the side table before really studying Kaplan. "What did you screw up?"

"Who said I screwed anything up?" Kaplan asked.

"I did."

Vinnie smiled as he watched Charleston work on Kaplan. Yeah, Kaplan had toppy vibes of his own, but no one could compete with Charleston. For a second, it looked like Kaplan might try, though. He stared at Charleston, returning his gaze without a blink, which was impressive. Vinnie never had managed that feat.

Eventually he looked over toward his agents. "Take perimeter," he ordered them. Vinnie had never seen two men jump to obey so quickly. They really, really wanted to get out of the room. Vinnie smiled sweetly and waved at Jordan as they left. Jordan managed a shake of his head that was either amusement or resignation, but Agent Asshole just stuck with pure disgust.

When the door closed, Charleston asked again, "What happened?"

Kaplan sighed. "You were right about Steger."

"No I wasn't," Charleston said. "I told you that your trap wasn't going to catch him because he wouldn't be involved in this. Turns out, he is in it just as deep as Thompson. Hell. He was a good officer at one point, but he doesn't even have the defense of being crazy."

"Yeah, but you called it when you said he wouldn't ever go on trial." Kaplan leaned back, resting his head on the back of the couch and stared at the ceiling.

Silence fell for several minutes before Charleston asked, "He shoot himself?"

"Nope. He just wouldn't stop taking shots at two of my men, even when there was no way he was getting out."

Charleston's expression turned grim. "Anyone else hurt?"

Kaplan sat up. "That's what took me so long. I have an agent in serious condition, but the doctor says that he'll pull through fine as long as there aren't any complications."

"So, Steger's dead?" Vinnie clarified. He wasn't sure why, but he really just needed someone to come right out and say that the asshole was dead. Actually, he'd feel a whole lot better if someone showed him the body and let him poke it. Maybe. After nearly being dead himself, Vinnie wasn't sure he was ready to see his first dead body.

"Very dead," Kaplan said with some sort of grim satisfaction that made Vinnie just a little leery.

"And Thompson?" Vinnie could feel his guts knot up just from saying the name. Fuck. He hated being so off-balance.

Kaplan didn't answer. He just put his head back against the couch and closed his eyes.

"You lost him." Charleston didn't sound amused.

"I lost him," Kaplan agreed. Reaching up, he rubbed his hands over his face. "I'm getting too old for this shit."

"You're younger than I am," Charleston pointed out, "and if you suggest I'm too old for this shit, I'll kick your ass and prove how young I still am."

Kaplan still had the heels of his hands pressed into his eyes, but Vinnie could see him smile. "Yeah, you're so badass you dangled yourself out there like bait." Kaplan sat up, and the humor vanished from his voice and expression. "Thompson is crazy as shit and obsessed with you. It's time to really put you in witness protection, Kalb."

Charleston shook his head. "No."

"Don't be an idiot."

"I'm not running from this."

"You're the one who told me that you couldn't stop a determined assassin, remember?" Kaplan demanded.

Charleston looked thoughtful for a second. "I said you couldn't stop a skilled and determined sharpshooter. Thompson isn't skilled enough to take me, but if I vanish, he's going to go to ground."

"Then let him. We'll track him some other way."

"Not going to happen."

"What? You think I can't do my job?" Kaplan glared at Charleston.

Instead of getting upset, Charleston just shook his head and looked mildly amused. "Don't try that on me, Kaplan. Three years we've been working together on this. I've seen you use that same trick to manipulate other people often enough that I'm not going to fall for it."

Kaplan sighed. "It was worth a try." His body sagged, and Vinnie was guessing that he had just accepted defeat.

"So, you've been trying to catch this guy for three years? And he only came out because of me?" Vinnie wasn't sure how to feel about that—a little creeped out, maybe. As much as he liked attention—all kinds of attention—this was disturbing. Surprisingly, there was such a thing as getting too much attention, and Vinnie had just landed in the middle of it.

"He never could understand why men submitted to me." Standing up, Charleston walked over to the wall beside the window. Using a finger, he lifted the edge of the curtain just enough to look outside. "He forced people or paid people or tricked them, but in the end, he never got what he wanted, and that's why I had to help Kaplan bring him down."

"So, are you like a kinky FBI agent now?" Vinnie was seriously getting confused. If Charleston was just a witness, he wasn't really acting like it. Then again, as a teacher, Charleston was very un-teacher-like.

"He's FBI; I'm just a really pissed off captain." Charleston poked his thumb toward Kaplan.

"Hell, I'd love to have you in the agency," Kaplan said. "After people had to work with you for a while, they'd start thinking that I was warm and fuzzy. But to answer your question, kid, Kalb is a witness who chose to have a really shitty cover so that the bad guys would come after him."

Charleston shifted so he could look out the blind and study a new strip of darkness out of the corner of the window. "I've never lied to you, Vinnie. I left a lot out, but I never lied."

"Good thing, because you stink at lying, Kalb," Kaplan

complained. "You should have just lied about how you found out about the scheme at all. You never should have risked getting your ass kicked out of the service," Kaplan said quietly.

"It was more than just a risk; it was a certainty." Charleston let the curtain fall closed again, but for a second he just stared at the wall without turning around.

"That's just one of the reasons the military sucks. Kicking a guy out because he's gay is just stupid." Vinnie often wondered if his own father had sent him into military schools just because he knew that Vinnie was gay. Oh, little Troy Martello had done his best to leer at women, but looking back, he suspected that it had been pretty obvious that he preferred to leer at men. It would be just like his father to choose the one place where Vinnie would be least comfortable and most likely to get his ass kicked.

"They didn't ask, but I certainly told," Charleston said with a shrug. "I knew my career would end if I opened my mouth about my sex life, but some things are just not worth the price they cost."

Kaplan's unhappy expression gave Vinnie the feeling these two men had disagreed about this topic more than once. "After you gave three years of your life to this investigation, they'd damn well better give you that honorable discharge." Kaplan's tone of voice sent a cold shiver down Vinnie's spine.

Charleston turned around and gave Kaplan an amused look. "Trying to fight my battles for me?" he asked.

"Hell no. I'm just saying." Kaplan shrugged. "However, this is my investigation, and I am not using you for bait. Not anymore."

"Then I'll quit working with you and still stay here." Charleston crossed his arms and just looked at Kaplan. It wasn't a glare or a stare-down or anything overtly hostile, but Vinnie could feel the tension in the room. If he were to place a bet, he would bet that Charleston meant every word. The man wasn't exactly big on bluffing.

"I could call the general. You are still in the Army, Kalb, and I think that means you'll go where you're ordered to go until they kick you out because their heads are planted up their asses."

Charleston shook his head. "But the general hates me. If I point out that you want to move me because staying here is likely to catch the killer and result in my death, he's going to consider that a win-win."

Kaplan stared at Kalb longer this time, and Vinnie could feel the tension like a snake coiling around all of them. However, Kaplan eventually turned away. "You're a real pain in the ass, Kalb."

"Never claimed I wasn't. You don't get to be an officer without knowing how to make co-workers miserable and subordinates tremble in fear."

Kaplan leaned forward and rested his elbows on his knees. "Okay, let's say that you leave yourself on the hook, waiting to see if Thompson shows up."

"Yep, let's say that," Charleston agreed. Kaplan took a second to glare at him.

"Fine, what do you plan to do with Bernardi?"

Both of them looked over, and Vinnie couldn't keep his stomach from knotting. "Hey, feel free to…." Vinnie waved a hand. "I don't know… hover around me, provide twenty-four hour security, install bullet-proof glass on all my windows. Charleston can be as badass as he wants. I'm okay with panicky and needy."

"Can't afford any of that. The best I can do is put you up in a safe house for a few weeks. If this is going to take longer than that, we might want to consider Witness Protection." Kaplan made it all sound so reasonable that it took Vinnie a second to really understand what he was saying. He wanted to take Vinnie away from the life he had carefully built up, but Vinnie didn't want to give up his life.

He liked being Vinnie Bernardi. He liked it in a way that he had never liked being Troy Martello, despite all the money and the expensive toys and the big houses. He definitely did not want to give up his life or his job or his identity, not for Thompson. Vinnie hated that Thompson had already taken so much. He'd made Vinnie uncomfortable in his own skin for the first time in two years, and now he was threatening to take his identity. It wasn't fair. Yeah, he'd stuck his nose into the middle of this, but he'd just been trying to get Charleston's attention or maybe just indulge in a few good fantasies; he didn't deserve this.

"Kaplan, give us some time," Charleston suggested. "Maybe

morning would be soon enough to discuss all this."

At first, Kaplan just looked from one of them to the other. Vinnie pulled his foot up under him and started picking at a thumbnail. If he opened his mouth, all sorts of stupidity was going to fall out, and he knew it, so he stayed uncharacteristically silent.

"Right. I'll check in with you two in the morning. Kalb, give me until then to try and find some other way to get at Thompson, and please try and keep that one from annoying Addleman and Jordan to death."

Charleston didn't answer. He did hold out his hand, though. "Let me borrow your lock pick set."

"Do I really look like someone who spends a lot of time trying to break into places?"

When Charleston just continued to wait with his hand outstretched, Kaplan reached into his pocket and pulled out a little black case. "Don't lose it," he warned, and then he turned and headed back out through the kitchen where he'd come in.

Chapter
Twenty-Two

CHARLESTON waited until Kaplan left before he walked over to the couch and sat at the opposite end. Vinnie watched as he opened the lock-pick set and pulled out a small silver tool. "Come here," he ordered. For some reason Vinnie didn't understand, he jumped. Charleston looked at him for a second before gesturing at Vinnie's wrist.

Looking down, Vinnie looked at the cuffs locked around his wrists. "Oh, right." Feeling vaguely like an idiot, Vinnie scooted across the couch and offered Charleston one of his wrists. Charleston slipped the tool into the lock and worked silently, the metal pick making a soft ticking sound until the cuff finally opened with a loud click. Charleston pulled the cuff off and ran strong hands over the over-warmed skin.

A shiver went down Vinnie's back. Yeah, he'd always wanted Charleston's hands on him, his fingers stroking over skin that itched from having leather locked tightly around it. This just really wasn't how he imagined it happening. Vinnie was caught between wanting to revel in the touch and wanting to jerk his hand away.

"You're still unsettled, huh?"

Vinnie snorted. "I don't think I'll ever feel settled again. He wants to take my life away."

Charleston had a flash of confusion cross his face before he nodded. "Giving up Vince Bernardi—would that really be losing your life?"

"Yes."

Charleston didn't answer that, but from the sigh, he thought Vinnie had answered wrong. Vinnie could feel Charleston's disappointment gnaw at him.

"So, do you know Kaplan from one of the sex clubs?" Vinnie asked in order to change the subject. It really couldn't be normal for an FBI agent to be such good friends with someone who was just the witness/bait.

"Kaplan?" Clearly he had shocked Charleston.

"He's on the toppy side," Vinnie said, feeling like he had to defend himself. It really hadn't been a stupid question. Hopefully.

Charleston blew out a breath. "Honestly, I don't know. I haven't ever considered it." Charleston had loosened his hold on Vinnie's arm, so Vinnie pulled it back. Charleston chuckled. "I've tried to not consider it. These last three years, I've tried very hard to start not thinking about people's sex lives. That's what happens when you get ordered to spend all of your time with oversexed teenagers who spend so much time pushing your buttons that you just know they're asking for a good Dom."

"Was I that bad?" Vinnie asked. Usually he didn't really care what people had thought of Troy—in most ways that counted, Troy wasn't him.

"Bad, no. Tempting...." Charleston let his voice trail off. "I learned to just ignore the sexual signals people were putting out."

"So, you didn't notice that Kaplan really isn't too bad with the seriously dominant vibe he has going on?"

That made both of Charleston's eyebrows go up. "You should tell him that. Just make sure I'm in the room when you do," Charleston suggested. "Give me your other hand."

Twisting around on the couch, Vinnie gave Charleston his left hand. Using the pick, Charleston started working the lock on the second cuff.

The silence wore on Vinnie. Quiet had always made him worry, like if he wasn't controlling the conversation the other person might blurt out something. They could tell you they were sending you off to military school and marrying your nanny. Vinnie was well aware of the fact he still had father-issues. "It really sucks that you're putting your life on the line, and they're still kicking you out of the military. If gay people ran the world, it'd be a lot more fair," he blurted when the weight of the silence grew too heavy.

"I doubt that."

"What?"

Charleston glanced up with an amused expression. "People are people, Bernardi. If gays were in control, they'd be just as small-minded as everyone else."

"But you're a good person, and I'm guessing you're some kind of god of training and tactics, and they're kicking you out because you're gay. That's not fair. Do you really think a gay man would ever be that shitty?"

"Yep." Charleston kept working. "They don't have a choice about asking me to leave, Bernardi. In the service, people have to work with each other. If the men in my unit get to know me and then start to suspect that I'm gay, it's not going to matter to them. They've seen me in the field and they know who I am. If the first thing they hear is some rumor that I'm gay or deviant or suspected of being involved in human slavery, they're never going to let themselves trust me. Men need to trust their officers."

"Wait. So you support this Don't Ask, Don't Tell shit?" Vinnie was so shocked that he pulled his hand back before Charleston could open the lock. With an aggrieved expression, Charleston twisted around and leaned back on the arm of the couch so he could really study Vinnie.

"The way they have it set up now? No. It's stupid. They chase baseless rumors and kick good soldiers out of the service even when their behavior on base and within the unit is entirely appropriate. However, if a man or woman walks into a unit and shoves their sexuality or their religion or their kinks in everyone else's face, that's going to affect the unit."

Shock drove the air from Vinnie's lungs. "So, we should hide who we are to make other people more comfortable? Fuck that."

Charleston clenched his teeth for a second. Vinnie knew he was pissing the guy off, but there was no way he was backing off on this point. He was right. He knew it. After a second, Charleston seemed to find some sort of calm. "That stunt you pulled with Kaplan's guys, as amusing as it was, did it gain you anything?" Charleston asked.

"It amused me."

"Fine. You never need to see them again. However, are you going to act like that with the clerk at the grocery store? The minister at your church? The police officer who stops you for speeding?"

Vinnie twitched his shoulders and leaned back with an exaggerated sprawl. "I'm comfortable with myself, and if they don't like me, they can just fuck themselves."

The first few seconds after he said it, Vinnie was very smug in his own rightness, but the longer Charleston just stared at him, the less comfortable Vinnie felt. Eventually, he looked down at the cuff still locked around his left arm.

"If you really want to shock the hell out of some small-minded idiot, impress them, Bernardi. Be so damn good at whatever you do that when they find out that you're submissive or gay, you force them to face their own prejudice. I may be leaving the service, but there are men who will never look at gays the same way again. That's an objective worth planning for. Now give me your hand."

Vinnie surrendered his hand before his brain even processed the request. Charleston's hand caught him by the wrist, just above the cuff, and this time he held on tightly. The touch made Vinnie want to squirm, but their bodies were too close together on the couch for him to get away with it. Instead, he just stared at the pinstripe pattern on the couch, his guts twisting unhappily. The second cuff seemed more difficult to open than the first.

"Spit it out, Bernardi," Charleston said sharply.

Vinnie jerked in surprise, but Charleston had his wrist firmly enough that he didn't pull himself free this time. "What?"

Charleston looked up at him.

Vinnie rolled his eyes and decided that while he loved Charleston's dominant streak, sometimes it was just annoying. "It's just that doing that feels like lying."

Charleston let long seconds go by as he worked the lock. This one was obviously a lot tougher. "You have to decide how to live your own life, Bernardi, but the way I see things, my sexual orientation only becomes someone else's business if I'm interested in bedding them."

"So you just let them assume you're straight?" Vinnie had done that all through high school, and he'd felt slimy every single time he'd made some lewd joke about a woman's breasts or sneaked porn magazines into school.

"I don't care what they assume," Charleston said. "They can assume I'm from Pluto for all I care, but I'm not going to start a conversation with the fact that I'm gay or dominant or someone who has spent most of his life killing people for a living."

Vinnie's eyes snapped to Charleston's face, searching for some sign that the man was joking, but he was concentrating on the stubborn lock.

"I led an infiltration team, Vinnie, one of the best. We went behind enemy lines to scout high-priority areas and paint targets, and most of the time, we took out any opposition that might be there to ask questions about the American military presence in the area. I'm proud of what I did, and while I feel sorry for every life I took, I'm not ashamed of what I've done. However, I'm not going to tell people any of that in the first ten minutes I meet them." The lock finally gave with a little click, and Vinnie watched while Charleston unbuckled the leather. "If someone wants to know me, I won't hide any of those things, but shoving your beliefs in other people's faces isn't conducive to good unit morale." Charleston ran his thumb across the inside of Vinnie's wrist where the sweat had turned the skin clammy and red. Vinnie shivered.

"You had a hard night, and we're both tired."

"And Feathers McGraw is still out there somewhere," Vinnie added unhappily. There were a whole lot of disasters to try and figure out, too many for him to think about when he was still a little jumpy from the almost dying.

"Feathers McGraw?" Both Charleston's eyebrows were up.

"The bad-guy chicken from *Wallace and Gromit*," Vinnie explained. Charleston still looked confused.

"He was dressed like a chicken, but he was really an escaped penguin that talked his way into Wallace's house and convinced Wallace to totally trust him right before turning out to be a gun-wielding, psycho diamond thief." Yeah, Wallace had been a real idiot trusting someone like that.

Vinnie thought about stepmother number four. He'd come home from school to find all of her belongings packed and sitting on the marble inlayed floor in the front hall. He'd felt like someone had punched him because this was the stepmother he'd really loved—the only one he'd wanted to keep. She'd been waiting for him all day so that they could curl up and watch the show on tape before she walked out of his life.

That must have been ten or twelve years ago, but to this day, Feathers McGraw still scared him more than Freddy Krueger. Lying on the couch with Emma's arms around him as he silently cried, he'd truly hated his father for the first time—not felt disappointed in him or even like a horrible son. Nope, that's when he learned to hate Troy Martello, Sr. He supposed that's when he started hating Troy, Jr. too. "You can learn a lot from television. You should try watching some." Vinnie knew he sounded like a total nut job, but now that he'd brought the damn show up, he couldn't figure out how to drop the topic. It just felt like his brain was clogged with fat today.

The corners of Charleston's lips twitched. "Really? And what great lesson did you learn from Feathers McGraw?"

Vinnie didn't answer. What had he learned? He'd learned that people let you down, that they were evil, that people who should care about you didn't. Emma had promised to call, but she never had. He wondered if he would eventually be able to wash Thompson out of his life as completely as he erased his father and even Emma. He wondered if Kaplan was going to force him to make Vinnie Bernardi disappear. "I learned that sometimes the penguins are just out to get you," Vinnie said quietly.

Charleston chuckled, but it was a grim sound. "Sometimes they are, Bernardi. But in this case, Feathers McGraw is not going to get past me, not tonight." Vinnie didn't know what to say. He sat and stared at his reddened wrists until Charleston caught him in a strong arm and pulled him close. The sudden closeness made Vinnie's breath catch.

"Don't. I can't—" Vinnie's voice cracked.

"Why?"

"I'm going to cry. Stop." Vinnie squirmed, but Charleston shifted so that he could catch Vinnie in both his arms and hold him close.

"That's okay, Vinnie. You've earned it."

Vinnie gave one last feeble attempt to slip free, and then he felt the tears start. Instead of pushing against Charleston's embrace, he clutched at the man's shirt and shook. He'd lost too damn much. He couldn't lose himself. He couldn't lose Vinnie and RJ and Dan. He couldn't lose his shitty little apartment and the endless war against the cockroaches. He couldn't lose his last stupid hope that he would someday get Charleston. He couldn't. Vinnie's whole body jerked as the sobs pulled at him, but Charleston just held him tightly, refusing to let go even when Vinnie's nose started running.

Vinnie cried until his breath started coming more easily and he started feeling stupid. It wasn't like he'd been blown up. It wasn't even like Vinnie Bernardi had such a great life that he was worth clinging to.

"I'm okay. You can let me go," Vinnie mumbled into Charleston's shirt.

"What hurts most?" Charleston asked without letting Vinnie go. Vinnie lay in Charleston's arms and tried to come up with an answer, but he didn't have one. "I don't know."

Even though Vinnie expected Charleston to push, the man just nodded. "Okay. That's fair. It's late and I think we've both had a longer day than we expected. Let's get some sleep."

"So, when you say we should go to bed…." Vinnie let his voice trail off.

"In separate beds," Charleston said firmly.

"Right." Vinnie tried to sound disappointed, but right now, he was so tired, he really just wanted to sleep. Either that or he wanted to huddle under the covers and have a nice quiet, private nervous breakdown, one or the other.

"The bedrooms are through here," Charleston said, getting up and heading for the hall on the opposite side of the room. Vinnie followed. Hopefully everything would seem better in the morning.

Chapter
Twenty-Three

SUN streamed through the open windows, highlighting little floating motes of dust. For long minutes, Vinnie floated in that quiet place, caught halfway between awake and asleep. His eyes lazily tracked the progress of one particularly ambitious dust particle that rose toward the ceiling. However, no matter how much he tried, he just couldn't stay in that place. Outside, someone was running a lawnmower, and footsteps paced the hallway.

The footsteps sent Vinnie scrambling out of bed as his nightmares and the sound tangled together until he was half-convinced Thompson was walking down the hall. Vinnie was halfway to the corner before his brain told him that wasn't reasonable. Possible, yes. Reasonable? No. Still, he held his breath as the footsteps passed his door. Even then, he couldn't get rid of the nagging fear that Thompson was around the corner. Looking around, Vinnie realized that someone had delivered clean clothes at some point—a plain T-shirt, jeans, and sneakers. He pulled the shirt on and jammed his legs into the jeans so fast that he ended up hopping on one foot when he got the other tangled.

Footsteps returned to pace in the opposite direction, and Vinnie crouched down in the corner, pulling the sneakers on as fast as he could. The footsteps faded, and Vinnie leaned back against the wall and slowly slid to the ground, his heart beating fast enough to make him dizzy. Even though the terror was passing, Vinnie still hurried to finish getting dressed. If something happened, he really didn't want to face it in his underwear.

The door to his room had a tiny squeak, and Vinnie held his breath as he eased it open. Down the hall, he could see a sliver of the living room, and a woman with gray, curling hair was sitting on the couch flipping through a magazine; however, she spent more time looking around than she did actually reading it. And from the cheap suit, she was FBI. Vinnie eased his way out of his room, trying to control his heart beat. Obviously, some little part of him still expected Thompson to jump out at him.

"Hey," Vinnie said, breaking the silence as he walked into the living room. The woman looked at him with dark blue eyes that traveled up and down him. Vinnie wasn't sure whether he should be flattered or offended.

"Breakfast is in the kitchen, and let's get one thing straight," she said without any introduction. "You can give Addleman and Jordan shit as much as you want, but if you pull that with me, I will not be amused." She pointed at pencil at him, and Vinnie just froze.

"Yes, ma'am," he finally offered. She grunted and pointed toward the archway. "Kitchen's through there. Don't open the curtains, and do not open the back door for any reason."

"Got it."

She pinned him with a no-nonsense glare for a second before she started working a crossword puzzle in her magazine. "Kaplan asked me to come in as a favor to him. He did that because he knows I will kick your ass and handcuff you to the bathroom pipes if that's what it takes to make you behave."

"Oh." Vinnie wasn't sure what to say. He supposed he should be flattered that he could intimidate FBI agents, but right now, he was too busy being intimidated to really feel anything except a desire to get out of the room before he pissed this woman off. Vinnie hurried into the kitchen.

Most of the time, Vinnie was one of a dozen different bottoms at RJ's place, all trying to get the attention of half that many tops. He actually complained about the lack of dominant personalities in his life. Now he was surrounded by tops, and it wasn't nearly as much fun in reality as in fantasy. Tops made him edgy, and while one top was a good sort of edgy, too many tops in one room was definitely hard on the nerves. In the kitchen, Vinnie grabbed a cup of coffee and a donut with sprinkles before heading back into the living room. "Is Charleston still here?"

A grimace twisted her face for a second, so Vinnie was guessing that she was not one of his fans; however, she poked her thumb in the direction of the bedrooms. "Last door on your right."

Giving her his best smile, Vinnie started in that direction. "Thanks."

"Bernardi."

"Yeah?" He turned to look at her.

"If he wants to put his neck on the chopping block by going out for his morning run, that's his choice. You, however, are my responsibility. You do not pull that stupid shit."

Clearly Charleston had already been impressing people with his ability to completely and totally ignore all rules other than his own. Vinnie just gave another nod and darted toward Charleston's room before this new woman handcuffed him to the sink as a precautionary measure.

Without knocking, Vinnie pushed the door open. There, lounging on his bed like some king waiting to be served was Charleston, palming his cock and looking more feral than Vinnie had ever thought possible. The crisp white sheets were folded down and draped over his knees, and a gun sat on the bed stand next to him. Vinnie stopped. All his blood immediately flowed south as his gaze was caught by Charleston's hard cock rising up from his body.

Charleston's hand stopped and rested on his hip, giving Vinnie an even better view of a lovely cock rising from salt and pepper gray curls toward a stomach that still had a six pack.

"Do you not know how to knock, Bernardi?" Charleston asked, but he was still sprawled against the white sheets, so Vinnie didn't have enough blood to form coherent thoughts. Reaching down, Charleston grabbed the edge of the sheet and pulled it up over himself so that his erection was a bulge in white.

"I… um…." Vinnie poked his thumb back toward the living room.

"Problem?" Charleston grabbed his weapon and swung his legs

over the edge of the bed, his eyes searching the hall behind Vinnie. Unfortunately, when he stood up, the sheet slipped away and the last two brain cells still getting blood failed, leaving Vinnie open-mouthed and hard.

"She…. Um, she said you were in here," Vinnie finally managed to say. Charleston was standing next to the wrought iron headboard, and Vinnie's brain immediately imagined all the places to attach cuffs or scarves to that headboard. His little adventure with Thompson really should have scared him out of bondage but obviously not.

Charleston slowly put the gun back down on the end table and grabbed his pants off the chair next to his bed.

"Did you need something?"

"Wow. You're really an Adonis, sir."

Charleston pulled his underwear and pants on so quickly that Vinnie had to blink in surprise as he lost sight of one very nice cock. Even better, that very nice cock had been attached to Charleston, and the man was even more beautiful naked than he was with a sweat-soaked T-shirt clinging to his body, and Vinnie was very fond of the whole wet T-shirt look.

"Martello!" The name cut through Vinnie's lust-addled brain and he finally got himself to look at Charleston's face. The guy was still pretty god-like, even with his pants on. He was also a little pissed.

"Um, yeah?"

Charleston just looked at him.

"Oh, sorry, sir. I shouldn't have just broken in here."

"No, you shouldn't have. And don't apologize. If you make a mistake either fix it or move on."

"Right, sir."

Charleston crossed his arms.

"You were um…."

"Masturbating," Charleston provided. "I sometimes do that, Bernardi."

"Oh." Vinnie cleared his throat. "Well, yeah, I mean, you're a man, so I did assume you sometimes did. Feel free to hit me upside the head any time now, sir," he suggested.

Instead of a slap, Charleston walked over and ruffled Vinnie's hair. "Next time knock."

"Got it, sir." Vinnie watched while Charleston went over and retrieved his shirt. "So, should I leave you alone to... um... finish?" Vinnie kicked himself. He sounded like a geeky virgin trying to bed his first top. Vinnie hadn't been a virgin since he was fifteen, and he hadn't been a virgin to bottoming since he was eighteen and a guy picked him up in the parking lot of RJ's bar. "Or I could help you with that," Vinnie smiled winningly.

"You already have, but since you're up, we have other things to do." Sitting on the end of the bed, Charleston pulled his shoes on and tied them.

"I have?" Vinnie was not following that bit of logic.

Charleston finished the last knot and straightened up. "A young submissive half my age still thinks I look like an Adonis, and what's more, he chose to risk death to follow my lead, even when he had no idea where I was going. Yes, I think it's safe to say that you have already contributed to my morning distraction. Now, let's go find out where Dwayne is." The man looked surprising unwrinkled, and the running clothes folded and sitting on top of the dresser were definitely new.

"Wait, how long have you been up?"

"A lot longer than you," Charleston answered. With that, he was out the door. The brush of his arm against Vinnie's sent a little shiver through him, and for a second, Vinnie could only cling to the door jamb and try and talk some sense into his cock, which just wanted to come and come now.

"This year, Bernardi," Charleston called. The bastard had to know that Vinnie was hurting, but Charleston never did cut anyone any slack.

"Coming!" Vinnie trotted down the hall, wishing that his jeans were a little looser because this was not only painful but embarrassing. He hurried into the living room and then stopped right behind a lamp so the shade was strategically placed. Charleston's lip twitched, but he didn't make any comment as he faced off against the woman and a new agent, a guy with freckles and a really thick neck.

"He can come here or I can go to him, but one of those things is happening," Charleston told her firmly.

"You are a federally protected witness."

"I'm a witness. Period. If I choose to turn down federal protection, there isn't a damn thing you can do about it."

"I can take you into custody as a material witness." The woman was going toe to toe with Charleston, but there really wasn't a competition here. Charleston was going to win.

He smiled at her, but it wasn't a nice expression, not at all. "You go get your material witness warrant, and then we can talk. Until then, you have no authority over me. So, either you get Kaplan on the phone or I am walking out that door."

"Thompson is still out there."

"I know. That's the point." Charleston started heading for the front door, and Vinnie scrambled after him.

"Oh, no you don't. Bernardi stays right here." She reached out to grab Vinnie's arm, and two things happened at once. Vinnie shied away so fast that he slammed his shoulder into the wall near the door, and Charleston reversed direction, grabbing the woman's wrist as she reached out for him.

"Touch him, and I will help him press charges for assault." Charleston's voice was dangerously soft.

The woman yanked her hand back. "Sir, if you want to risk your neck, that's your choice. You're a trained soldier, and I have to assume you're armed. However, Bernardi is a civilian, and he is under our protection."

Vinnie stepped forward. Okay, it was sexy to have the big, bad top stand up for him, but he wasn't some pathetic little pushover. "Unless you have one of those material witness warrants for me, you can't hold me anymore than you can hold Charleston. As a citizen, I have a legal right to tell you to mind your own business."

Charleston smiled, his expression predatory. "Exactly. You're riding shotgun, Bernardi. Car's out front."

Vinnie walked past the woman, past her thick-necked partner who was now on the phone, past Charleston who seemed to be covering his escape. Outside, the sun was just over the tops of the houses, so it was still early by Vinnie's internal clock, but Charleston came trotting down the sidewalk, clearly ready to take on the world.

"Where to, sir?" Vinnie asked, hurrying after him.

"Where we'll find Kaplan. If we want our lives back, then we need to find out where he is on this case. Are you good with that?" Charleston stopped and really looked, and Vinnie realized that it wasn't a simple question. Instead of answering quickly, he thought for a second, nodding when he decided that he was. Yeah, he still felt raw and more than a little ashamed, but he wanted his life back. He wanted to keep Vinnie Bernardi, and that meant he was ready to fight for him.

Charleston continued to look at him for several seconds. Despite the fact that Vinnie felt a little bent around the edges, he met Charleston's approval because the man gave one quick nod before he turned and headed for the car. Vinnie followed. The longer he followed Charleston, the more he felt right standing about two steps behind the guy.

Chapter
Twenty-Four

THE hospital parking lot was full, but Charleston drove up and down the aisles, fruitlessly searching for a parking place. "There's a place out there," Vinnie said. On the other side of a line of trees, there was an overflow parking lot with a dozen empty spots. Charleston had driven by every single one without showing any sign of stopping.

"You see anything?"

"Yeah... lots of open spots." Charleston just looked over at him with that expression that said he was not even going to answer something that stupid. Vinnie cleared his throat. "Like what, sir?"

"A van with a broken door, a panel truck for a delivery company that has no business at a hospital, a car with a sniper hanging out the window. If I knew what I was looking for, Bernardi, I would have already found it." Apparently Charleston had decided that Vinnie didn't need the coddling and handholding this morning.

"Oh, you think Thompson's here?"

"I think Thompson is still focused on finding one of us, and the only lead he has is Kaplan. He'll be here."

Great. The poetry loving freak was here, and so naturally, Charleston had led them right to the one place Vinnie didn't want to be. Vinnie swallowed, but the fear still rose in his throat. "You poked hornet's nests when you were growing up, didn't you?" His joke sounded lame, even to his own ears.

"Yep," Charleston answered without a hint of shame. "If I'm going to be playing in the yard, I want to know if that nest has hornets in it or not, and I'd rather find that out when I'm prepared to run like hell."

"Logical," Vinnie admitted. What he didn't want to admit was that he was pretty much drowning in fear. Now as Charleston cruised through the aisles of cars, Vinnie searched them, looking for missing plates or broken windows or poetry scrawled all over the side of some Buick, graffiti style. Unfortunately, everything looked normal. Charleston must have thought so, too, because he pulled into a space and turned the car off.

"Bernardi, you good?"

Vinnie took a deep breath. "Not really, but I'm getting there. Is that good enough?"

"That's the best answer you can give," Charleston replied. Reaching across Vinnie, he popped the glove box. "Hide this, but you do not part with it, understand?" He handed over a pretty sizeable knife.

"Got it, sir," Vinnie agreed. He really seriously needed to start wearing looser jeans because there were a limited number of places this was going to fit, and Vinnie didn't particularly want to put a knife in any of them. Charleston got out on his side, and his eyes darted suspiciously to every corner of the hospital parking lot. The far wing was under some sort of construction, and orange cones and yellow tape blocked off a large section of the grounds. He seemed particularly interested in that.

Vinnie got out and slammed his door closed, knife still in hand. An older couple was walking several rows down, and Vinnie shoved the knife behind him. The last thing he wanted was to get arrested for brandishing some big frickin' knife. He was fairly sure that he'd fall to little emotional bits if he got locked in a cell again, even if it was a police officer doing the locking this time. Vinnie tried to fit the knife into a back pocket, but the bulge was more than obvious.

"Any day now, Bernardi."

"Coming." Bending over, Vinnie tried bracing the tip of the knife in his sneaker. Then he pulled his sock up as high as he could to keep it flat against his leg. He took a couple of steps toward the hospital; however, the weight of the knife made it jiggle loose with every step. "Shit," he muttered. Charleston stopped and looked at him with that one raised eyebrow that made Vinnie feel like a timer somewhere was counting down to zero and he had a limited amount of time to get his head out of his ass. He tried stretching the sock so that it was pulled tight over the end of the knife. When Vinnie stood up, Charleston was so close that Vinnie yelped and jumped back. The knife slipped free and clattered to the ground. "Shit."

Without a word, Charleston retrieved the knife from the ground and stepped closer. Vinnie knew he should be focused on the killer that wanted him dead. He should be searching the parking lot for signs of Thompson. Instead, his eyes were inexplicably locked onto Charleston, watching as he stopped an inch from Vinnie and then reached out and caught Vinnie by the waist of his jeans. Charleston's mouth was quirked in that almost smile that he wore so often, and Vinnie gasped as Charleston slid the knife down his jeans and into his underwear, tucking it up beside Vinnie's cock. Then Charleston pulled his hand out and cupped Vinnie's crotch, rearranging both cock and knife until the position suited him.

"That's how you hide a knife in tight jeans, Bernardi," Charleston commented.

"Um. Okay." Vinnie's family jewels didn't like anything sharp or pointed moving into the neighborhood, even if it was sheathed, but when Charleston looked at him like that, sticking a knife down your crotch seemed suddenly reasonable. This time Charleston actually smiled before he turned heel and headed for the hospital. Vinnie hurried after him, trying very hard to not feel the leather pressing up against his cock or think about what he must look like with a nice bulge in his jeans, only part of which was the knife. Vinnie had a sudden urge to make a joke that went along the lines of, "Is that a knife in your pants or are you just happy to see me?"

In the hospital, Charleston moved through the crowds with a decisiveness that caused people to move aside for him, not even questioning his presence. Vinnie just followed in his wake. One nurse called out, but Vinnie gestured toward Charleston's retreating back and made a few noises about being sorry, but if he didn't keep up with the boss, his life wasn't going to be worth spit. Before she could protest, Charleston had turned the corner, and Vinnie dashed after him.

"He's on the fourth floor," Charleston said when he stopped at an elevator long enough for Vinnie to catch up.

"How do you—"

"One of the rules of staying alive is to always know where all the players are. If you don't know where someone is, you're going to get surprised at the wrong time."

Vinnie looked at Charleston. "Are you sure you're not a cop?"

"I'm just good at staying alive when a lot of people want me dead," Charleston countered.

"That's no joke." Kaplan came striding around the corner. "Which is why I had two agents watching the parking lot after you took off from the safe house."

"Were those your guys on the picnic tables by the construction?"

Kaplan sighed. "I really hate the way you spot my agents. Have you considered pretending to be fooled just to make me happy?"

"Nope."

Vinnie shifted to the side so he wasn't blocking the hall and just watched the two men. This was definitely not a relationship Vinnie understood, but they seemed to genuinely like each other, even if they weren't particularly nice to each other.

"Delia was not amused with your antics this morning, Kalb."

"She'll live," Charleston said without any sympathy.

"What the hell are you doing?" Kaplan demanded. "Are you really trying to get yourself killed? I mean, I know that the military has been your life, but I didn't think you were suicidal. However, now, with all the mistakes you're making, I'm ready to shoot you myself. Going out running is not playing bait—it's playing victim."

Charleston shrugged. "I was armed."

"I figured." The anger seemed to drain from Kaplan and leave fatigue in its wake. "Do I want to know where you got a weapon?" Immediately, he held up his hands in surrender. "No, no, don't tell me. You do what you want to, and most of the time, I don't want to know what that entails. You get the job done, and that's enough. However, what the hell are you doing dragging Martello into this?"

"Bernardi," Vinnie corrected the guy. Kaplan looked at him coldly, but Vinnie just glared right back. He wasn't Troy Martello, and he wouldn't let anyone shove him into that unhappy little box again. Hell, if his father had his way, Vinnie'd be off fucking every woman he could and drinking himself stupid at frat parties, all to prove the virility of the Martello name, and Vinnie was not playing that game, not anymore. He was Vinnie Bernardi, and he was going to fight for that name.

Eventually, Kaplan just turned back toward Charleston, obviously waiting for an answer. "Thompson is going to want him back. That's why I left him at a safe house with two agents," Kaplan said. "I certainly didn't have any illusions about Delia being able to keep you out of trouble."

"I don't trust them." Charleston managed to make that sound more like a fact than an insult, but Kaplan was still clearly taken by surprise. "I don't trust easily, Kaplan, so don't look so shocked."

"Delia is one of my best."

"Good for Delia. I still don't trust her. If Thompson is going to target Vinnie, I'm going to make sure he has to go through me to get him."

"You two are dogs growling over a bone, Jeff."

"Yep," Charleston agreed. Kaplan glared at him.

"That was not a compliment. And how exactly do you see this working? Do you plan to haul Bernardi around with you everywhere you go?"

"Yep," Charleston agreed again.

"Hey, I do have legs of my own, and I am perfectly capable of choosing who I trust to protect me," Vinnie protested. If he was going to be the bone in this scenario, he was at least going to be a bone with a voice. "I know Thompson is out there, and I trust Charleston. And as much as I don't want to offend Delia, because she seems like the kind of woman who would knock you down and cuff you to pipes given half a chance, I don't know her. I can't trust someone I don't know."

"Spoken by the man who let the suspect cuff him to a bed." Kaplan's words cut so deep that for a second, Vinnie couldn't breathe.

"And you've never been led astray by your cock," Charleston said sarcastically. "How about wife number two? Just based on what you told me, I said she was trouble. I could smell that disaster coming over the phone from five hundred miles away, and you still had to go there."

Kaplan grimaced. "She had nice legs. Really nice legs."

"At least Vinnie has the excuse of being young. What excuse do the two of us have for our pathetic love lives?"

Kaplan shook his head. "That's below the belt, Kalb."

"Yep, it's a real kick to the balls," Charleston agreed.

"However," Kaplan straightened up, "that doesn't change the fact that you shouldn't have brought Bernardi. Hell, my director is ready to ship him back to his father and let the old man get him out of harm's way."

"What?" Vinnie stepped forward, his hands curled into fists at his sides. "My father is not part of this, and if you think I'm going to let myself get shuffled off into a corner, you have another thing coming. I may be trying to play nice because Thompson is a terrifying asshole, and I believe that Charleston can bring him down, but that does not mean that I'm going to go along with just anyone." Vinnie only realized he was still advancing on Kaplan when Charleston caught him by the arm and held him back. "You can tell that director that he can take all his plans about sending me to my father and shove them right up his ass. I am not a minor, and if it comes right down to it, I'll tell the director, my father, and everyone else to fuck off."

Kaplan looked from Vinnie to Charleston and back. "And here I thought my ex had a temper." He shook his head.

Charleston shrugged. "We both prefer a little fire in our partners."

"Until we get burned," Kaplan said wearily. He glanced over at Vinnie. "I'll clean that up a little before I pass the message on. However, you need to understand the kind of risk you are putting yourself in." Kaplan took out a photocopied piece of paper. The copier had left faint black lines along one side, but the handwriting was precise and beautiful, long flowing strokes of calligraphy that the author had clearly put a lot of effort into.

My love reveals objects
silken butterflies
concealed in his fingers
my love invents worlds where
jeweled glittering serpents live.

I will have the boy wrapped in silk, and under my
fingers, words shall appear, the most beautiful ever written.
And Kalb will vanish in time, a fallen soldier neither
important enough nor respected enough to make even a
footnote in the history of the world.

"Okay, that's creepy." Vinnie handed the photocopy to Charleston. "This guy has some pretty major screws loose."

Neither man answered him. Charleston read the letter and Kaplan just watched the people pass by. He only spoke once Charleston looked up from the page. "Our psychiatrist believes he's escalating and near a breaking point. He's going to go on a killing binge soon. There's too much pressure built up, and Steger isn't around to control him anymore."

"Which is an even better reason for Bernardi to stay with me," Charleston said firmly.

Kaplan, however, did not look convinced. "Despite rumors to the contrary, you are not perfect, Kalb."

"Prove it."

"God, you are an arrogant bastard."

Charleston smiled. "Yep, and I've earned the right to be one, Dwayne. How's your injured man?"

Kaplan didn't answer right away. He stared at Charleston, but Charleston was studying the hallways and the small crowd that had gathered to wait for the world's slowest elevator. One guy was punching the button over and over, which seemed pretty normal to Vinnie, but it made him nervous that Charleston seemed obsessed with watching the gesture.

"He's in stable condition," Kaplan finally answered. "The bullet in the abdomen is going to put him in bed for a month or two, and probably put him on the injured reserve list for the next six months, but he'll recover."

"Anyone I know?"

"Hewlett."

"Damn." Charleston finally looked away from the impatient guy and focused on Kaplan. "Is his wife okay? She's what, seven months along?"

"Eight. She's fine, although next time I have to talk to a pregnant woman, I'm taking a paramedic team with me. She had a small panic attack that made us think she was going to deliver right there. I can handle psychopaths with high explosives a lot better than I can handle one pregnant woman."

"That might explain your divorce," Charleston grinned at his friend, and Vinnie had to bite down on the jealousy that he could feel creeping up.

Charleston turned toward Vinnie, shifting so his back was to the wall. "Hewlett was the first one after Kaplan to think I was innocent."

"He just figured that you were such an uncompromising bastard that if you did it, you'd be more than willing to tell us all about it," Kaplan said. "And now it's time for you to get yourselves back to the safe house or the guy who did do this is going to put a bullet through one or both of you. I'd love for you to prove your innocence beyond all doubt. If nothing else, it'd feel good to get proved right. However, I would just as soon you not prove it by getting yourself killed."

"Face it, there are days you fantasize about being able to shoot me." Charleston moved back from the elevator, pressing Vinnie toward the wall and looking around nervously. Kaplan seemed to have caught his nervousness because he took a step into the middle of the hallway, forcing people to walk around him.

"Yep, I do," he said, but his voice made it pretty clear that he wasn't paying attention to the words. "Elevators are down."

"Yep." Charleston's hand moved to his waist; he hooked a thumb in his belt near where he had his gun hidden.

"Could be the construction," Kaplan suggested.

Charleston didn't even bother to answer that—he just gave Kaplan the same sort of incredulous look he normally saved for some of Vinnie's stupider comments.

Reaching out, he caught Vinnie by the shoulder and pulled him close. Vinnie leaned back into Charleston's strong body. Before he could ask what was wrong, the fire alarm screamed and sprinklers all down the hall spluttered and then sprayed water into the air.

Chapter
Twenty-Five

NURSES appeared, walking quickly down the hall, their shoes slapping and echoing as the water gathered on the linoleum. Kaplan pulled out his gun and held it down at his side. "That bastard's here," he said.

"Did you just now figure that out?" Charleston shoved Vinnie toward the wall, standing between him and the gathering crowd.

A security guard came striding down the hall. "The exit is straight this way. Everyone needs to leave quickly and quietly, please." He pointed at the far end of the hall. Nurses started coming out of rooms, pushing patients that trailed a dozen IV lines that all looped up to bags the nurses were carrying.

"He has to know we won't just follow the crowd," Kaplan said.

"So should we really freak him out and follow the crowd?" Vinnie asked.

Charleston looked over. "That would be an interesting tactic." He seemed to think it over for a second before shaking his head. "I don't like the thought of being in the open with all those innocent people around. Thompson isn't a good enough shot to avoid civilians."

"He won't try and miss them at all," Kaplan said. "So, we head into the building and see if we can find a central panel where he could have set off the fire alarm. Sprinklers wouldn't go off for a simple pulled alarm."

"Security office?" Charleston pursed his lips.

"Sounds like a plan." With his gun still at his side, Kaplan started down the hallway, twisting and turning to work his way through the thickening crowd.

Charleston caught Vinnie's wrist before he could follow, and Vinnie opened his mouth to make all his arguments about why he shouldn't get left behind. However, before he could say anything, Charleston pulled him close. "Hang on to my belt and keep your outside shoulder as close to me as you can so that the crowd doesn't push between us. I'll angle my body close to the wall so we can push along the wall, but if you don't hang on, the crowd might sweep you away, got it?"

"Yes, sir."

Charleston turned to face the crowds of people who were just now showing the first signs of panic. With his shoulder close to the wall, he shoved people toward the middle of the hallway as he worked his way deeper into the building. Vinnie tried to press close, but someone hit him hard in the shoulder and Vinnie was thrown back, pulling Charleston back with him. Charleston glared coldly, and Vinnie moved closer and angled his body so that his right shoulder was nearly touching Charleston as they moved upstream against the tide of bodies.

Using the wall, Charleston was able to slowly move into the center of the hospital. Not even two hundred feet down the hallway, Vinnie spotted Kaplan still trying to swim upstream against the crowd. A crying woman ran into him and pushed him back a good six feet before he was able to shake free of her. Cursing, he made his way to the side of the hall, catching Vinnie's jeans and pulling himself into their odd little train.

Over the crying crowd, Vinnie could hear someone yelling, "Just move steadily toward an exit. Do not push." Yeah, that was wishful thinking. As far as Vinnie could see, everyone was pushing. Wisps of gray smoke gathered along the ceiling, and the smell of something burning seemed to be driving the common sense out of most people's heads. A nurse was pushing a man in a wheelchair, and patients and visitors alike pressed so close that a man tripped on the wheel and fell and then couldn't get back up.

"Kalb!" Kaplan had to scream over the growing noise. Kalb glanced back for just a second before focusing on the end of the hall again. "Kalb, we have to get these people out one of these office windows."

"Do it!" Kalb yelled back, but his words were nearly lost in the roar of the crowd.

"Kalb!" Kaplan pulled on Vinnie's jeans, trying to pull him away, and Vinnie put his head down and pulled for everything he was worth, hanging onto Charleston's belt. "Kalb!" Kaplan called again. Kalb just kept moving, and Vinnie struggled, nearly slipping as Kaplan nearly pulled his legs out from under him. "God damn it, Kalb, stop being so stubborn!" Vinnie was going to have bruises around his waist from Kaplan's pulling but then Kaplan was just gone, pushing his way into a side room, and Vinnie took a deep breath as he was released.

"You okay?" Charleston called back.

"Right as rain," Vinnie answered. A large man carrying a little girl slammed into Vinnie, mashing him into the wall. Vinnie gasped and went to one knee, nearly pulling Charleston down with him. "Okay, maybe not that right, but I'm holding my own," Vinnie corrected himself as Charleston pulled him back to his feet.

"That you are, Bernardi."

Vinnie grinned, even if the compliment was so brief that Charleston had already turned and started working his way farther into the hospital. He could definitely get used to all these compliments Charleston was showering on him. Funny enough, he'd had teachers and stepmothers who had complimented him every time he took a breath right, but they'd never made him feel the compliment quite as much as Charleston could, probably because Charleston just did not give compliments easily.

By the time the crowd had thinned out, the smoke had thickened substantially. "Sir, tell me we aren't doing something really stupid," Vinnie asked. Following Kalb through the panic of a false alarm was easy. Following him when the psycho fruitcake had clearly set the fucking hospital on fire was something a little harder to do.

"We aren't," Charleston answered simply. He had his gun out now, and the few people who still hurried by looked at them with near panic in their eyes. "He's here, and we're going to end it."

"Sounds good, as long as you mean by shooting him in the head."

Charleston glanced back, and Vinnie just shrugged. Yeah, it wasn't very nice of him, but this asshole had tried to blow him up and now he'd set fire to a hospital—Vinnie was okay having a few murderous thoughts.

With a shake of his head, Charleston continued down the hallway. The sounds of crying and random shouts still echoed down the halls, but now the corridor was empty. Somewhere from the direction of the smoke, the staccato sound of footsteps running made Charleston bring his gun up. Vinnie pressed himself against the wall and rediscovered prayer as a man came around the corner. Fear slammed into Vinnie before his brain could process the fact that it wasn't Thompson. A security guard in a black uniform slid to a stop when he saw Charleston's gun, and Charleston quickly pointed it at the ground.

"I'm with the FBI. Is there anyone still back there?"

"I don't know. I just checked patient rooms." The man kept his eyes on Charleston's weapon.

"Go out and find Special Agent Kaplan. Tell him I'm heading for the utility area and I have Bernardi with me."

The guard's eyes finally came up to look at Charleston's face. "Yes, sir," he offered, and then he was running down the hall again.

"You're with the FBI?" Vinnie asked.

"I'm with Kaplan—close enough." Then Charleston was moving again.

Charleston passed an office door, and before Vinnie could even blink, a body flew at them from inside. Both of them were carried across the hall before all three of them hit the far wall and then collapsed in a tangle of limbs. Vinnie heard something hard hit the tile floor and then slide, the sound muffled by the water that had collected on the floor.

He struggled to get up, but a heavy weight pushed into the back of his leg, pinning him in the half-inch of bitterly cold water. Limbs flailed and bodies squirmed, pressing him to the floor. Thompson. Vinnie could feel the fear crawl through his belly as Thompson and Charleston struggled. A knee caught him in the side, and Vinnie managed to roll away as he tried to get himself out of the middle of their wrestling match.

Thompson had both hands around Charleston's throat, but

Charleston was driving his thumb up into the underside of Thompson's jaw. Scrambling back, Vinnie searched the hallway for the gun he had heard clattering against the tile. A hospital cart lay on its side, a dozen trays with ruined food spilling out from the shelves. A wheelchair was upended, one wheel lazily turning as the sprinkler rained on it, and a soggy red robe looked eerily like a giant bloodstain. However, he couldn't find any gun.

"You're dead!" Thompson screamed the words as he leaped to his feet. His eyes were wide and his wavy hair was plastered against his head so that it looked skull-like. "You're dead!"

Charleston launched himself at Thompson, landing a punch to the kidneys, and Thompson stumbled back. Charleston followed him, landing two more body punches, and then they were grappling again, both of them slamming into the walls as they struggled. Vinnie edged back as they fought their way closer to him. Looking around, he searched for a weapon, grabbing a plastic food tray.

Thompson shoved Charleston back, and before Charleston could counter-attack, Thompson pulled out a gun. Charleston froze, his hands still up and ready to attack.

"You see?" Thompson took a step forward, and Charleston fell back, his feet splashing through an inch of water. "You see? I won. I won, and you lost." Thompson was shrieking his words, and Vinnie gripped his tray, well aware of just how useless it was against a gun. "Say it! Say that I won!" Thompson demanded. He jerked the gun up, and Vinnie stopped breathing, sure he was about to see Charleston shot.

Over Thompson's shoulder, Charleston made eye contact with Vinnie, staring at him with those blue-gray eyes that always seemed to have some hidden storm within them. Thompson followed his gaze, looking over his shoulder to study Vinnie. When Charleston tensed, clearly ready to attack, Thompson turned his attention back toward Charleston.

"Say it! Say I won. I won, and I am going to shoot you and take that lovely boy and turn him into an immortal piece of art. I will carve the truth into his flesh."

Vinnie's tray fell from his hands onto the tiles, plopping into the water and splashing him.

"I'm going to carve beauty into his young body."

Feeling like an idiot, Vinnie reached into his pants for the knife. How the hell had he managed to forget a big honking knife shoved down his pants? Thompson continued to wax poetic about blood and Vinnie's back as Vinnie inched closer, the knife now in his hand.

All he had to do was shove the blade into Thompson's unprotected back. He visualized himself doing it, shoving the knife in so far that it vanished into Thompson's body, but Vinnie's arm was shaking with some emotion Vinnie couldn't name. It wasn't fear, but it was a close cousin. He could feel his rabbit heart pound as he clenched the knife tighter, ordering himself to do it. He had to. But Vinnie's body rebelled. He stood within two feet of Thompson utterly frozen.

"Goodbye, Kalb. Have a nice death," Thompson said, raising the gun a half-inch.

"Goodbye, Thompson," Charleston answered. The words, the calm and familiar tone, seemed to open a flood within Vinnie, and he threw himself forward. Hitting Thompson in the back, Vinnie slammed the knife into the man's ribs.

A shockwave traveled up his arm, and the world seemed to go unfocused as they both slowly slid toward the earth, red spreading like the arms of an octopus reaching out into the water gathered in the hall, but Vinnie wasn't sure exactly who was bleeding.

Chapter
Twenty-Six

"BERNARDI!" Hands shook him. "Vinnie. Vinnie, sit up." Vinnie could feel his body being forced upright. He could see his hands, the red slowly running off his fingers as the sprinklers rained down on him. He could see Thompson, his wide eyes staring out at nothing, his leg still twitching even though it was pretty clear that he was dead. He was dead, and Vinnie's knife was stuck in his back.

Hands ran across his body, small flares of warmth when Vinnie felt so damn cold. He couldn't think. He was pulled close, a hand stroking over his hair, and Vinnie finally gasped in a breath, unaware that he'd been holding it. The hall smelled of smoke and floor cleaner and the metallic scent of blood. Watery blood that leaked from Thompson's body and traveled in small rivers and tributaries down the hallway.

"You did good, Vinnie. Come on; we've got to go. Buck up, soldier. You just need to get outside." Charleston pulled him up, and Vinnie followed Charleston's direction, his eyes still focused on Thompson's body. Now that he was standing, he could see the unnatural twist of the man's back, the way his arm was caught under him. If he was alive, that would hurt, but now, it just didn't matter anymore. None of it mattered anymore.

Charleston yanked on his arm hard, pulling him away from the awkwardly sprawled body and the spreading pool of red. "Focus, Bernardi."

"Right, sir. Focusing, sir." Vinnie forced himself to look at Charleston, to focus on that face which still had that same implacable expression, that same determination. The rest of the world had somehow changed, and Vinnie could feel that shift in his gut, but Charleston was the same. "Um, sir?"

Charleston had turned to head down the hallway, but he turned back.

"Was I shot?" Vinnie rubbed his right elbow. His whole arm hurt all the way up to the shoulder.

Concern flashed across Charleston's face, but then he just shook his head, his expression all business. "You're okay. It was the concussion from your knife hitting bone."

Vinnie's stomach flipped and he nearly vomited at the simple description of such a horrible act. He'd killed a man. "You'll be fine, Vinnie," Charleston said. A bubble of hysteria pushed up through Vinnie's belly. "Now move your ass," Charleston added. However, he didn't trust Vinnie to get his ass moving on his own; he caught Vinnie by an elbow and hurried him down the hallway. The air was hazy and hot, even with the sprinklers raining down, and even as close as he was, Charleston looked almost fuzzy. When Vinnie looked over his shoulder, Thompson and his inelegant tangle of limbs had vanished in the smoke and mist.

The hallway was silent. However long it had taken them to find and kill Thompson—and Vinnie realized that he had lost all sense of time—it had been long enough for the hospital to be evacuated. There was a hollow roar above them, and Vinnie looked up in confusion. Charleston's hand caught him by the arm and kept him moving.

"Head for the end of the hall," Charleston said, pointing at the glowing exit sign. Vinnie took one step before he realized Charleston was turning back the other way.

"What are you doing?" Vinnie watched as Charleston raised his foot and slammed it down on a cart, ripping the flat portion away from the leg.

"Get out of here, Bernardi."

"Not without you, sir."

Charleston turned to give him a cold glare, but Vinnie just glared right back. "Whatever you're doing, tell me how I can help so we can get it done faster."

"You can help by getting out."

"Not happening, sir." Vinnie could feel his guts churn, but he wasn't leaving Charleston behind.

For a second, Charleston seemed frozen in time. Then he turned back and brought his foot down on the second side of the cart. This time, the leg didn't break away cleanly. "Fuck." Raising his leg again, he repeated the gesture.

"Find me an ax or a crowbar," Charleston ordered.

Vinnie looked around for a second and then took off toward the lobby area. He'd seen one of those glass fire boxes with the hose and an ax. The smoke made his eyes water so bad that he nearly ran past the box before he saw it. Grabbing a chair, he smashed the glass and grabbed the ax inside. A gray figure drifted closer, and for a second, Vinnie thought he was seeing a ghost. Finally his brain processed the fact that it was a fireman in full gear. From the far end of the lobby, the man called out something, his mask garbling the words, but Vinnie just turned his back and darted back down the hall.

"Got it, sir," he called. Charleston had separated the leg of the cart from the rest and now stood near the elevator doors. "So, what are we doing?"

"The elevators had stopped before the fire," Charleston said. He held out his hand for the ax, and Vinnie handed it over. "When I get the doors pried open, get the bar in there." He put the sharp end of the ax in the center crack and then leaned hard against the handle. Slowly, a line appeared as the doors parted. Kneeling down, Vinnie put the bar up against the opening crack. The second Charleston had forced an opening, Vinnie jammed the end in.

Charleston pulled the ax out and dropped it to the ground. Then he pushed on the improvised lever while Vinnie pulled, and they slowly forced the doors open. "Get the metal plate," Charleston said, jerking his head toward the part of the metal cart he'd ripped free. Leaving Charleston to hold the door open, Vinnie grabbed it and jammed it into the opening.

Sticking his head into the now open shaft, Charleston looked up. "It's definitely between floors. It looks like it's between the second and third floors."

Two figures appeared out of the hazy air, firefighters dressed in heavy clothing. "You need to evacuate," the first one ordered. His helmet muffled his voice and created an odd echo. Vinnie thought Charleston would argue, but instead he just nodded.

"Which exit works best?" he asked. The firefighter pointed toward the lobby area.

Charleston caught Vinnie by the arm and pulled him away from the elevator. "Someone stopped the elevators before the fire alarm went off. I think you have people caught between floors," he said.

One of the firefighters moved to where the elevator doors were still pried open and looked into the shaft. The light on his helmet stabbed into the darkness. "We've got it from here," he said. Charleston nodded again and then moved quickly toward the exit. Another firefighter met them half way to the exit, escorting them out into the crowds of people encircling the hospital. Large fire trucks were pouring water into the west wing of the hospital where the fire was leaping from windows. The yellow construction tape had been ripped down, and someone had shoved a plow into a ditch to get it out of the way. The machine sat oddly tilted, the front shovel pointing at the sky and one wheel completely off the ground. Ambulances crowded into the open spaces, and police officers swarmed the entire area, their line of blue holding back the hordes of reporters. Vinnie froze. Scanning the chaos, he just absolutely froze.

A paramedic hurried up to them. "Any injuries?" Vinnie just stared at him.

"Check him out. He took a nasty hit to his right arm and he's a little dazed." Charleston nudged Vinnie forward.

"I'm fine," Vinnie protested.

"Bernardi, let him check you out, or I'll strap you down to the stretcher and let him do a prostate exam," Charleston ordered in a tone of voice that suggested he really wasn't kidding. Vinnie shut his mouth and didn't argue when the paramedic urged him to sit on the curb. With his blue-gloved hands, he felt around Vinnie's neck and arm before shining a light in his eyes.

"If you can make everyone this cooperative, I could offer you a job riding ambulance," the guy told Charleston with a laugh. "Okay, I'm not seeing any serious injuries, but you do have some symptoms of shock, so I'd like to run you in to the hospital."

"I just ran out of a hospital," Vinnie protested, but he did it softly. He really didn't need Charleston to strap him to the stretcher.

"A funny guy. Great." The medic didn't sound like he was amused.

"I need to find an FBI agent. Any idea where law enforcement set up?" Charleston asked. The medic poked a thumb toward the corner of the east wing.

"Charleston?" Vinnie looked up in panic. He could feel his chest start to tighten, and even though he knew it was stupid, he had to grab his own knees just to keep from clutching Charleston's leg.

"Whoa, there. I'm not going anywhere. I'm sure I can bully someone into running a message. I conned you into running my attendance for an entire year, after all." The twist was back in Charleston's smile, and Vinnie could feel the pressure in his chest ease. Charleston raised his arm toward two firefighters dressed in uniform who were standing off to the side. They were both a little older, and one had on a headset, so Vinnie was guessing they were supervisors.

At first they ignored Charleston, but whatever look he was giving them worked because the one without the headset finally wandered over. "Yes?" he asked, his voice curt enough that it would have made Vinnie retreat without saying a word. Charleston, however, wasn't that easily bothered.

"We ran into the probable arsonist inside. I lost my sidearm when he attacked, and his body is still in the hall leading to the security office. We need to coordinate with Special Agent Kaplan from the FBI. He was on-scene when the alarm was pulled."

For a second, the guy just blinked. Yep, Charleston did have a way of really dumping a lot of information into a very short period of time. He'd done that in school, only back then, he'd expected the students to memorize the entire history of the 5307th Composite Unit Provisional after one telling of some obscure story about Burma. It was nice to know that everyone had some trouble keeping up with Charleston. After a bit, the guy seemed to finish processing everything Charleston had said.

"Your name?"

Charleston paused for a second, but then he answered, "Captain Jeff Kalb. The suspect is Captain Thompson of the Third Infantry Division."

"And you?" The man looked down at Vinnie. Vinnie's entire mind went totally and utterly blank.

The medic rescued him. "He's suffering some shock. I think it's probably best to ask him these questions later." Charleston didn't comment, but he rested his hand on Vinnie's shoulder.

"I'll coordinate with local police and see if we can't find your Agent Kaplan," the firefighter said, turning away to go talk to the man on the headset.

"We should move you to an ambulance where we can monitor you more closely, but I don't see that any of them are open right now," the medic commented.

"I'm fine." Vinnie leaned forward, his arms resting against his thighs.

"Sure you are." A blue hand pressed to the side of his neck as the medic took his pulse again.

"Charleston, would you tell this guy I'm fine?" Vinnie begged.

"Nope."

Vinnie sighed and let his head fall down to rest on his knees.

"Hey there, Mr. Bernardi, stay with us." The medic poked him in the neck and Vinnie looked up long enough to glare at him. "Your eyes are overly dilated, and I'm concerned about your body temperature. I need you to stay alert and keep talking to us."

Vinnie looked up at Charleston, intentionally deploying his best puppy gaze because all he wanted to do was sleep. He wanted to sleep and pretend that the day had been one big nightmare.

"Forget it, Bernardi. You're on your own when it comes to medics." As gruff as Charleston sounded, the man sat down on the curb so close to Vinnie that their shoulders touched. "The military teaches you to never fuck with a medic." Charleston reached over and patted Vinnie's leg, and when he was done, he left his hand there. Vinnie didn't understand why his eyes were suddenly so very hot.

"I didn't—I mean, I know I said I wanted him dead, but I didn't mean to kill him," Vinnie said softly. The medic looked down at him with huge eyes, but Charleston just patted his leg again.

"You should have seen me as a raw lieutenant after my first blood. You're doing fine, Vinnie, and you don't have a single thing to feel sorry for."

"Maybe I should have just hit him with the tray."

"Blunt force to the back likely would have led him to instinctively pull the trigger," Charleston said, his voice as clinical as if he was discussing one of his military history lessons. This was a lot more real than history, and Vinnie felt a little flash of frustration that Charleston wasn't more emotional. It was like Vinnie couldn't be emotional and flail if Charleston was being calm. "Since the gun was pointed at me, I'm rather grateful you dropped the tray."

"But…." Vinnie stopped.

For a long time, they sat on the curb and watched the chaos. Vinnie noticed that the medic stood a little farther away from him now, and that annoyed him for some reason, even though he wanted space.

"My first time, my captain took me out and got me shitfaced drunk."

Vinnie rolled his head to the side to study Charleston, but the man wasn't showing any emotion—not shame or pride or even grief at having killed someone.

"You feel like getting drunk?" Charleston asked.

Vinnie sighed. "Will it make me forget?"

"Nope. But in the morning, you'll be so busy trying to keep your brains from leaking out your ears that you won't care."

Vinnie tried to give a weak laugh, but it sounded more like a sob, even to his own ears. "Thanks, but I'll skip it."

"Wise man. Wiser than I was at twenty."

"I doubt that."

"I don't," Charleston said. Vinnie didn't understand that comment, but then Charleston stood up, ending any more conversation. When Vinnie looked over to where Charleston had his gaze pointed, Kaplan and an older man in a uniform were striding across the parking lot. Charleston stood there, his back straight as he waited for them to reach the curb.

Chapter
Twenty-Seven

VINNIE kicked off his sodden shoes, watching with disgust as they landed with a wet thunk on the office's hardwood floor. Once he'd done that, he had no idea what he was supposed to do. Jordan had gotten stuck with bringing him back to the local FBI offices while Charleston disappeared with uniform guy and Kaplan.

"Take a load off," Jordan suggested, gesture toward the couch.

"I'm all wet. I'll make a mess."

"Consider it revenge for the fact that Kaplan stuck you with me," Jordan suggested. He smiled, and Vinnie realized he was a nice looking man. He didn't hit the gaydar at all, and Vinnie tended to ignore people who weren't gaydar-compatible, but Jordan would even be cute if he used a little eyeliner to accent his dark eyes.

"I don't mind being with you."

"Ah, but you would have gone with Kalb if the others would have let you," Jordan pointed out. Vinnie didn't even bother denying that. Kaplan had promised to come back and take Vinnie's statement, but the open aggression between Kaplan and uniform guy and Charleston and a woman who showed up later wearing the ugliest skirt suit in the world.... It had made him want to cling to Charleston's side. Instead, Charleston had told him to head back with Kaplan's agents.

"I'm sure you don't want to be stuck with me, either," Vinnie said. For the first time, he felt a little frisson of guilt at having tortured Jordan and his stick-up-the-ass partner.

"Better here than watching the various agencies all try to claim credit for finding Thompson." Jordan really studied Vinnie then. To avoid the gaze, Vinnie went over and sat on the couch, sliding a bit because his wet clothes on the slick leather was not the best combination. However, Jordan kept staring, and Vinnie had never been good with silence.

"Do you want me to tell you what happened?" Vinnie asked.

"Oh no." Jordan held up his hands. "If you give me your statement, I'm going to end up in a pissing match with the CIA and CID. Do I look suicidal? I let the boss handle the jobs that really piss the rest of the world off."

"Piss them off?"

Jordan walked over and sat on the couch. "Hell, yes. Half the intelligence agencies had someone tasked with bringing Thompson down, and an Army officer in exile and a stripper did what multiple government agencies couldn't. Someone is going to be miserable over that fact."

"I should probably enjoy that," Vinnie said slowly. Two days ago, he would have loved it if something he did got middle class people with their middle class jobs in trouble. Now… now he just felt empty.

"Do you mind if I ask you something?"

Vinnie looked over, pretty sure what Jordan was going to ask. "Do you want to know why I tortured your partner with all that sex talk?"

Jordan seemed to breathe in and out at the same time for a millisecond, leading to a brilliant case of choking on air. "Um, no. I can figure that one out. Addleman is my partner, but he can be a real asshole."

"Oh. Then, what?"

Jordan studied the carpet for several seconds. "What's it like to have to kill in the line of duty? Oh"—he quickly raised his hand—"I know you aren't technically on duty, but you clearly see Kalb as a partner, you trust him at your back, and I just…." Jordan rubbed a hand over his face. "I can tell from your expression that I'm mangling this. Never mind."

"No… it's just… well… yeah, kinda," Vinnie finally agreed. "Right now, I'm not really sure how I feel."

With a nod, Jordan stood up. "I get that. I shot a suspect once, and the whole time he was in surgery, I felt almost like I wasn't real, like the whole situation wasn't real."

"He didn't die?"

Jordan shook his head. "No, he pulled through. The only other time we've been in a spot that tight, Addleman took the shot, and he isn't exactly one for discussing feelings."

Vinnie remembered how the man had turned purple and nearly exploded from rage just from Vinnie's inappropriate teasing. "He does seem a little emotionally constipated."

"Oh yeah. But you know, he's a good guy to have at your back."

Vinnie didn't answer, but he couldn't imagine wanting Addleman and his stick-filled ass at his back. If Jordan trusted him, he couldn't be all bad, though. "Is anyone going to be mad at Delia?" Vinnie suddenly asked. He didn't like the thought of the woman getting shit for not keeping him and Charleston at the safe house.

"Agent Youngdahl? She'll be fine. She's actually another senior agent and not technically on the case, so she won't even get splashed by all the shit that's about to roll downhill."

"That's good." And with that, Vinnie didn't know what else to say. The room was either getting colder, or his wet clothes were finally soaking through his skin and chilling him to the core, but Vinnie didn't say anything. He really just wanted some quiet, and as long as Jordan was willing to stand by the door and just watch from a distance, Vinnie pretended that he was alone with his storming thoughts.

"You can go find us warm, dry clothes," Charleston said loudly as he slammed through the door fast enough to make Jordan jump. Kaplan was right on his heels, and Addleman several steps behind him.

"Kalb," Kaplan said. Charleston turned and stared at the three FBI agents. While they all had on suits, Charleston still had the wet, dirty clothes he'd been wearing in the hospital.

"Give us some time," Charleston said firmly. He crossed his arms, and Kaplan looked around the room, frowning when he saw Vinnie on his couch… either that or he was frowning at the mess Vinnie was making.

"A few minutes. Addleman, go find them some clothes. Jordan, see which safe houses we have available." Kaplan jerked his head toward the door, and both agents headed out without comment. "Tell me you're not going to do anything stupid," Kaplan asked, and he almost sounded like he was begging.

"Both men I planned to kill are dead, and I didn't manage to kill either one," Charleston pointed out.

Kaplan sighed and looked from Vinnie to Charleston and back. "This is breaking about a dozen regulations, and I'm only doing it because there are no suspects to take to trial and because you're a mean bastard, and I just don't have the energy for a pissing match with you," Kaplan finally said. Turning around, he headed for the door. "You have a few minutes." When he headed out, he closed the door behind him, and Vinnie was left alone with Charleston.

"How are you holding up?" Charleston asked.

He made it sound so casual. How was he holding up? He was losing his mind. His guts were twisted in knots, and he wanted to sink into the ground. He was pretty sure he was about a mouse hair away from running screaming in circles. "Um… okay?" Vinnie finally answered since the real answer didn't want to come out. He felt like if he said any of that, he'd immediately fall into little tiny emotionally distraught pieces.

"Bullshit," Charleston answered.

"Yeah, well some days just aren't worth getting out of bed for," Vinnie struggled to grin.

"Was today?" Charleston looked at him, but Vinnie didn't have an answer, not in a few seconds or even a few minutes. Time dragged on, and Vinnie squirmed helplessly, but he couldn't get his mouth or his brain to supply any sort of answer.

Charleston's eyebrow did that twitch thing that meant his patience was limited. "I don't know," Vinnie answered.

Charleston nodded. "Better. It's never an easy choice—killing a man. But if you hadn't gotten out of bed, think how the world would be different."

"Thompson would be alive," Vinnie said quietly. His right arm ached—throbbed actually.

"Yes, and he'd be trying to kill me and take you. According to the FBI profiler, he'd be out looking to find some sub to tie up and torture to death. And based on the fact that he dumped gallons of gas into an empty wing at a hospital and set fire to it, I think we can safely say that he would have caused significant damage if we hadn't taken him down."

Vinnie just gave a quick nod. He knew all that. He knew it, and his heart still ached and he could feel his ribs tighten every time he thought about Thompson's sightless eyes. They sat in silence, and Vinnie watched a small puddle form at their feet. If the FBI used real wood for their floors, all this water was going to really ruin something. The silence pressed in on Vinnie, and he welcomed the weight of it. Always before, he'd filled the world with words—to distract or entertain or manipulate. But now he just sank into the silence that filled the air and the feel of Charleston's hand on his knee.

Vinnie expected more talking or lecturing or maybe just a kick in the ass, but they sat in silence. Slowly, Vinnie leaned over so that he was resting some of his weight against Charleston's shoulder, but other than that, they were silent.

The door opened. "You two decent?" Kaplan asked without putting his head in.

Charleston rolled his eyes.

"No, we're naked, and I'm tied over your desk," Vinnie shot back. The joke felt awkward in his mouth, but that's what Vinnie Bernardi would say. Charleston's lips twitched.

"You're a real pain in the ass," Kaplan said as he came in the room, a pile of dry clothes in his arms.

"He is, isn't he?" Charleston agreed, but he sounded fond of pains in the asses as he said it.

"It's a talent." Vinnie shrugged.

"How are you holding up?" He tossed the clothing toward Charleston.

"I'm not running in circles and screaming," Vinnie pointed out. It was the only answer he had.

Kaplan nodded and walked over to the desk and sat on the edge of it. "You did good, kid." Charleston patted Vinnie's knee, and Vinnie wanted nothing more than to believe them.

Charleston tightened his fingers around Vinnie's knee for a second, holding him tightly before he loosened his hold and turned to Kaplan. "You recovered the body?"

"Yep. The crime lab wants to take some samples to lock down the forensic evidence, but I told them they were going to have to wait."

"I appreciate that."

Kaplan nodded, and for a second, the two men exchanged some indecipherable expression, and Vinnie was too tired to even object to being left out of the loop. Something had happened with the uniformed guy, and Vinnie was guessing it wasn't good. Charleston had that look on his face—the one that promised that the next person who stepped out of line was going to be running laps until their hair fell out. Lots of teachers never seemed to show their stress until they snapped, but Vinnie had become an expert in reading faces and knowing when someone was pushed to a breaking point. Of course, usually he pushed people anyway, but he tried to just wait as Charleston sorted the clothing Kaplan had given him.

"Where to from here?" Charleston finally asked.

"Your informal statements are being typed up. You'll need to give separate statements, review them, make corrections, and sign. Forensics wants your clothes bagged and delivered to the lab."

Vinnie looked at Charleston, that familiar fear of being separated from him crawling into his belly. He wasn't this needy or clingy. He made fun of needy, clingy men. Vinnie Bernardi did not cling… except when he had an overwhelming urge to cling. He sighed at his own patheticness.

"I'll stay with Bernardi," Kaplan said, "but this is not optional. The forensic department said that the gas can used in the fire had Thompson's prints all over it, so we have a military officer involved in arson, attempted murder, and probably murder if we can prove to the court that he was the Poet Killer. We need to do this by the books, Kalb, because people are not happy."

"I think I noticed."

Kaplan sighed and shrugged. "That kind of kill would be hard enough on a trained agent, but Bernardi has no training. You had no business taking him into that building, Kalb. The general didn't say anything that I wasn't thinking. Hell, he even said it nicer than I would have."

Charleston leaned back and looked at Kaplan without a trace of regret in his face. "We took him down."

"You put a civilian in the middle. Accusing you of using poor judgment was kind considering the kind of regulations he could have thrown around if he wanted. I should have been with you—not Bernardi."

Charleston glanced over, and Vinnie wanted to defend Charleston's choices—he did, but he could still see Thompson's wide eyes staring at him, the red dripping from his fingers as the sprinkler rained down on him.

Charleston's gaze softened. "If you'd been with me, Dwayne, Thompson would have shot you on sight and then had his fun with me. He wouldn't have turned his back to you—he sure as hell wouldn't have let you get a knife in him. If I was going to take backup, I was going to take Vinnie. The kid is tougher than you think, and more importantly, Thompson always was an idiot around subs. He never understood that a submissive could be just as strong and just as dangerous as any top."

"You planned for me to kill him?" Vinnie struggled just to get the words out.

Charleston was shocked when he looked over. "Hell, no. I planned to take the bastard out myself. I just trusted you to have my back if something went wrong. I've met your father. He eats hard-asses for lunch, and you can twist that man up so fast that he can't tell up from down. If you could handle him, and if you could handle being in that cell, you could handle anything Thompson threw at you."

Pride filled Vinnie, but it still couldn't chase all the horror away. He still felt uneasy at having to tell his story without Charleston there to lean against. "So, I just need to say what happened?" Vinnie asked Kaplan.

"Yep, that's it. Just read the typed copy of the informal statement and add in details and make corrections as you need to."

Vinnie remembered the last psychiatrist he'd gone to. "Your head shrinker isn't going to make me tell him stories about inkblots, is he?"

Kaplan just looked blankly at Vinnie, and Charleston laughed. "If he does, you can have fun completely fucking with him," Charleston offered.

Vinnie smiled. "That might not be bad." As quick as it came, Vinnie's smile faded. It was good to know that both these men believed Vinnie did the right thing, but that didn't make all the guilt vanish. It just helped make it fade a bit. "I can do this."

"Yeah, you can." Charleston stood up and let his hand rest on Vinnie's shoulder for a second. "However, right now you're dripping all over the place. You can use the bathroom first." Charleston shook out the clothing Kaplan had tossed him and handed over a pair of sweats and a T-shirt that said FBI on the back.

Vinnie took the clothing and headed for the bathroom. The faster he changed and got the talking over with, the faster he could go back to his own life.

Chapter
Twenty-Eight

VINNIE followed Charleston up the narrow walk to his house at the edge of the academy grounds. He felt three years younger just being on the property again. At least when he was sitting in that tree and spying, he had that edge of fear to keep him from feeling like a little duckling following momma duck around.

"Come on," Charleston invited him, throwing his door open as he went in. Vinnie looked around for a second. It was late Sunday night, maybe even Monday morning at this rate, and the place felt empty… or maybe it was Vinnie who felt empty. After giving his same story to three different sets of investigators, he felt like he'd been drained of all words. He'd fallen asleep a couple of times in the middle—crashing on Kaplan's leather couch while people argued about procedure and jurisdiction—but he basically had been running since Friday when the world had started to crash around him.

"Hey, I'm getting invited into the inner sanctum," Vinnie joked. Charleston turned on a lamp revealing a simple living room with an old couch facing a stereo with no television at all. In the corner, magazines were neatly lined up with the spines showing and a weight bench in the corner had a white towel draped over it.

"Nice house," Vinnie said, more to be polite than out of any admiration.

"No, it's not." Charleston headed through a door into a kitchen. "It's the place where I'm stationed until they decide what to do with me." He came back with a beer in one hand and a soda in the other. Vinnie looked at the beer with great longing, sighing when Charleston offered him the soda instead. Walking over to the couch, Vinnie dropped down, happy enough for a little caffeine in any form. Already he was so tired he wouldn't be able to sleep, which didn't make sense, but he knew it was true.

"So, are you going to go back to being Captain Jeff Kalb?" Vinnie asked. He wasn't sure how he felt about that. Charleston was Charleston. He couldn't imagine the man having any other life. However, the guy with the uniform had appeared twice over the last weekend from hell—vanishing both times that Vinnie showed his face. It made a man a little paranoid to walk out of a bathroom and send a general running out of the room. Paranoid or proud. Vinnie wasn't sure which he was feeling.

Charleston cracked open his beer and sprawled over about three-quarters of the couch. "Don't know. The people who hate me are probably still trying to maneuver me into a dishonorable discharge, and the officers who either support me or just hate the system will try to get me honorably discharged."

"The general?" Vinnie asked.

"Oh, he'd love to give me a dishonorable discharge. But until that political fight is over, I'll be here."

"Still being Charleston?"

He took a long drink of his beer, and Vinnie tried to not notice the way his neck curved and moved as he swallowed. He finished and then shrugged. "It's not a bad person to be."

"Would you consider staying Charleston?" Vinnie held his breath as Charleston looked over. He didn't want to feel so clingy, but he just felt like he needed to have something he could cling to. He didn't really know Kalb. Kalb had stood silent while people argued around him, but he knew Charleston.

"Charleston is just a part of me, Vinnie. I can't stay in this role forever. For one thing, sooner or later, I am going to kill some student and hide the body in the woods." Charleston said it with such a deadpan tone that it took Vinnie a second to grin.

"Not going to happen, sir. You put up with me." Vinnie felt a flash of pride at the smile he brought to Charleston's face.

"As much as I don't mind people seeing me as Charleston, one of these days, I do want to reclaim the rest of myself. There's a difference between putting a part of yourself to the side for a while and losing it."

"Some parts I would rather lose," Vinnie said.

"I don't know. I kind of liked Troy," Charleston said. Vinnie nearly slid off the couch in shock. "He was a kid, Vinnie. He made a kid's mistakes, but he never turned into the sort of manipulative asshole his father was. That man was all charm and no substance, so I don't know how he managed to raise a kid who had balls and a lot more integrity than his old man."

Vinnie shook his head, oddly upset by the turn this conversation had just taken. "Troy Martello hid who he was. He was a coward."

Charleston angled his head and really studied Vinnie for long time. "When you meet someone, do you plan on telling them within the first five minutes that you were forced to kill a madman who was about to shoot someone?"

Bile rose in Vinnie's throat. "No," he answered quickly.

With a nod, Charleston reached over and put a hand on Vinnie's knee. "You're growing up, Bernardi. Troy never hid anything. Everything he ever felt flashed across his face, and he was not all that successful in trying to hide his sexual interest. True, he was a more private person. Locked up in a military academy full of homophobic kids, he chose to save himself some grief by keeping feelings to himself. However, the important thing is that I truly believe that Troy would have stepped forward to protect a gay student in a heartbeat." Charleston stood up. "You can have the couch, Vinnie. There are linens in the closet over there."

Vinnie looked where Charleston was pointing, and by the time he looked back, Charleston was walking slowly toward his bedroom. Vinnie fingered the arm of the couch, too tired to go after sheets and too tired to sleep. Instead he drank his soda and stared at the empty wall. Some tenant before Charleston had hung a picture on the wall, and there was a dim gray box where it had hung. Vinnie knew he should think about everything that had happened, everything he'd heard everyone say. Charleston and Kaplan and the Asian psychiatrist with the bad hair—they'd all been talking at Vinnie, and he couldn't even seem to remember anything they'd said. It was water sliding past him, and he was too tired to try and gather it up.

Without intentionally going to sleep, Vinnie eventually just drifted away. The empty bottle slipped from his hand and rolled several inches before hitting the leg of the side table with a soft clink.

Morning turned out to be closer to afternoon when Vinnie finally opened his eyes. They felt crusty, and when he raised his hand to rub them, a blanket slid off him and pooled on the ground at his feet.

"Rise and shine, Bernardi." A cup of coffee was thrust into his hands the second he pushed himself upright, and Vinnie blinked at a very blurry Charleston. Either that or his eyes weren't fully open.

"Are you always this cheerful in the morning?" Vinnie loudly slurped at his coffee and then nearly choked to death when he discovered that his coffee had more hair on its chest than he did. "Holy shit. You did use water, right?" Vinnie squinted up at Charleston. Wait. The man had on a running suit… a sweaty running suit.

"Yes, Bernardi, I used water, about ten hours ago when I made it."

"How long have you been up?" Vinnie watched while Charleston stripped off a sweaty T-shirt and grabbed the towel off his weight bench to dry himself. Either the man was completely oblivious about the fact that he was hot, and Vinnie didn't think anyone could be that oblivious, or he was showing off.

"Long enough to teach five classes and take my chosen few on their afternoon run." Charleston tossed the towel on top of the sweaty T-shirt on the bench and headed for his bedroom, his bare chest making Vinnie's libido do interesting things. Very interesting. He hadn't been this incapable of controlling his own body since seventh grade when he pretty much kept a textbook glued to his crotch all year. His father had been married to Karen or Kathy or someone that year, and the poor woman had assumed Vinnie had just taken a sudden interest in books.

"Your run?" Vinnie felt like his brain was in first gear.

"My run. The one you used to enjoy spying on." Charleston came back out of the room, and unfortunately, he was buttoning up a blue shirt.

He stopped in the doorway and looked at Vinnie for a second before he walked over and sat on the coffee table. "Life goes on, Bernardi. It's Monday, so no matter how much you grieve in private, you have to get on with life."

"Grieve?" Vinnie set his coffee down on the far end of the table from Charleston and rubbed his eyes.

"Grieve, Vinnie. You killed a man. Every time I pulled the trigger on one of my targets, I grieved for them. Sometimes I was sorry that they'd had such a shitty life that they'd chosen the wrong path; sometimes I was sorry they'd followed an evil leader. It didn't matter. Every kill I made—I grieved for the son of a bitch I killed. So, you go ahead and feel bad that you had to kill Thompson or that Thompson's childhood was so piss poor that he couldn't jack himself out of the gutter he fell in. But while you're doing that, you remember this: you recovered from your childhood, so Thompson could have recovered if he would have gotten some help."

Vinnie stared at Charleston. He wanted to make a joke out of it, to laugh off the suggestion that he would grieve for Thompson. He wanted to be like the guys on television who killed the bad guy and went out for celebratory drinks afterwards. Instead he found himself nodding.

"So, ready to get on with life?" Charleston asked.

With a weak grin, Vinnie nodded. "Have to eventually."

Charleston reached out and patted his shoulder. "It gets easier. So, what plans does Vinnie Bernardi have for Monday afternoon?"

At first Vinnie waited, hoping that Charleston would offer something… anything. However, Charleston just sat on the coffee table and watched Vinnie, waiting for an answer with that unreadable expression of his.

His apartment was an option, but the sheets on the bed were still stained with his come mixed with Thompson's. Handcuffs dangled from the headboard and his window was broken. He didn't want to face that anymore than he wanted to face the wrath of RJ. He was just too tired for any of it.

Standing up, Vinnie headed for the bathroom. "Hey, you don't need to worry about me. I'm a cat. I always land on my feet, and I still have seven or eight lives left." Vinnie grinned at Charleston. Before he could blink, Charleston was up and on him, standing so close that Vinnie could feel the heat from his body, and he could feel the wall behind him even though he didn't actually remember plastering himself to the wall. He was still a little bothered by the fact he was an inch taller. Charleston just felt so much larger than life… and larger than Vinnie.

"Don't!" Charleston slapped his hands against the wall on either side of Vinnie, trapping him.

Jumping, Vinnie tried to hide his fear and his desire. "Don't what? Hey, I am just trying to get out of your hair, the way you want." He held his hands up in surrender.

"First, don't tell me what I want. Second, don't try and hide behind this mask of yours the second the emotions get too real. I saw the real Vinnie out there at that hospital. I saw the real you last night, so don't retreat into this illusion, not with me, Bernardi."

That stopped Vinnie. For a second, he couldn't come up with a response to that. He felt exposed… raw. Carefully smiling, Vinnie shrugged. "No mask here. I'm just tired, and I want to go…" Vinnie stopped again and swallowed. The emotion poured from Charleston, scaring him. Vinnie knew how to deal with rage or disappointment or lust, but whatever Charleston was feeling, it was more visceral, more primal, and Vinnie's mouth went dry with fear.

"Tell me what you want," Charleston whispered.

The tone pulled at Vinnie's needs, but he didn't plan to spend his whole life clinging to the man. Vinnie felt like a big enough loser already. "Hey, you're not responsible for me."

"Tell me anyway," Charleston insisted. Vinnie hated that. He hated the way one word from Charleston made him want to give in no matter how much common sense told him to stick to his guns. It was like the potato incident all over again, only this time Vinnie was going to end up losing more than a night's sleep if he gave in. He was already doubting himself again, and seeing Charleston reject him… not a pass, not a come-on or a leer but *him*… he couldn't take that.

"Let's not go there, okay?" Vinnie said, his voice edging toward anger. "I just really need some space right now."

"What do you want, Vinnie?"

"What the fuck do you want me to say?"

"Something honest."

Vinnie looked at Charleston, trying to figure out the rules to whatever game they were playing. "I've been honest. I want you, but either you're not honestly interested or you've got a funny way of showing it. So, since you won't jump my bones even after I walk in on you masturbating, I think I want to find some food, pee, and go home, only not in that order."

"Oh, I'm interested. If you think I'm not, you're an idiot, and I know you're not an idiot, Vinnie."

Vinnie sighed. "Okay, yeah, you're interested. But you're interested in the 'look but don't touch unless it's in a totally platonic sort of way', and I'm really not interested in you as a father figure. I mean, I really appreciate how helpful you've been, but if you're going to torture me by walking around half naked, I have to tell you, my self-control is really not that good."

"Look but don't touch?"

"Don't touch except for the fatherly sort of comforting. I get that. I don't want that, but I get that," Vinnie said wearily.

"You really are an idiot."

Vinnie glared.

"Bernardi, I'm not comfortable with a partner who is so cut off from his feelings that he won't even have a serious conversation, but I would say that you've done a lot of growing in the last few days. Of course, even if you were still a green kid, I probably would have bedded you eventually. I just wouldn't take that risk with Thompson out there."

"But…?" Vinnie stopped.

"I don't tease, Bernardi. So, you've been playing this game for a long time, but it's time to piss or get off the pot. I want to hear what you want."

"I…." Vinnie wet his lips. "To be tied to your bed," he answered.

Charleston's smile grew slowly. Pressing closer, his body pinned

Vinnie, holding him captive and surrounding him with the scent of honest sweat and soap. "That's the first time you have been honest. You've tried manipulation and charm, but that is the first honest thing you've said." Charleston was leaning in so close that the words were warm against Vinnie's neck.

Vinnie breathed faster, his heart thumping painfully fast, but still, Charleston didn't move. He stood, crowding Vinnie and watching him with eyes that were dark and dilated. "What do you want?" Vinnie finally asked.

Charleston straightened up, dropping his hands to his side. "That's the right question, Bernardi. I want you tied so tightly that you can't move, and then I want to take a flogger to your back until the red marks merge together. I want to hear you cry out, Bernardi."

Vinnie stood still, his legs wobbling weakly. The tying up was good, the flogging was tolerable, but Vinnie still couldn't quite believe that Charleston wanted him. Charleston was his holy grail, his impossible quest, and a little part of Vinnie was screaming in terror that he was about to ruin a friendship and destroy his very best fantasies by trying and failing to get the real thing. They looked at each other. Charleston backed off until he stood several feet away, but Vinnie felt trapped by the man's presence. "Why?" he whispered.

"I want you to trust me."

Vinnie frowned. "I do."

Shaking his head, Charleston backed away another step. "No you don't, Vinnie. You still have all your masks in play. Right now, you're thinking about how to play this and looking for exits."

"No I'm not." Vinnie's voice got thready as he lied. Charleston frowned.

"You can't know if you trust me until you give yourself to me and see what happens, but if you aren't ready for that, you can leave." Charleston voice was calm and accepting as he backed away another step.

"But... you turned me down."

"I turned down your offer to manipulate me into bed, Bernardi."

Charleston sighed and then stepped closer. Raising his hand, he rested his palm against Vinnie's cheek, and the heat soaked into him. "You want to control this, and I do not share control. I respect safewords, and I respect your right to leave when you want to; however, if you're in my bed, you will not control what happens."

"So, you want me to just surrender? Hey, I'm great at surrender." Vinnie twitched his body.

"No, you aren't," Charleston said. "You're great at manipulating, but I can teach you to submit. I can teach you to drop these masks and trust me with your body and your secrets." Charleston gave a crooked, wry grin. "I think I've proved that I can keep a secret or two."

"Or four or five," Vinnie agreed. His mouth was dry, and he tried to swallow, but he couldn't seem to manage to get it right. He started coughing. The coughs drove the air from him, and he started getting light headed before Charleston guided him to a chair and sat him down. The next thing he knew, hands were holding a glass of water to his lips. Closing his own hands around Charleston's he drank, trying to wash away the tickle that threatened to choke him.

"You okay now?"

Vinnie nodded unhappily. That was just about the unsexiest thing he could have done under the circumstances. Streaks of water stained his wrinkled shirt from where the water had slopped over the side of the glass, and he figured he was probably blotchy and red. "Do you really want—" Vinnie stopped. Seriously, he was not so pathetic as to ask that question.

"I do want to control you," Charleston answered Vinnie's unasked question. "I want to tie you down and watch your skin slowly redden as you lose yourself in the pleasure and the pain. I want to lie next to you and feel your muscles strain under the skin as you try to lie still because I've ordered it."

Vinnie looked up at Charleston. "So, not just a fuck and run?" he asked with a little laugh that sounded weird, even to his own ears.

Charleston put his hand on Vinnie's shoulder. "I've killed, Bernardi. I've shot men, I've held the knife and felt their warm blood down my arm, and I've thrown the grenade. I know my own power, and what I want is to hold you helpless and prove to myself that I have more in me than death."

"You do," Vinnie whispered, and he believed it.

"Then give yourself to me. Don't try and manipulate me, just give yourself to me."

"Okay." The word slipped out before Vinnie even had time to think about it. Maybe Charleston understood that because his expression was still guarded.

"Finish your water. If you mean that, I'll be in the bedroom. Leave your clothes here."

"And if I change my mind?" Vinnie asked, and a little part of him wanted Charleston to tell him he didn't have a choice. That would be easier.

"The front door's unlocked, Bernardi." With that, Charleston turned around and headed through an open door into the bedroom and vanished.

Chapter
Twenty-Nine

VINNIE shook as he edged closer to the bedroom door. He'd been naked dozens of times, often strutting and preening as he showed off his toned body and hard cock. Now he felt twelve years old and just as vulnerable. A little part of him wanted to run, but one of Charleston's favorite sayings was echoing in Vinnie's head. "If you do what you've always done, you'll get what you've always had." Vinnie knew what he had, and there were parts of his life that he loved, but he didn't love himself. He was flailing and lost, and he was just so damn tired that he wanted an out. Friday night he'd done what he always did: he went home with some Dom who he thought he could twist and manipulate. True, that hadn't exactly turned out the way he wanted it, but none of his relationships were exactly good. So he had to do something different. This… this was different.

When he looked around the corner, Charleston was sitting in a chair with a book on his knee. He looked up as Vinnie hovered near the doorjamb. For heavy minutes they looked at each other and Vinnie pressed himself closer to the wall, most of his body hidden behind it.

"Do you feel safe here?" Charleston eventually asked, his voice curious rather than confrontational.

"Of course I do. If I didn't, I wouldn't be naked."

Charleston closed his book and carefully set it on the floor beside his chair. Vinnie searched the corners of the room, but there weren't any overt signs of bondage equipment. The bed had a heavy headboard with thick posts good for tying someone down, but that was the only sign that

Charleston was kinky. Vinnie had himself convinced he was going to find a full-blown dungeon. He'd never had a Dom ask him for power. Usually it was a carefully negotiated dance, one that Vinnie was very used to winning. Yes, he would do bondage. Yes, he would do some light pain if his partner enjoyed it, but he set the limit at twenty strokes, and nothing that broke skin. He would do cock sucking; he wouldn't do barebacking. Vinnie had the whole spiel down, but Charleston was asking him to just trust.

"Then why are you hiding?" Charleston leaned back in his chair. Vinnie only realized Charleston was wearing glasses when the man took them off and set them carefully on the book.

Vinnie shrugged and strolled into the room with an exaggerated roll of his hips. If Charleston wanted a show, Vinnie could give him one.

"Stop."

Vinnie froze, one hand half raised toward the footboard. Slowly he lowered his hand and looked at Charleston, once again feeling about twelve and very vulnerable. "What?" Vinnie asked when Charleston just looked at him for several seconds.

"You are a beautiful man. You don't need to show that off. However, I asked you a question, and that requires an answer. Why were you hiding?" Charleston leaned forward in the chair, resting his elbows on his knees. This really wasn't Vinnie's idea of a good time, but he'd agreed to not manipulate Charleston, and he really wanted to obey. The problem was that he didn't know what to say.

"I don't know," he finally answered. For a second, Charleston studied him before leaning back in his chair.

"How do you feel?"

"Uncomfortable," Vinnie admitted. If Charleston wanted the truth, Vinnie could do that. He just wasn't all that sure Charleston was going to like what he heard.

"Honesty is good." Charleston praised him, and Vinnie blushed at just how easily Charleston's words cut through his defenses. "How uncomfortable are you?"

Vinnie let his hand drop to his side. "Pretty fucking

uncomfortable."

Instead of answering, Charleston stood up and started walking around the room, his eyes watching Vinnie. Even though Vinnie had nothing to apologize for in the physical department, he still instinctively sucked in his gut. Now if he could find a way to suck in and hide his neuroses, that would probably be more helpful. Without touching, Charleston examined every inch, circling until he sat on the side of the bed opposite from his reading chair. "What would make you feel more comfortable?" he finally asked.

"Uh." Vinnie's brain stalled for a second. "Moving on with the sex would help."

"This isn't just about sex," Charleston said. Pulling one leg up under him, he looked supremely comfortable in his own skin. Vinnie was starting to resent him for that.

"But we're going to have sex, right?" Vinnie asked hopefully.

"If I feel like it," Charleston answered, which wasn't actually an answer. Vinnie shifted from one foot to the other.

"What are you feeling?" Charleston asked again.

"Like an idiot just standing here," Vinnie said.

"I'm enjoying just watching you. If you're going to submit to me, shouldn't you be focused on what I want?"

Vinnie's eyes had been exploring the far corners of the room, but now he looked right at Charleston, half suspecting that was some sort of joke. Charleston just wanted to look?

"That makes you even more uncomfortable," Charleston noted.

"Well, yeah. I thought you wanted to tie me up and take a whip to my backside and fuck me."

"I want to dominate you," Charleston said. From the tone he was correcting Vinnie, but Vinnie couldn't figure out how that was any different from the list Vinnie had given. "Drop and give me thirty." Charleston barked out the order, and Vinnie was halfway to the ground before he remembered he wasn't one of Charleston's recruits anymore. However, by that time, it was just easier to go ahead and get in position. The first fifteen or twenty were easy, but then Charleston walked over and put his foot in the middle of Vinnie's back, pressing down so Vinnie had to work for the last ten. Sweating, Vinnie finished his last pushup and collapsed to the ground, breathing hard.

"Up."

Still panting, Vinnie pulled himself up using the post of the footboard and waited to see what Charleston wanted next.

"How do you feel?"

"Tired and still frustrated about not getting any sex." Oddly, Charleston smiled. Vinnie gave up trying to understand anything. When he'd been going to school at the academy, he thought Charleston had some esoteric military code of ethics, but no one could be as weird as Charleston. The man had his own rules.

Standing up, Charleston ran a hand down Vinnie's shoulder, capturing the wrist in his hand for a second before moving around to Vinnie's back. His hands moved over Vinnie's back slowly, exploring each curve and muscle before sliding across sweat-slicked skin to new territory. When Charleston slid his hands down and over Vinnie's ass, Vinnie had one second of hoping they were moving on to the main event, but Charleston just continued down to the legs. Running his hands on either side of each leg, Charleston explored Vinnie the way an owner might examine a horse. Vinnie wasn't sure if he should be turned on or just creeped out, but his cock was hard and starting to ache, so clearly parts of him were fine with this sort of personal exam.

"Lay on the bed," Charleston said. Vinnie looked over his shoulder at Charleston, not asking but wondering where this was leading. "Right after you drop and give me thirty," Charleston added. Vinnie opened his mouth to protest. He was here for sex, not physical training, but Charleston's eyebrow quirked, and Vinnie found himself on the floor counting off another set of pushups. This time Charleston didn't push him down, but Vinnie's arms were tired, and he struggled to get the last few. He collapsed at twenty-three and lay panting on the ground, but Charleston just watched, silent and unmoving. After a few minutes, Vinnie pushed himself up on trembling arms to finish. Once he was done, he collapsed onto the floor again.

"Are you ready to obey every order, or do I have to keep going back to this familiar territory?" Charleston was sitting on the edge of the bed, and he rested his foot on Vinnie's ass.

"Sir, yes sir."

That got an eye roll from Charleston. "On the bed."

This time Vinnie didn't hesitate or look to Charleston for some sort of explanation; he got up and sat on the bed. "Um, on my back or my stomach?" He looked over at Charleston, half cringing as he waited for the order to do more pushups. He was going to hurt tomorrow, and not just in a good way.

Charleston reached over and ran a possessive hand over Vinnie's arm, squeezing the bicep. "Questions are always allowed, Vinnie. On your stomach in the middle." Vinnie nodded and then awkwardly crawled onto the bed trying to not kick Charleston, who still sat on the edge and watched as Vinnie settled himself on his stomach and tucked his hands in under his head. He might have spread his legs in invitation, but he couldn't with Charleston sitting there. The bed was a queen, so he didn't have that much room. Instead he studied the blue checked pattern on the flannel sheets and tried to ignore just how much his cock really, really wanted to come.

When Charleston ran a possessive hand over Vinnie's calf, he sucked in a surprised breath.

"Problem, Bernardi?"

"No, sir. I just didn't expect you to touch me there."

"If you're giving me control, I can touch you wherever I like."

Vinnie nodded. That was true, but most of the time, his tops pretty much went straight for the ass once they had him secured. This was new territory for him.

"Do you prefer handcuffs, leather, or rope?"

"I thought this was all about what you wanted," Vinnie said. The second the words came out he bit his tongue. "Sorry, sir. That was…. Feel free to gag me."

"That's the second time you've asked me to gag you."

"Considering how often I get myself in trouble with my mouth, trust me, you want to gag me."

Charleston brought down his hand on Vinnie's upturned ass. The loud slap had a slight echo to it, and Vinnie jumped as the heat warmed his ass. "Ow."

Charleston raised an eyebrow.

"It stung," Vinnie defended himself. His ass didn't hurt, but it did have a certain heat and throb in it that he wanted to rub away. Instead he kept his hands under his head.

"You still haven't answered."

"Answered what?" Vinnie looked over his shoulder, confused and uncomfortable again.

Charleston reached down, and Vinnie flinched. This time, though, Charleston ran his hand over the stinging cheek, soothing it. "Handcuffs, leather, or rope?" he repeated.

"Oh." Vinnie blushed as he realized that he had changed the topic. Normally he was really a lot better at playing submissive. "I usually don't have a lot of time for rope. I get frustrated. Leather is the best but expensive, so most of the time, I stick with handcuffs. Wrap a scarf around the wrist before you tighten the handcuff down, and that keeps the metal from pinching too much."

The amusement on Charleston's face made Vinnie blush even more. Great, now he was telling Charleston how to tie him up. Fuck. He was totally off his game today.

"I prefer rope, so most of the time, that's what we'll use. You need to learn a little patience, anyway."

"Yes, sir." Vinnie buried his face in the flannel sheet and groaned at the thought of having patience when his cock was hard enough that a few good strokes would send him over the edge into a killer orgasm. However, he had promised to submit, and this was him submitting. He realized he wasn't exactly graceful in his submission, but he was trying.

Getting up, Charleston went over and opened a drawer. Pulling out a long length of rope, he started pulling it through his fingers, straightening it out and letting it fall to the ground. Vinnie watched it, fascinated with the way it coiled and moved. Charleston was going to tie him up with that. Fear and desire tangled in his guts.

"What's your safeword?"

Vinnie swallowed, and even that delay was enough to make Charleston narrow his eyes slightly. "Armageddon," Vinnie quickly offered up. Charleston nodded. "Sir?" Vinnie bit his lip, not sure he wanted to distract the man now that he was getting on with the good part.

Charleston stopped running the rope through his hand and just looked at Vinnie, obviously waiting.

"If you're asking me to give everything to you, should I have a safeword?"

For a second, Charleston just looked at him. Then he slowly gathered all the rope in one hand and walked over to sit at the edge of the bed near Vinnie's shoulder. Running his hands over Vinnie's back, he took several minutes before answering. "Vinnie, what is a safeword?"

Vinnie looked up at Charleston, and he knew he had his "stupid teacher" look on his face—the one that used to get him kicked out of class without even saying anything, but he just couldn't help it. Charleston cleared his throat and almost looked like he might smile. Vinnie was shocked at the warm wave of victory he could feel just from inspiring that small moment of happiness.

"Everyone has their own definition, Vinnie. If you're going to submit to me, then we need to make sure we're using the words the same way."

"Fuck." Vinnie turned his head to hide it in his arms. "A vocab lesson. I always sucked at those."

"Oh, I don't know." Charleston patted his ass. "You always remembered well enough after a few hundred pushups. So, no more distraction. Answer the question."

Still hiding his face, Vinnie blinked as he realized he had changed the subject. "Okay, a safeword is something I use when I don't like how you're doing something, and I want you to stop." Turning his head to the side, he looked up at Charleston to see if the man was accepting his answer. The look Charleston gave him bordered on pity, but before Vinnie could ask why, Charleston had shaken his head and the expression vanished.

"The word means something different to me. For me, a safeword means that we've reached a place where you don't feel capable of continuing. Maybe you feel unsafe or you're hurting too much, or maybe something unexpected has happened like something I've done reminds you of something unhappy."

"So, I say it and you stop."

Charleston nodded. "Yes, I do. I stop and we talk about what you're feeling and why you can't continue. We then decide if this is something you can't physically do, in which case we'll avoid doing it again, or we'll find a way to try and approach the activity from a different direction. However, if you use your safeword, you have to talk to me about why."

Vinnie looked up, horror curling in his stomach. This was harder than handing his body over to someone. Sometimes he suspected that he didn't actually care all that much for his body, but what Charleston was asking…. Vinnie didn't know if he had that to give.

"Are you okay?" Charleston rested a hand on Vinnie's shoulder, and Vinnie was glad he was lying on his stomach. This way, Charleston couldn't see how his cock had wilted at the idea of having to offer up feelings and thoughts that Vinnie had always kept to himself. If he used a safeword, it was because he wanted the scene to stop, not because he wanted to talk or had to stop. Fuck, he'd once safeworded out because once he was tied up, the top had stripped, revealing the most pathetic cock Vinnie had ever seen in his life. The thing had been sad. All Vinnie's desire had pretty much drained away, and Vinnie had safeworded and fled to the bathroom. The top was furious, but Vinnie had insisted he had a sudden case of violent stomach cramps.

"Do you need to think about this?" Charleston made it sound perfectly reasonable. Vinnie was naked in the middle of the man's bed and Charleston already had the rope out, but maybe Vinnie should take time to think about this. Most men were not happy if a bottom backed out that late in the game.

"I'm just not…." Vinnie turned to stare at the sheet.

"You don't trust me enough to turn that kind of control over?" Charleston finished in a matter-of-fact tone.

"No!" Vinnie turned to his side, realizing too late that Charleston would be able to see his sudden lack of interest. Surprisingly, Charleston didn't even blink at Vinnie's soft cock nestled in the curled hairs. "I trust you," Vinnie insisted, reaching out to tentatively touch Charleston's hip.

"I concealed my name, my history...." The way Charleston put it, Vinnie should distrust him, and that wasn't true.

"I always knew who you were, even if I didn't have the right name. I trust you." Vinnie rolled back to his stomach. "I just feel uncomfortable."

"About the fact that you can't run away?"

"For one."

Charleston nodded. "You can leave any time, Vinnie. I just won't let you leave without facing whatever fears are making you run."

"And that would be the uncomfortable part." Vinnie turned his face to the mattress and buried his eyes again. "I have no trouble sharing the body. I just prefer my fears to remain hidden and buried in a big dose of unhealthy self denial."

That got a chuckle out of Charleston. "At least you're honest about your state of mental unhealth."

"Oh, I'm not really good at honesty. Not even with myself."

"That's where you're wrong. You're more honest with yourself than you give yourself credit for. However, if you're not willing to bring that honesty out into the open, maybe I should give you a ride over to RJ's."

Vinnie snorted.

"Bernardi?" Charleston's tone made it clear that he expected some sort of explanation.

Vinnie shrugged. "She was really pissed about my scene at her place, so she already promised to tie me to the stage and whip me for it. You know, most subs would love to be stuck choosing between two Doms with their respective whips."

"But you aren't." Charleston paused. "Do you have any other friends I could take you to?"

Vinnie nodded. "Yep, but I'm not going to give you their names," he told Charleston.

"Oh?" That one word sounded incredibly dangerous in Charleston's mouth. Vinnie knew he was playing with dynamite, but if he chickened out now, he was never going to get this chance again, and he was tired of trying to satisfy himself with fantasies.

"I know that I'm not good with getting things out in the open, but I want to. So, we do this your way. I'll only safeword if I really need the scene to stop, not if I decide that I don't like the look of your penis and I'd just rather go home and watch Star Trek reruns."

Charleston blinked in surprise, clearly caught off guard by Vinnie's answer. Vinnie shrugged. "It only happened once, but looking back, I was probably using my safeword to push people around."

"If people weren't so easily manipulated, you wouldn't have gotten into the habit," Charleston said, and that almost sounded like an excuse, which was ironic because Charleston hated excuses. He never put up with them. Before Vinnie could revel in the moment, Charleston added, "Just don't think you'll ever get away with pulling that shit on me, Bernardi."

"No, sir," Vinnie quickly offered. "I wouldn't dream of it. Well, I'd dream of it, but I wouldn't expect it to actually happen."

"Good guess, Bernardi. So, you dreamed of it? Tell me."

Vinnie could feel his face get hot. Shit. "It'd be a lot easier if you told me a fantasy—I'm good with role play. I could be anyone for you."

The slap on his ass made Vinnie jump in surprise. This time Vinnie didn't cry out, but his butt did sting. "I didn't say we would act out your fantasies. I ordered you to tell them to me," Charleston said. Vinnie's face got even hotter as one fantasy rose to the surface, but his cock was already hardening. Resting his forehead on his arm, Vinnie took a deep breath.

"You're a mob big-shot, and I walk in on you doing something particularly mobbish. Your guys want to kill me, but you decide that I'm pretty and want to keep me instead."

Vinnie didn't bother looking at Charleston, so his hands gliding over Vinnie's naked back were a surprise. Strong fingers massaged the muscles, and Vinnie shivered under Charleston's touch.

"Go on," Charleston urged him.

"Um, that's pretty much it. You keep me and make me do lots of things I end up loving. And after what happened with Thompson—"

"Shhh. No, don't get those two things confused in your head, Vinnie." Charleston knelt next to Vinnie, his hands on Vinnie's shoulder and his mouth so close to Vinnie's ear that his breath stirred the small hairs at the back of his neck. "What do I do to you, Vinnie? Do I hurt you? Do I love you and hold you? Are you a pet on your knees at my feet?"

"All of the above," Vinnie confessed.

Charleston made a humming noise and went back to stroking his calloused hands over Vinnie's bare skin, touching everywhere. Fingers ran though Vinnie's hair and a thumb traced over his closed eyes, and Vinnie lay there, shaking with a need to do something and not able to think of one thing he could do. This was Charleston's show, and Vinnie was here to submit—to submit everything.

Chapter
Thirty

CHARLESTON continued his massage until Vinnie was limp and helpless, so relaxed that he couldn't move without the bed being set on fire.

"Good?" Charleston asked.

Vinnie hummed in pleasure. "This is not really how my dates usually go,"

"Do you like how your dates normally go?" From the smug tone in Charleston's voice, he already knew the answer to that. Vinnie didn't. True, he'd liked Thompson even less than normal, but no matter how high his hopes were going into the sex, he always came out disappointed. On good dates, his body ached deliciously, but his brain still managed to come up with all the ways that he was dissatisfied. Even if Thompson hadn't turned out to be a psycho, Vinnie still wouldn't have been happy two minutes after the guy left.

"Try something new, Bernardi," Charleston said. He laid the rope against Vinnie's back. It was soft, long coils of it lay against Vinnie's shoulder and arm, and Vinnie just waited as Charleston settled himself, straddling Vinnie's thighs so that Vinnie was trapped.

For long minutes, Vinnie could feel the slide of the rope against his skin as Charleston worked, but nothing seemed to happen. Keeping his hands tucked under his head, Vinnie had to order himself to not get impatient. At least, he had to order himself to not *act* impatient. He had the feeling that Charleston was the sort of top that would not appreciate a backseat driver. Hell, if Vinnie acted impatient, Charleston would probably take twice as long. Vinnie wasn't sure why that felt sexy, but it did. So instead he lay still and suffered as Charleston handled the rope, letting the long length slide against Vinnie's arm, heating the skin.

"This is killing you, isn't it?" Charleston sounded amused.

"Like you wouldn't believe," Vinnie agreed. "I really want to start squirming or making suggestions about how to make this go faster." Vinnie looked over his shoulder and gave Charleston a half smile. "I might even be pointing you toward the handcuffs."

"So, you want to annoy the man who's about to take a whip to your backside?"

"That doesn't actually sound smart, does it?"

"Not really," Charleston agreed. He shifted back so that he was sitting on Vinnie's calves. "Sit up, hands behind your head."

Pushing himself up, Vinnie watch curiously as Charleston looped the rope around his shoulders. A knot held a two-inch loop right between his nipples, and Charleston wrapped the long ends around Vinnie's back before bringing them back to the front and threading them through the loop. It was almost hypnotic, watching as Charleston slowly worked the rope around his chest, crossing over the shoulders, and then back through the loop over and over. The two ends were so long that each pass seemed to take forever, and Charleston's hands brushing against Vinnie's warm skin made his cock ache with need.

Even though his hands weren't tied, Vinnie kept them behind his head, trembling as the ropes tightened with each pass. After several thicknesses were wrapped around his chest and two around each shoulder, Charleston started testing each strand, tugging and pulling to make the harness tighter and tighter. Vinnie groaned.

Charleston chuckled without pausing in his work. Unlike handcuffs that could be quickly unlocked, this sort of intricate rope work was going to take just as long to undo, and Vinnie shivered at the idea of being sated and exhausted at the end of the night and still having Charleston's hands all over him. Most tops were finished about the time they came, but then Vinnie wasn't surprised to find that Charleston wasn't like most tops.

"On your stomach." The order was curt, the same tone Charleston had always used when ordering Vinnie to do pushups or run the track. Vinnie dropped onto his stomach without even blinking. "Good boy." Charleston patted his side like he was a dog, and as much as Vinnie wanted to feel resentful or degraded, he just felt warm. He curled his hands into fists and struggled to keep himself still because he desperately wanted to hump into the sheets and finish the orgasm that he could feel creeping up on him. The rope pattern pressed into his chest, and Vinnie had to fight an urge to sit up and explore it with his fingers.

Charleston shifted forward, this time resting his weight on Vinnie's shoulders. His pants brushed against Vinnie's bare skin, pressing the rope even tighter against his body.

"Comfortable?"

Vinnie groaned, the weight making it hard to breathe and the need to come making him so hard he wasn't sure he cared.

Charleston brought a hand down on Vinnie's bare ass, the sound cracking through the air. Vinnie yelped. "Questions require answers," Charleston said calmly.

"Define comfortable," Vinnie snapped. He flinched, half expecting another swat. The heat might feel good after a few seconds, but Charleston's hand could really make it hurt. Instead of a swat, Charleston's hand ran possessively over Vinnie's ass, smoothing away the sting.

"Can you breathe easily?"

Vinnie let his breath out once he figured out he hadn't earned punishment. "I can breathe, but it's a little harder than normal," he answered before Charleston could get impatient.

"Do you feel out of breath?"

"No. Well, not other than the normal out of breath because I really need to come sort of way."

Charleston leaned back. "Is that an attempt to get me to hurry?" His eyebrow quirked.

"What? Me? Would I do that, sir?"

"Yes." Charleston gave him another swat, but this one was all heat with no sting. Vinnie smiled. "Stretch your hands over your head, fingers toward the bed posts."

Vinnie moved into position. Charleston looped the rope and created a loose knot that he put around Vinnie's arm before he started working it down. When the knot was close to Vinnie's shoulder, he started tightening it, tugging it into position. Vinnie watched one after another as Charleston created knots and then worked them down his arm until he had a line of twelve knots, all matching and all connected to loops leading from his chest harness. It was almost meditative, watching Charleston's strong fingers repeat the same motion over and over.

Vinnie's skin tingled with every brush of Charleston's fingers, and the rope pressing into his flesh made him more aware of his arm, as if his arm had suddenly become sexualized. He longed for touch, and every time the edge of Charleston's shirt brushed over an elbow, Vinnie shivered. Finally, Charleston finished. He tied the rope to the bottom of the bedpost and then took the end of the rope and tied a second knot near the top of the bedpost with a slip knot. Charleston would be able to pull that top knot free easily, but with the rope anchored to the bottom of the bed post, Vinnie was completely helpless.

Flexing a muscle, Vinnie watched the skin press up against the rope, bulging on either side until he relaxed. Charleston started humming softly as he ran his fingers over the other half of the rope and then stroked Vinnie's left arm. He worked slowly and methodically to repeat the same pattern, and Vinnie almost felt like he was drifting. Sometimes that happened in class; he'd be focused on the teacher droning on but not really listening, and it was like he just slipped away to some half-state where he wasn't asleep but he really wasn't awake. The world slipped past as Charleston hummed, time punctuated only by the brush of his fingers.

Still drifting, Vinnie watched Charleston tie off the second rope. His arms were in a V, each hand just an inch shy of touching the bedpost, and Vinnie just waited. Charleston slid down until he was resting against Vinnie's thighs, pinning him. Vinnie groaned as Charleston ran strong hands over his back and ass, thumbs pressing deep into the yielding muscle. Sleep pressed close as Charleston ran his hands down Vinnie's sides.

"You're going to mark beautifully."

"Hmmm." Vinnie knew he should probably have some sort of answer, but he felt like a lazy old cat that had been lying in the sun too long. Charleston chuckled and got off the bed.

The loss of Charleston's warmth pulled Vinnie closer to the real world. He tried to lift himself up to see over his shoulder, but he was tethered so tightly that he couldn't twist around. He was comfortable as long as he lay still, but he clearly wasn't going to be doing any moving with his top half.

"What are you getting?" Vinnie asked, watching as Charleston pulled something out of the closet.

Charleston didn't answer. He just gave Vinnie an indulgent look and a little shake of his head, like Vinnie had done something bordering on disrespectful but Charleston was amused and he wasn't going to step in. Sometimes when the other teachers called Charleston in to discipline Vinnie, Charleston would get that expression, and Vinnie had always loved it. It meant that Charleston was on his side, even if Vinnie still had to do pushups because some stick-up-his-ass teacher decided to take offense to Vinnie's sense of humor.

"Right. Just submit." Vinnie sighed and relaxed, focusing his eyes on the pretty line of knots down his arm. "I thought I was pretty good at submitting, but I'm starting to think I'm in danger of failing the final exam."

"No final exam, Vinnie. If we both enjoy this, there's no reason why we can't practice until we get it right."

"Practice, that sounds good. Practice sounds very good." Vinnie mumbled.

"Are you falling asleep on me?"

"I'm considering it," Vinnie confessed.

Charleston snorted. "So either you're trying to manipulate me into moving faster, or you have decided you trust me."

"I trust you." Vinnie thought about that. "And I wouldn't mind you going faster, but mostly I trust you."

Charleston shook his head. "We should talk about your lack of good judgment."

Vinnie opened his eyes and focused on Charleston. He was standing next to the bed, his shirt off and his pants showing a noticeable bulge in front. A scattering of graying hair across his chest turned into a faint line that led down the center of his muscled stomach where it disappeared under his waistband. Vinnie had a sudden urge to take a pen and draw on Charleston's stomach to make an arrow pointing down. Buried treasure, this way.

"Whatever you're thinking, don't." Charleston popped him on the top of the head, and Vinnie settled his head back onto the bed, still smiling. His smile faded as Charleston brought his hand up. He had a whip in his hand. It was black with several long strips trailing down from a wrapped wooden handle. Vinnie sucked in a breath as Charleston ran the long tails over his skin—over the rope encircling his arm.

The leather slid over his skin, soft and tickling as Charleston traced the line of Vinnie's back and then over a leg. Vinnie struggled to hold his leg still and wished Charleston had tied his legs. If this were any other top, he'd make that suggestion, but it wasn't any top. It was like this was Charleston's show. Vinnie was one of the props, one of the actors sent here or there by a director. Charleston let the whip's tails brush over the bottom of Vinnie's feet before he finally pulled it back.

"You're going to take marks so nicely."

Taking in a large breath, Vinnie prepared for a hard hit. Instead, Charleston barely brushed the whip past his ass once and then again.

"I know I'm not usually into the whips, but I can take more than that," Vinnie protested. He didn't like pain, but even worse, he didn't like people assuming he was some wuss who couldn't take a little pain.

"Yep," Charleston agreed. "And you will." However, Charleston's next pair of hits were still just faint kisses of leather across Vinnie's back. He swung the whip one way, catching Vinnie on the left side and then back hitting him on the right side. "It's like the knots, Vinnie. Just let go." Charleston's words were little more than a whisper.

Vinnie looked at the line of knots up his arm, each pinning him to the bed. He flexed his arm and felt the rope press deep into him, and that same feeling of distance and calm seeped back in through all his impatience and anxiety. The whip started moving with a rhythm as predictable as the knots against his skin. Left... right... pause. Left...

right… pause.

Vinnie twitched as the whip caught a ticklish spot, the tail running past it so that his whole body shuddered. Immediately, Charleston's palm rested against his flank. Charleston's thumb caught the same spot, and Vinnie giggled, the sound escaping before he could control it. Charleston smiled and then went back to the whip.

The pattern became a drumbeat that lulled Vinnie, but now he could feel the heat gather. No one hit was all that hard, but they came so often that the sting was like nettles against his skin. Vinnie hissed in a breath, his body's reactions out of his control. He twisted as the sting caught him on the left thigh and then a sharper sting against the right.

"You're turning very nice colors." Charleston stopped, draping the whip over his shoulder with a casual flip of the tails. He ran his hands over Vinnie, and this time, Vinnie strained as the heat of Charleston's body almost burned him.

"It doesn't feel like I thought," Vinnie said.

"How did you expect it to feel?"

"Painful."

Charleston just made a little humming sound and climbed onto the bed. Straddling Vinnie's calves, he started running his hands over Vinnie's body. Fingers spread out and pressed deep, and the heat of Charleston's hands burned. The strokes became stronger as Charleston worked, his thumb running along the sides of Vinnie's spine, and the massage sent little pangs and twinges through Vinnie's body, making his muscles twitch and his skin turn to goose bumps as it cooled the moment Charleston's touch passed.

"Very nice," Charleston said as he moved off the bed and took the whip from his shoulder where he'd draped it like a decoration on one of those fancy shoulder pads on military uniforms. Moving to the other side of the bed, he reversed the order. Now the whip hit on the right side, high on his back. Vinnie gasped. Heat rushed to his skin, and his whole back tingled for a second. The matching strike on the left side brought even more heat and a sharp sting. Now Charleston brought the whip down hard enough that every slapping blow made Vinnie gasp. He breathed in time with the whip, his body turning into a furnace.

Sweat made his hair stick to his neck and slicked his arms, and now Vinnie fought the ropes. His body demanded movement, and he pulled and strained, but the rope never gave an inch, and Charleston still rained down a steady pattern. A particularly hard hit on the swell of his ass made all Vinnie's thoughts scatter. For a second, he couldn't remember how to breathe. Charleston stopped and ran dull fingernails over the abused skin. Vinnie cried out, the heat soaking so deep into him that he could feel his whole body coil with need.

"Breathe, Bernardi."

Vinnie did. He couldn't avoid obeying that voice, so he breathed as the whip fell. With every stinging blow, Vinnie cried out and moaned and strained against the ropes. He tried to rub his cock against the soft sheets only to have a strong hand grab his ankle and pull him flat against the mattress, and then the whip returned. Vinnie struggled to hold on to any thoughts, but the world slipped away, like a picture he could see even if he wasn't part of it. All that existed was his body and the fall of the whip and Charleston's odd humming. He could feel his body building toward a climax, his head as dizzy as the time he'd gone sky diving and pretended to be casual even as he nearly pissed his pants. "Yes," he cried on each blow.

The whip stopped, and Vinnie cried out. "Please. Just a little harder."

"Kneel up." Charleston's hands at his hips were unyielding, and Vinnie obeyed with a little whine. His body was raging, and he just needed a little more to tip over into bliss. Just a little more. But Charleston was forcing his ass up into the air so that Vinnie's hot cock dangled in the air, the heat lost.

"Please," Vinnie begged. "Please don't stop."

"I won't. I promise." Charleston landed a slap on Vinnie's butt, and Vinnie cried out and humped the air as every line of heat the whip had left once again came to life, like a fire that had found new oxygen. Charleston spanked him again, and Vinnie pressed into the touch, needing more and more. The headboard creaked from the force of Vinnie's weight straining against it, but Charleston kept every stroke the same. The sound of flesh hitting flesh echoed against the walls like a heartbeat, and then that vanished.

For a second, Vinnie was too winded and too confused to protest. He tried to twist around, to see why it had stopped, but the ropes around his chest held him tight.

"Shhhh," Charleston soothed him, a hand sliding over his hip. Vinnie tried to obey, but his body had turned into a hungry beast that just demanded more. He arched his back and mewled, too lost in his own head to even feel embarrassed about the noise coming out of him. Metal clinked, fabric rustled—Vinnie's brain couldn't decipher the sounds as Charleston moved behind him. All that mattered was coming.

A slick finger breached him, sliding in so fast that Vinnie didn't have time to brace for the cool feel against his heated backside. He gave a strangled cry and pulled so hard the headboard screeched in protest. The only response was Charleston taking away the finger so that Vinnie felt emptier than ever. Before Vinnie could even form a word, thighs pressed up against the back of his legs, and Charleston thrust inside in one hard stroke. The heat and the pressure made Vinnie scream his pleasure and his need. His cock hurt. The need to come was coiled so tightly that he couldn't breathe, and his cock threatened to just fall off. One finger ran up the underside and then circled the crown, which was wet with precum, and Vinnie screamed again, his whole world graying as he came in a shattering orgasm.

Panting, he sagged and let the rope and Charleston's hands on his hips hold him while Charleston started rocking in and out slower now. The post-orgasm haze was punctuated with sharp waves of pleasure and tingling almost-pain when Charleston ran hot hands over Vinnie's hotter back and ass. Every thrust of Charleston's body pressed him up against the back of Vinnie's thighs where whip lines lay like embers against his hot skin.

Some distant part of Vinnie wanted to do something to make up for the fact that he'd come first, leaving Charleston to have to take his pleasure from a sated and blissed out partner, but that would require effort. Vinnie didn't seem to be able to find energy for anything. He existed, but anything beyond that required effort that he wasn't capable of. He felt Charleston finish with a little grunt and then pull out. Vinnie simply waited, his ass still in the air as Charleston disposed of the condom and then came back to the bed to rearrange him.

Charleston pulled his legs out so he lay flat on the bed and moved him up an inch so the ropes around his chest weren't straining so hard. He draped a sheet over Vinnie's waist and lifted his head to slip a pillow under it. Vinnie just blinked owlishly.

"How do you feel?" Charleston brushed a sweaty lock of hair back from Vinnie's forehead.

"Good." Vinnie closed his eyes. Charleston's fingers soothed him.

"You're not going to be able to sit comfortably for days."

"Hmmmm." Vinnie was too worn out to stop and figure out the meaning of words like "sit" and "days."

Charleston chuckled and carefully settled himself next to Vinnie, his arm draped over Vinnie's shoulders. "Have you ever felt this way before?"

"Not even close," Vinnie honestly answered.

"How many times have you honestly let go of the control?"

Another time Vinnie might have fought answering that question. As a bottom, the whole goal was to let go of control; however, he sucked at it. Right now, though, the whole world, including his past, was nothing more than a flat oil painting with no power to hurt him. Only he was real... him and Charleston. "Never," he answered without shame.

"Do you like giving up control?"

Vinnie laughed. "Oh yeah."

"Why don't you, then?"

"I don't trust people. Not really."

Charleston didn't answer immediately. He stroked Vinnie's cheek and ran a finger under the ropes, his touch making the skin tingle and sting. "Why do you trust me?"

Vinnie opened his eyes and blinked at Charleston, trying to find words to describe something that was so fundamentally true that it was like describing the color of air.

"I know you," Vinnie finally said. "I know your rules. I understand your rules."

Charleston shook his head. "You're going to call yourself a fool when you wake up tomorrow and look at all the marks on your body."

"Nope. I'm going to like seeing them," Vinnie said confidently, and he knew he was right.

Chapter
Thirty-One

IN THE morning, Vinnie usually dragged himself into consciousness with great resentment about the time that the last of the morning news shows had given up and courtroom dramas had taken over the television. If he found himself up before ten, he pretty much hated life. This morning, however, he found himself drifting toward awareness when sunrise was just faintly staining the blinds and most of the room was still dark. Charleston was already up and moving, silently performing pushup after pushup next to the bed, his bare back slick with sweat and the muscles shifting under his skin.

Vinnie reached out, his body feeling strange, like he shouldn't have control over it, and he felt some sort of faint surprise when his arm responded. Faint lines criss-crossed his skin where the rope had pressed into it, and Vinnie shivered at the evidence of yesterday's games. Game didn't quite describe it, but Vinnie didn't have any other word for it. Leaning over, he reached out so that his fingertips brushed across Charleston's shoulder when the man raised himself up at the top of his pushup. Charleston looked over and smiled but continued to work.

Wanting more, Vinnie shifted closer to the edge of the bed. His back ached liked he'd strained every muscle in it, and he groaned.

"Problem?" Charleston asked, his voice thick with the effort of doing his own pushups. Vinnie wondered what number he was on.

"No, sir," he answered. He certainly wasn't going to whine about a little aching, especially not when the ache felt so damn good. It was like the stretch he felt after a really big top had taken him hard and fast—and

Vinnie's ass was feeling that ache, too, but this extended to his entire body. All of him ached. All of him remembered what it had felt like to be under Charleston's whip.

"You might want to look in a mirror before you say that." Charleston kept doing his pushups without pausing, but Vinnie could hear the command in the suggestion. Sliding over to the other side of the bed, Vinnie carefully climbed out. The length of rope Charleston had used was coiled neatly at the side of the bed, and Vinnie could feel his muscles tighten in anticipation just from the sight of it. His cock, already half-hard, started rising to the occasion. Clearly he was going to have to avoid home improvement stores unless he wanted to be arrested for being a perv. Rope was definitely going to make him embarrass himself from now on.

Turning away from the coil, Vinnie padded into the bathroom and looked over his shoulder. The mirror showed him a patchwork of long red lines and short curling curves. Some places where lines met had quarter-sized red blotches and the few scant inches that weren't marked up looked shockingly white in the middle of all that red. The marks continued down over his ass and onto his upper thighs. Bending over, Vinnie checked his inner thigh, but all the marks had fallen on the back and outside of his legs.

"You're pretty marked up." Charleston appeared in the bathroom doorway.

"Oh yeah." Vinnie smiled. When Charleston didn't return his smile, Vinnie could feel all his pride slowly ebb. "Sir?" Vinnie stomach curdled at the thought that Charleston wasn't happy.

Instead of answering, Charleston reached out and caught Vinnie by the back of the neck and pulled him close. Vinnie wasn't sure what to expect, but the noogie was a surprise. After a quick knuckle rub over Vinnie's head and a second of holding Vinnie captive while he squirmed, Charleston let him go. Now Charleston was smiling.

"Someone has a lot of practice with the whip. You could charge money for that, sir."

"That would make it prostitution."

"Well, yeah, but think how much money you'd have." Vinnie

smiled at Charleston. In return, he got one of those indulgent looks.

"I think I'll stick to the amateur leagues."

"I wouldn't call you an amateur. You must have a whole lot of experience taking a whip to someone's backside." Vinnie made the comment while carefully keeping his gaze focused on the mirror. Charleston reached out and flicked him on the ear hard enough to make it sting. "Ow." Vinnie rubbed his ear.

"Ask, but do not play games with me, Bernardi," Charleston warned. Vinnie smiled. The man was just as much of a hard-ass bastard with his lovers as he had been with his students.

"Okay. How many men have you whipped, and please tell me I'm in the top... oh, I'd be happy if I was in the top fifty percent of that group."

Charleston's eyebrow quirked.

Vinnie held his hands up defensively. "You said you wanted honesty. This is me being honestly insecure."

Charleston crossed his arms and leaned against the door jamb. "I haven't actually whipped that many men. Whipping was a treat, something I could only do when the sub had a leave planned, because I couldn't leave marks that might be seen in the barracks. Usually I used pressure points and stress positions to bring someone down."

Vinnie nodded. He wouldn't exactly call it going "down," but Charleston had managed to temporarily push him out of the real world. Vinnie still felt a little like he was floating at the edge of reality without quite engaging with it totally. "And am I in the top fifty percent?"

Charleston seemed to think about that. Vinnie called himself an idiot for the way his stomach knotted with worry, but he wanted to be good. He hadn't been able to hold back his orgasm, which yeah, was pretty normal. But usually Vinnie was also really careful to stay attentive to his top until the guy finished. Last night he'd been so very out of it, he hadn't really been useful at all at the end.

"You beg nicely," Charleston said, which was totally unexpected.

With a blush, Vinnie closed his eyes tightly. "Okay, that's actually one thing I try not to do."

"I know. That's why I enjoyed it so much," Charleston said. "The fact that you totally let go of all control makes you one of the best I've ever had in my bed. Even if you don't choose to come back to my bed again, every sub after you will hate having to live up to that standard."

"But…." Vinnie studied Charleston. "Why wouldn't I come back?"

Charleston sighed and turned around, and headed for the living room, but Vinnie followed. The waist of his sweat pants were dark with sweat and he rolled his shoulders, so Vinnie was guessing he'd just done a whole lot of pushups. "Vinnie, this was enjoyable."

"Well, that's better than you starting with this being not enjoyable, but I'm not liking the sound of this."

Grabbing a bottle of water off the end table, Charleston sat on the arm of the couch and just looked at Vinnie. For the first time, Vinnie was suddenly uncomfortable in his own skin. He wished he was dressed, but he really didn't want to put on his tight jeans, not with his backside still marked by the whip.

"I loved last night." Charleston stated it so simply that Vinnie didn't process the words right away.

When he realized what Charleston had said, Vinnie slowly smiled gave a cocky shrug. "I am pretty damn good."

Charleston sighed at sat on the couch. "Sit," he said, pointing at the floor in front of the couch. Vinnie felt his face get warm. Okay, so they were clearly still playing the game this morning. Vinnie edged closer and then awkwardly lowered himself to the floor near Charleston. He angled his body so that his right hip pressed into Charleston's leg.

"Vinnie, I'm old, cranky, and about to get my ass booted from the only career I've ever known. I'm also demanding, unforgiving, and unlikely to ever change."

"Can I just say I'm weirdly turned on by all that?"

"You're turned on by discovering that you can have sex without having to control everything," Charleston countered, flicking Vinnie's ear with a finger.

"That too," Vinnie agreed. "But finding that out wouldn't have changed the fact that I had some pretty well-used fantasies with you in the starring role. I made you an Arab slave-owner and a mob boss, and I still managed to underestimate how bossy and controlling you could be," Vinnie said with a half-shrug that made his back ache.

"Vinnie." Charleston stopped. Reaching out, he ran a thumb over one of the marks. Vinnie hissed from the stinging pain, but as weird as it felt, the sting also reminded him of that quiet he'd found under Charleston's hands, the place where all the past became just some image with no power to hurt him because the whip and Charleston's hands were all that existed. Vinnie scooted closer and leaned his shoulder against Charleston's knee. The sun came in through the half-open blinds, bars of light slowly crawled across the floor toward Vinnie's feet. Vinnie just watched them.

"I never got to keep a sub, you know," Charleston said quietly. "By the time I discovered how much I really needed to dominate someone, I was in the service. The army was always my master and the first master of every sub who ever laid down for me." Charleston's voice was distant, and Vinnie reveled in the rare moment of sharing. Charleston wasn't one for telling stories about his past, and Vinnie had the feeling that wouldn't change, even now that he didn't need to protect a secret identity. Laying his cheek against Charleston's thigh, Vinnie just closed his eyes.

Charleston ran his fingers through Vinnie's hair and then down to trace the rope marks on his shoulders. Vinnie shivered as fingertips traced the sensitive skin.

"You have to make me one promise, Vinnie." Vinnie tilted his head to look up at Charleston. "You have to be willing to use your safeword. If you need space, if you need to back away and find some room, you have to promise you will use your safeword because there aren't going to be any orders that send you off to the other side of the world, and I have never been good at letting go on my own."

Vinnie swallowed, stopping just before he gave some flip answer about never wanting Charleston to let go. He'd been let go too much already. But Charleston didn't take flip answers about serious subjects. "I promise," Vinnie said.

Charleston studied him for a long minute before nodding. "Okay. So, right now you've made a mess at work. Since taking a whip to your backside is now my job, we need to go see if we can get things straightened out with RJ."

Charleston patted Vinnie's shoulder briskly, clearly meaning that it was time for them to get moving. Vinnie's back gave twinges of almost-pain, and Vinnie pushed himself up, forcing his abused back to twist in such a way that his whole body rediscovered the fire from the night before. Time to get on with life.

Chapter
Thirty-Two

"WELL, look who the cat dragged in." Vinnie flinched away from RJ's tone, but Charleston's fingers wrapped around his arm. Her eyes narrowed. "Friend, you'd better have permission to touch him, or we're going to have a short and very painful discussion."

"I do." Charleston didn't bother to explain or justify his actions, but then again, he never had. The whole verbal flailing was more Vinnie's thing.

"Vinnie?" RJ asked.

"Hey, RJ. Um. Yeah, Charleston's fine. He just insisted that he had to come if you were really going to...." Vinnie stopped. He had no idea why this was so fucking uncomfortable, but it was.

"So, are you looking out for him now?" RJ stood up and stepped toward them.

"Better than you did."

That made RJ narrow her eyes, and Vinnie could see Dan shift behind the bar. Danny might go home and let a man tie him up, but when he was at the bar, he followed RJ without question or hesitation. Vinnie wanted to warn Charleston of that, but Charleston's fingers dug into the soft of his arm the minute he started to open his mouth.

"Really?" RJ asked, her voice dangerously calm.

Charleston gave a sharp nod. "Yes. I fucked up by sending him in here and not checking on him for several hours. You told him you were going to whip him and then sent him home for a few days."

"Would you have taken a whip to him while you were angry? If that's the kind of top you are, you are not walking out that door with him, no matter what permission he's given you."

"I can—" Vinnie stopped when he was met with matching and very sharp orders to shut up. He shut up.

Charleston looked RJ up and down, and his expression made it very clear that he didn't like what he saw. If there was any way to piss RJ off faster, Vinnie sure hadn't seen it. "I wouldn't have sent him away after making that kind of promise."

"I give a submissive a chance to reconsider before I take them down." RJ sounded just as angry as Charleston, and Vinnie just waited in horror as two forces of nature slammed into each other like storm fronts.

Instead of getting angry, Charleston nodded in agreement. "That's admirable, but you sent Vinnie out into the arms of the first person who could give him instant gratification."

"You?" RJ spit the word out.

"No. He ended up in bed with a man the military calls the Poet Killer. Thompson has tortured dozens and killed a couple as he carved them up."

RJ froze, her whole body caught in a pose that suggested she was about to throw a punch. She might be little, but Vinnie had seen her lay into enough men that he really didn't want RJ and Charleston going at it, especially not over him. However, Charleston still had his arm in a tight grip, so he couldn't do a whole hell of a lot. Slowly, RJ looked toward him. "What?"

Vinnie flinched away from telling her the truth. It wasn't her fault that he'd been slightly on the side of totally self-destructive, but the way Charleston had phrased things, he'd made it sound like RJ was to blame. "Why?" RJ finally asked. She sounded so confused that Vinnie's stomach dropped and his heart tripped along so fast that he couldn't catch his breath. "Fuck. I told you that your place here was safe." Charleston stepped forward so that he was between them, blocking RJ's view.

"He never told you his real name," Charleston said in a matter-of-fact tone that didn't seem to match the swirling emotions in the room.

For long seconds, she refused to stop staring at Vinnie, and he shifted uncomfortably. Eventually, though, she looked over at Charleston. "Didn't seem important. A person is whoever they want to be."

Charleston pursed his lips and waited a second before answering. "He's Troy Martello, Jr. His father owns the Martello Systems Corporation."

"Well, shit." Vinnie couldn't see RJ because he'd ducked his head to avoid her gaze, but he could hear the weariness in her voice, and it cut through him. She had a right to be angry; almost from day one she'd made it clear that lying was the only sin she wouldn't forgive.

"His father is a real son of a bitch, always promising Vinnie a safe place," Charleston said. It was true enough. Vinnie had gotten to the point that he hadn't trusted two words his old man had said; however, he hadn't realized until this moment that some little sliver of him hadn't trusted RJ. Maybe he couldn't trust until he gave someone the power to hurt him and they chose not to, but standing in the same room with Charleston and RJ, he realized that he'd been afraid when he'd run out of the bar on Friday. He'd been afraid that he'd fucked up so badly that RJ would throw him out, and he cared about this place more than he wanted to admit. He shivered, his emotions sweeping through him, and Charleston's hand found his back, pressing into the whip marks. The dull pain pushed the world father toward the edges of his awareness, centering him on Charleston.

"So, he's used to being given things and promised things," RJ concluded.

"And having his father then vanish only to end up on the front page of a tabloid with his starlet of the week," Charleston agreed. "He doesn't trust people to follow through."

"I never said that," Vinnie protested, but he said it so softly that he wasn't sure either of them heard him.

RJ sighed. "Vinnie, I never made a promise I wasn't going to keep. I have the whip here, and I'm just as ready to take you home and deal with whatever you have rotting inside you."

Vinnie cleared his throat and tried to find a voice loud enough to be heard. "I know." His throat felt raw. Actually, his whole body felt raw and tender. He couldn't even seem to find one joke about this whole situation.

RJ's voice turned firm. "So, either you need to take him in hand, or I'm not only going to chain him to my wall, but I'm going to be keeping him tied up until he learns that some of us mean what we say."

Charleston stepped forward, and Vinnie felt suddenly exposed. He could fight off a psycho, but facing RJ and letting her see just how messed up he was inside… that was far harder. Fuck, he really was a headcase. Part of him just wanted to go darting off. He could walk down the tree-lined street to his apartment and go inside and watch a movie and pretend that everything was okay. But he'd tried that and it hadn't worked. Straightening himself up, Vinnie stepped to Charleston's side.

"He's mine. If he wants to keep working here, that's fine, but you will not punish him." Charleston stopped inches from RJ. It was like seeing the immovable object meet the irresistible force. Either that or it was like watching two immovable objects try to move each other.

RJ studied Vinnie, and Vinnie squirmed under her gaze, but he refused to drop his eyes. He did, however, press his shoulder against Charleston's. She narrowed her eyes and studied that touch. "He shouldn't be here so soon after you had a scene with him," she commented.

The edge of Charleston's mouth twitched as he almost smiled. "I thought you deserved to see the real Vinnie since you were all that was holding him together for the last two years."

Dropping into a chair, RJ propped her boot up on the rail of a second chair with a heavy sigh. "Obviously I wasn't doing that good of a job. Fuck. If I'd known he had that bastard as a father, I would have known to look a little deeper under all that puppy-charm that seems to leak out of his pores."

Charleston sat down in the chair opposite RJ. Vinnie stood awkwardly, not sure what to do. After catching Vinnie's arm in a strong grip, Charleston pulled down on his wrist slowly and powerfully until Vinnie finally sank to his knees at Charleston's feet. Looking down, Charleston gave him a smile and reached around behind Vinnie's neck to pull him close. Vinnie leaned against Charleston's leg and closed his eyes.

"He's good at masks," Charleston said. "And sometimes we need to hold onto masks to protect ourselves, but Vinnie is pretty hard to find under all the submissive charm."

"Very." RJ leaned forward. "So, why should I trust you to take care of him?"

"Other than the fact that he's already submitted?" Charleston sounded amused.

"If he'd come today, I would have put him against the wall. By the time I was done, he would have not only ached in his body and soul, but he would have given me his name, his deepest fantasy, and his submission."

"You sound sure of yourself."

"I am." RJ didn't bother explaining beyond that, but Vinnie figured she was telling the truth. There was only one thing he didn't understand.

He looked up at RJ. "Why didn't you make me submit before?" he asked softly. Charleston's fingers threaded through his hair.

RJ leaned back. "I meant what I once told you, Vinnie. Cocks are fun to play with, but I really don't want one in the middle of my living room. And you are so very sweetly submissive, I figured if I took you down, you'd be kneeling at my feet for the rest of your life. That's what happened with Dan and his master."

"Yep," Dan agreed. "The first man to really make me give everything up became my world." Dan looked Charleston up and down. "Of course if you aren't as good to Vinnie as Evan is to me, that doesn't mean that I won't beat the shit out of you and take Vinnie away from you." Vinnie stiffened, fully expecting Charleston to explode. Instead Charleston laughed. It was a beautiful sound, and part of Vinnie resented that Dan had inspired it. Vinnie glared over at his friend, but Dan just looked amused.

Charleston gave an aborted half-laugh and ruffled Vinnie's hair. "Not the shy sort of submissive, are you?"

"Me?" Dan snorted. "I'm more the kind to curse and struggle as

Evan whips me raw before fucking me. I'm also the kind to kick more than a few asses that are asking to be kicked."

"I bet."

"That doesn't seem to be your kind," RJ commented. Vinnie looked over, and she was staring down at him with the softest expression he'd ever seen on his face.

"No, I like them trying to obey, even when they can't," Charleston agreed.

"He likes the whip, doesn't he?" she asked with that same look in her eye.

"Yep."

RJ nodded, sighed, and then stretched her neck first one way and then the other. "Life fucking hates me. I need to find some cute little lesbian with a whip fetish. So, is Vinnie still going to be working here?"

"Does he have a job?" Charleston asked the question, but it was Vinnie holding his breath as he waited for an answer.

"Does he want one? Unless you're a Rockefeller, it seems like he has more money than everyone else in this room combined."

Vinnie shook his head. "No, that was Troy Martello. I haven't been him in a long time, RJ."

She looked down at him with a sort of fond exasperation. "Two years, Vinnie. I have chewing gum I've kept around longer than that, so don't act like you've forgotten what it means to be the son of a rich man." She laughed and shook her head. "And I have you scrubbing toilets. If you've found a Dom who can put you in your place, I'm not seeing why you'd want to come back around here."

"Because you guys are here," Vinnie said with a frown. RJ looked from Vinnie over to Dan and finally to Charleston.

Charleston's hand moved so that it rested against Vinnie's neck. "Maybe someday he'll be ready to be Troy Martello again. Right now, Vinnie has enough to deal with without having to open that can of worms. So, what do you say we just try and salvage his job here after Friday's disaster?"

RJ seemed to think about that for a while. "If you tell me his head is out of his ass and he isn't going to start a bar fight or act like an ass onstage, I want him back."

Charleston chuckled and ran fingertips over Vinnie's neck. "His head is out." Vinnie blushed as they discussed him like he was a dog that had needed obedience training, but his cock was starting to warm up to the idea nicely. Instead of looking at them, Vinnie closed his eyes and rested his head against Charleston's thigh.

"It does seem like it," RJ agreed. "How closely are you planning on holding on?"

"At first? Very. He's going to get insecure, and we all know that Vinnie makes some very unfortunate choices when he feels insecure."

RJ's snort suggested she agreed. "Evan and I have managed joint custody of Danny pretty well."

"Oh?" Charleston's fingers wandered down to trace circles under the neck of Vinnie's shirt, and Vinnie struggled to stay still.

"I make sure that Evan knows Danny's schedule down to the minute. If he needs to be out of town or is busy, he tells me, and I have Danny bunk here."

"And when he screws up?" Charleston asked.

"I've learned not to," Dan said.

"Yeah, but I still remember when you were young and chasing the most dangerous tops you could find," RJ said with amusement in her voice. "I thought we were going to find you in a ditch after someone accidentally killed you because you didn't know how to use your safeword."

"I wasn't that bad."

"Yes, yes you were," RJ disagreed with undisguised fondness for him even if he had been a big screw up. That gave Vinnie some hope. "That's why Evan and I came to the agreement. If Danny did anything unusual here, I told Evan. Most of the time, it wasn't important, but if Evan wanted to punish him, that was his choice. If Evan wanted something done here, like Danny chained to the bar, I made sure that happened."

Vinnie opened his eyes to look at Dan. Dan saw Vinnie's shocked gaze and shrugged. "It's been a long time since I screwed up badly enough for that, but the old timers will still remember me being leashed to the bar with a huge chain and padlock."

"What did you get in return?" Charleston asked.

RJ smiled. "Simple. From the time Danny walks in that door to the time he leaves, he's mine. He obeys every rule I set or I punish him."

"I won't let you touch Vinnie." Charleston's tone made it clear he was not going to compromise on that.

RJ looked down at Vinnie. "Then I reserve the right to watch as he's punished if he fucks up again."

Charleston seemed to think that over, and Vinnie waited, hopeful that he could still salvage his life. He wanted to work here. Dan and RJ and Tom and the other dancers were his friends, and he didn't want to lose them, but he'd give them all up if that's what Charleston asked of him. "Deal," Charleston agreed. "Do you want to see him punished for Friday?"

RJ frowned for a second, and Vinnie could tell that she hadn't quite made up her mind. As much as he'd loved the feeling of Charleston's hands and whip against his back, he didn't want to be punished. He didn't want the reminder of how much he'd screwed up, and if Charleston punished him, he'd feel it for days. "I am sorry," Vinnie said softly.

RJ looked down at him. "Then tell me why you did it."

Vinnie looked up at Charleston and blushed. God, this sounded stupid, but he supposed she deserved an answer. "I was trying to get Charleston's attention," Vinnie whispered. He could have been arrested, and if he had been, his fingerprints would have blown his secret identity. And that wasn't nearly as bad as the idea that RJ's bar could have been closed down altogether. It'd been a stupid risk to take just to attract someone's attention.

"You're right, he does make bad decisions when he's feeling insecure," RJ said.

"Yep," Charleston agreed. Closing his hand around Vinnie's neck, he pulled him close.

"Dan, bring us a couple of beers. We're going to work out Vinnie's schedule so the boy knows that he has two pair of eyes making sure that he doesn't act that stupid again." RJ put her boots on the ground and leaned forward onto the table.

"You got it." Vinnie smiled as Dan grabbed a couple of mugs. Since his knees were starting to ache, Vinnie shifted around and sat at Charleston's feet, sand clinging to his hands as he moved. Brushing them off on his pants, he leaned against one of Charleston's legs and rested his cheek against the knee. Whatever agreements they came to, he'd deal. Vinnie watched Dan deliver the beers, and then he closed his eyes, not even bothering to listen to them arrange his life.

After a second, Charleston's hand rested against his shoulder, and Vinnie felt himself drifting back into a place where the world existed only as some distant picture that couldn't really touch him. It felt like a safe place to be.

LYN GALA started writing in the back of her science notebook in third grade and hasn't stopped since. When she found the Internet and the world of gay romance, she found her true calling. When she isn't writing stories of happy men doing very dirty things she's teaching in New Mexico.

URBAN
SHAMAN

LYN GALA

http://www.dreamspinnerpress.com

BDSM Titles from DREAMSPINNER PRESS

http://www.dreamspinnerpress.com